THE
ALMOST
BOYFRIEND

THE
ALMOST
BOYFRIEND

CHRISTINA
BENJAMIN

CROWN ATLANTIC
PUBLISHING

Copyright © 2017 by Christina Benjamin
All rights reserved.
Published in the United States by Crown Atlantic Publishing

ISBN 978-1546818045

Text set in Adobe Garamond

Version 1.1
Printed in the United States of America
First edition paperback printed, May 2017

To all my Irish girls, especially Nana.

PROLOGUE

Rule #1: Friends don't kiss.
Rule #2: Friends don't lick each other.
Rule #3: Friends don't shop for underwear together.
Rule #4: Friends absolutely don't fall in love.

Rules are amazing. Rules keep order. Rules set boundaries. Rules are absolutely necessary for boy/girl friendships. Rules are not meant to be broken. The problem is some people aren't very good at following the rules. Even the ones they make. Especially when it comes to boys.

These are Samantha Connors' rules. And she broke every single one of them . . . well, almost.

CHAPTER
1

Sam

"Sam, it's a long flight. Are you really not going to talk to me the entire time?"

Samantha Connors flipped her thick brown hair and gave her father her best icy glare before returning to stare out the window from her comfy first-class seat. There was nothing to see but clouds. She turned up the volume on her ear buds and closed her blue-green eyes trying to force the tears back as she listened to Adele wail unjustly. Adele was always Sam's go-to songstress when she was upset. Listening to Adele lyrics was like crying on the inside—just how Sam liked it, so no one could see her pain.

But some things were too big even for Adele to remedy. And Ireland was one of those things. It's not that Sam had a problem with the country. She actually thought Ireland was quite lovely. But she didn't want to move there. Not now. Not when she could finally see light at the end of her teenaged tunnel.

It was her senior year of high school and her father had destroyed it by making her move with him to Ireland. She'd fought him every step of the way, which wasn't like her at all. Sam and her father usually coexisted without much friction. But Boston was Sam's life! And he'd taken that from her— *basically giving her a license to behave like the angsty teenaged daughter she'd never been.*

Sam had begged her father to let her stay and finish out the school year so she could graduate with her friends, but what little good that did. Here she was, sitting on a six-hour flight to Dublin, with only Adele to keep her company.

Her father scratched at the graying temples of his wavy brown hair and fidgeted with his glasses before tugging gently at Sam's left ear bud until it came free. "Are you still mad at me, honey?"

She scowled at him. "You think?"

"Sam, listen. I know you think moving to Ireland is the end of the world, but once we get there, you'll remember how much you used to love it."

"Dad, I was eight the last time I was in Ireland. I used to love Barbie and karaoke. But I'm not that girl anymore. I'm seventeen. I've grown up. When are you going to see that?"

"I'm not blind, Sam. I know you're not a little girl. But I still want you to be part of this family."

"Dad! There's only two of us. I'm pretty much a founding member of this family. That's not going to change. But I want to make my own decisions, start my own life. You have to let me be an adult."

"You're *almost* an adult," her father reminded her. "I still get to call you my little girl for ten more months."

Sam blew out a frustrated breath, rolling her eyes as she shoved her ear buds back in. 'Almost' was her father's favorite word and every time he said it, Sam pictured herself choking him in various ways.

I'm almost done working, Sam—she was wrapping her computer cord around his throat.

I almost made it to your soccer game, Sam—she was unlacing her soccer cleats to tie around his neck.

I almost got you a puppy, Sam—a leash would make a good noose.

I almost bought you a car for your good grades, Sam—stuffing her report card into his mouth would do the trick.

But that was just her father. He'd always been that way. 'Almost' really meant 'never' when he said it. And he never followed through on his promises. Until he did.

I almost care that you don't want to move to Ireland, Sam, she thought bitterly. Of course he hadn't said that, but he might as well have.

And for as many times as Sam fake-strangled her father in her mind, she didn't really mean it. She loved him, in her own weird-teenaged-daughter kind of way. Her father was all she had. Growing up, he'd been forced to play both father and mother to her, and he'd done a good job.

Sam's mother died when she was eight—that's why they'd moved from Ireland to Boston to begin with. Her father never remarried. He never even dated. He pretty much buried himself with work, occasionally lifting his head enough to raise her.

Sam knew she wasn't being fair. Her father was actually pretty great most of the time, and so was their relationship.

They cohabited rather effortlessly. Her father was reasonable and Sam was flexible. She was allowed to date, just not get too serious. She could go out on school nights, as long as he knew where she was. He didn't police her fashion or friends, so she chose them wisely. He gave her free reign on the Internet. *That started when she got her period.* Sam thought her father was going to shrivel up and die when she started asking him questions about tampons. "Why don't you Google that, honey?" had been his response.

And last year, Sam's father even told her he didn't have a problem with her drinking after prom—knowing that's what everyone did—he just made her promise not to get in the car with someone who'd been drinking.

Her father always told her he was happy to treat her like an adult as long as she acted like one. And that worked for Sam. Her best friend, Megan, repeatedly whined about how strict her parents were. "I wish they could just be chill, like your dad."

But sometimes, Sam thought she wouldn't mind being parented a bit more. Her father couldn't spend a lot of time with her because his tech firm kept him busy. But it was hard to be mad when she knew he only worked so hard so he could send her to the best schools and give her everything she wanted—*well everything except for a car and a puppy*—and he'd probably been right that she didn't really need those things. Boston had great public transportation and with Sam's sports schedule and her father's work, neither of them were really home enough to take care of a puppy.

Sam knew her father did his best. Losing her mother wasn't easy on him either. He never talked about her. And after a while, neither did Sam. She reasoned that they both were just trying to make things easier on each other. Perhaps that's why he was so easy-going and she was so mild-mannered. 'Don't rock the boat', was pretty much the motto for their relationship. And it was perfect, until Ireland got thrown in the mix.

Ireland was ruining everything.

Sam tried every possible option to get out of it. She tried reasoning, she tried yelling, she even tried crying hysterically. But nothing worked. She felt like a heat-seeking missile and Ireland was the only thing with a pulse for miles.

But there wasn't much Sam could do about it now. She was already on the plane. Short of finding a time machine or an independent fortune, Sam wasn't getting back to Boston until she graduated from high school. But by then, it would be too late. Her friends would have already moved on and forgotten about her. Well, maybe not her best friend, Megan Fields, but everyone else surely would. Especially Sam's almost boyfriend, hunky lacrosse player, Ryan Kennedy.

Sam didn't have many regrets in life, but Ryan was one of them. She'd flirted back and forth with him for the past year, but she never really felt a rush to move past that. She liked keeping her options open. It never seemed to bother him either. Ryan seemed happy with their random hookups at parties.

Sam's mind wandered back to the last conversation she'd had with Ryan.

"So you're really moving to Ireland?" he'd asked.

"Yep. Are you gonna miss me?"

"Do you want me to miss you?"

"I want you to want to miss me."

"Well, I'm certainly going to miss this," he said kissing

her with way too much tongue.

Sam had been thinking about giving Ryan even more than kisses to miss, but Megan interrupted them. Sam forgot she'd invited her brazen best friend over for packing and pizza. Sam asked Ryan to stay and join them, but he politely excused himself. She really hadn't expected him to stay—*packing wasn't something an almost boyfriend did anyway.*

"So, are you dating him or not?" Megan asked when they were alone, trying to pull her glossy black hair into a ponytail—it was still too short from the trendy bob she got at the start of summer.

"Almost."

"You can't *almost* date someone, Sam. Either you are or you aren't."

Sam rolled her eyes at her best friend. "Well, I'm moving so it doesn't really matter, does it?"

"Of course it does! Do you want to date him, or not?"

"I don't know. Sometimes I do. But sometimes it just seems like too much work."

"Work? I don't think falling in love is supposed to be work. It's supposed to be something you can't help but do," Megan said dreamily.

Megan was a hopeless romantic and it always drove Sam crazy. Mostly because Sam was more hopeless than romantic. She took a big bite of pizza and frowned at Megan. "How are you such an expert about love all of a sudden?"

"Hey, I've had seven boyfriends, I'll have you know."

"Book boyfriends don't count, Meg." Megan was also a giant book nerd—*probably where her hopeless romanticism came from.*

"Says you!" Megan shot back indignantly. "But seriously, you need to figure out what you want, Sam. You can't just go around *almost* loving people."

"I don't do it on purpose. But Ryan is impossible. If I knew he loved me it would be different. I mean, I can't tell if he actually likes me, or just likes trying to get in my pants."

"Yeah, sorry about that. I feel like I interrupted the whole getting-into-your-pants scenario," Megan replied sheepishly.

"It was probably for the best. Getting hung up on Ryan right before I move to Ireland doesn't seem like the best idea."

"Yeah, you need to keep your options open for all the hot Irish boys!" Megan swooned.

"Why would I do that? I'm coming back to Boston as soon as I graduate."

"You say that now, but you might end up falling for some gorgeous prince!"

"Meg, I'm moving to Dublin, not Cinderella's palace."

"I'm just saying, you never know."

"Well I do. I've been to Ireland before. The boys are exactly the same. The only difference is they're all named, McSomething or O'Somebody and they call soccer, football."

"You forgot about their sexy Irish accents."

"The only accent I wanna hear is a wicked good Boston one," Sam said, with thick Bostonian diction. "Besides, I'll be back before you know it."

Now it was Meg's turn to roll her eyes.

"Seriously Meg, the first semester always flies by, and who knows, maybe my dad will see the light by then and let me come home. But if not, I'll be back by summer. Nothing has to change."

"I sorta hope it does."

"What? Why?"

"Listen, you know I'm Team Sam for life, but your dad has a point. This could be a great opportunity for you. A year in Ireland may not be your first choice, but if it's gonna happen, you might as well embrace it. This is our last year to be young and stupid. Soak it up, Sam—all the way. That means no more *almost*."

Sam leaned her cheek against the cool glass of the plane window, trying to see through the clouds. Meg and her father were wrong. Ireland wasn't going to be some great adventure. *How could it be, when everything about the tiny green island reminded her of her mother and what she'd lost?*

Maybe Megan was right. It was time for Sam to stop being so 'almost' about her life. She knew everything she wanted was in Boston and it was time she went all in to get it.

Devon

Today's the day, Devon thought when he woke up. *The day the girl of my dreams is coming back to Ireland.* Looking forward to this day was keeping Devon alive. The past year had been a nightmare for him. Everything he'd thought he could count on started to crumble like a house of cards. It all started with his father's diagnosis. *Inoperable brain tumor. 12 months to live.* Those words rattled around in the empty space in Devon's chest. Nothing had been the same after he heard them. Not school, not his friends, and certainly not his future.

But today everything was going to change. Devon's second chance at happiness was coming back to him. He still remembered the hope that filled his chest when he heard his childhood crush was coming back to Ireland. Sam Connors. *Christ, how he'd loved her.* Well, as much as an eight-year-old boy knows how to love. It'd been ages since he'd seen Sam. He'd pretty much moved on with his life thinking he'd never see her again. But he never forgot her. *No one forgets their first love.*

CHAPTER

2

Sam

"So where to?" Sam asked when she climbed into the car her father rented. They'd shipped the bulk of their belongings ahead on a container ship, so luckily they each only had a carry-on and got through customs quickly.

"First off, switch sides," he said laughing. "If you thought I was scared of letting you drive in Boston, you're nuts if you think I'm letting you drive in Ireland."

"Sorry," Sam mumbled. "Old habit." She had forgotten the steering wheel was on the wrong side here. And they drove on the wrong side of the road too. *Ugh, everything was just wrong in Ireland.* "Ya know, I might actually need to learn to drive at some point in my life, Dad."

"I know that. But let's figure out where you plan to land after your last year of high school. Then we can talk about driving."

"Boston, Dad! I'm going back to Boston. You're only delaying the inevitable by dragging me here."

"We'll see," he replied.

He was right about that. Her father was about to see a brand new side of Sam. And he wasn't going to like it. The six-hour flight gave her more than enough time to come up with a thousand ways to get back to Boston. And the one she settled on was genius. It was almost too simple. She was going to morph into the teenage-daughter from hell. Drinking, Sex, Drugs—nothing was off limits. If she went off the deep end, she could blame it all on Ireland, and her father would have to see reason and send her back to Boston. Now all she had to do was find the right guy to use to make that happen. And she just so happened to have her sights set on the perfect pawn—Devon James.

Sam could never forget Devon, no matter how hard she tried. It had been nine years since she'd last seen him, but that didn't stop her from having nightmares about him. He'd made her summers hell. Every year they got stuck at the same summer camp while their parents worked together. Which meant 24/7 with Devon following her around putting spiders in her hair and calling her Spam. One day he'd even pulled her skirt over her head and everyone saw her flowery underpants.

Then, as if he hadn't hurt her enough, he'd kissed her! It was the day she left Ireland to move to Boston. She'd been crying in the back of her father's car while he said goodbye to Henry James, Devon's father. Devon had slipped into the car and held Sam's hand. For a moment, Sam had been so shocked by his kind gesture that she stopped crying. And that's when Devon kissed her. She shoved him away and screamed for her father. And that was it. She'd never seen Devon again, but she couldn't forgive him for stealing her first kiss.

While she was packing, Sam had found a framed picture of her and Devon from camp. She tried to throw it out, but of course Megan saw it and wanted to know everything about the dark-haired boy with the bowl cut and caterpillar eyebrows.

"That's Devon James. He's my dad's business partner's son. He's the worst."

"He looks like Neville Longbottom!" Megan exclaimed.

"Who?"

"You know, from Harry Potter?"

"Oh, yeah." Sam laughed. "I guess he kinda does."

Megan wanted to be a film writer. She was always comparing everyone to characters in books and movies. Most of the time Sam had to read the same books just so she could carry on a conversation with her best friend. It sort of gave them their own secret language, which was dorky and endearing all at once.

"Don't worry." Megan had told her. "Neville gets hot in the end."

"Megan, this isn't a fairytale. This is my life! I don't care if Devon is hot. He used to call me Spam. He's a dick."

A dick I'm going to use to get myself back to Boston, Sam thought giddily. She was having entirely too much fun scheming ways to make Devon look like a villain. Sometimes her wicked imagination scared her. Perhaps she spent too much time talking fiction with Megan. She wished Megan were with her. She'd have a million fantastical ideas about how to set Devon up.

Sam's father interrupted her scheming. "Look, Sam, can we put this argument on pause?" he asked. "It's been a long day."

She smiled. "Sure, Dad." *Why not give him one last day of his agreeable, loving daughter?* "So, where to?" she asked.

He pulled out his phone and turned on the GPS. "The James's house."

"What?" Sam felt panicky as she glanced at herself in the side view mirror. She was suddenly regretting her choice of comfy travel clothes. "Why?"

"There are some things I need to discuss with Henry."

She groaned. "Can't you drop me off first?"

Sam felt grubby from the flight and the last thing she wanted was for Devon to see her looking like a train wreck. Her brown hair was in a messy bun, she didn't have any make up on and she needed to shower the airport film off before she would feel presentable enough to see anyone—which she was hoping wouldn't be until classes started the following week.

"Dad! I look like crap. I can't see anyone looking like this."

"The James's aren't *anyone*. They're almost family."

"*Daaad,*" she groaned.

The last thing Sam felt like doing was sitting through a meeting with her father's business partner. And if she ran into Devon looking like this he might not take the bait, ruining her scheming before it even started.

"Samantha," her father said sternly. "Henry is my oldest and dearest friend. After we lost your mother . . ." Sam watched her father's dark eyes pool with tears and her throat dried up.

This was why they never spoke about her mother.

This was why she could never truly argue with her father.

This was why she didn't want to come back to Ireland.

They weren't ready for this. The memories were still too raw here. They'd been on terra firma for a solid sixteen minutes and already her father was losing it. He took a deep breath and seemed to regain his composure. "Henry and his family have been there for us through everything. And now it's our turn to repay the favor."

"Okay, Dad," she murmured.

Scheming be damned—Sam would have agreed to just about anything if it meant her father wouldn't get teary eyed. *She wasn't a monster.* It was bad enough that Sam looked exactly like her mother—same wild brown hair, sea glass eyes, oval face and porcelain complexion that freckled in the sun. She often wished she looked more like her father so he wouldn't look at her like he did—with a searing mixture of love and pain. She was a constant reminder of what her father had lost. But DNA aside, the waves in Sam's hair were the only apparent trait she'd inherited from him.

Sam reached over and squeezed her father's hand while he collected himself.

"And I expect you to be polite and courteous," her father continued. "Their family is suffering enough. They don't need to worry about us."

Sam nodded. "Of course, Dad."

Henry James was her father's college roommate-turned-business partner. They'd founded a software company, Cor-Tec, right out of college and it had become rather successful. Henry ran the UK headquarters, while her father ran the ones in the US. And Henry was the reason she'd been dragged to

Ireland. He was ill and needed her father to help out with their international clients. But now that they were driving to the James's house, Sam wished she'd paid better attention during her father's initial conversation about Henry's health.

It's not that Sam was heartless; she just didn't remember what exactly was wrong with Henry. When her father had first mentioned going to Ireland to help take the reins while Henry recovered, Sam thought he meant only he was going. And maybe he had at first, but somehow, taking the reins for a while turned into a permanent move, leading Sam to think things must be pretty bad for Henry.

As they escaped the congested traffic of Dublin and headed out to the rolling green countryside, Sam tried to piece together what she remembered of Henry and his family. She remembered they lived in a cute stone cottage in the middle of nowhere. She remembered his wife had blonde hair and her name was Gretta or Gretchen—*something with a G.* She sort of remembered a pretty flower garden she used to chase butterflies in. But the only thing Sam remembered perfectly was Devon.

She shook thoughts of him from her head as they drove up to a sprawling stone mansion. Perhaps her eight-year-old mind didn't quite remember things accurately. The James's house looked like a castle!

"Is this where they've always lived?" Sam asked as they were buzzed through the massive iron gates.

"No, they moved about four years ago, when the business really took off."

"Oh. So the tech biz is big in Ireland?"

"It's big everywhere, Sam," he replied giving her a weathered look.

Her father hated that Sam wanted nothing to do with the business he'd built from the ground up. The truth was, she didn't really get what he did. She knew he built software, but beyond that, her eyes glazed over whenever he started talking tech. She didn't really know what she wanted to do, but tech wasn't it. It seemed boring. All she ever saw him do was stare at his laptop and yell on the phone. Neither of which appealed to her. She changed the subject. "Our house in Boston sure didn't look like this."

Her father laughed. "They don't make houses like this in downtown Boston."

"What about here? Do we get a McMansion, too?"

"No, I'm afraid not. I just rented something close by. It's cozy, but it's just the right size for the two of us."

"Isn't it just the three of them?" Sam asked staring at the massive stone fortress in front of her. It was larger than her old school—and Stanton Prep was nothing to scoff at.

"No, I told you Henry and Gretta got divorced. He remarried and has three more children now. They needed a little more space."

"I'd say. This place is ridiculous."

"Sam, please don't be rude."

"Sorry. What's Henry's new wife's name again?" she asked trying to focus.

"Cara. She has twin girls, Tallulah and Isabella. And a son, Charles."

None of this sounded familiar. Maybe Sam had thought ignoring everything pertaining to Ireland would make it seem less real. "Right," she said. Her chest squeezed anxiously. Ireland certainly seemed real now. Sam gave herself a mental pep talk. *Well, I'm here. Might as well put my plan into action.*

"What about Devon?" she asked as her father parked and a butler-looking man approached their car. "Does he still live with Henry?"

"Yes. He'll be taking over his father's position in the company. I'll be working with him as much as his schedule allows, so you'll probably see him around a lot."

Perfect. Well, almost. It would be perfect once Devon won her a ticket back to Boston.

Devon

When Devon saw the small white BMW rolling up the drive to his house, he nearly choked. *She was here.* Sam Connors was finally here! He'd dreamt about this day for so long, he had to pinch himself to be sure it was real. "Of course it's real, ya arse," he muttered to himself.

When Devon's father told him that Thomas and Sam would be arriving today, Devon had immediately grabbed his dog, Eggsy, and gone out for a run. He would've gone crazy waiting around the house with his thoughts racing circles in his head.

Ever since Devon had kissed Sam, nine years ago, she'd become this unattainable creature that he pined for. It was quite ridiculous, really. Sam probably didn't even remember him. But that didn't change the fact that he'd been in love with her. Sure it was eight-year-old-boy-love, which manifested as bullying and name-calling, but still, he couldn't get her out of his head.

The day Devon found out Sam was moving to America had been the worst day of his life. He'd gotten some idea into his mind that if he kissed her, she'd stay—like life was some big fucking fairytale. *Christ, what a wanker.*

Of course it didn't work out. She cried and shoved him away and that was that. He'd never seen Sam again. *Well sorta.* He of course kept tabs on her through Facebook and such. It's not like he was stalking her. *He wasn't some creepy git.* But she was his first kiss—*it's something a boy holds on to.*

Or at least he did for a while. But the past few years, Devon had been so busy with school and football that he didn't have time to think about Sam. He didn't have time to think about anything. *Okay, well that might be a wee bit of an exaggeration.* It was mostly the partying and girls that kept Devon busy. But come on, he was a strapping young lad. A footballer. Devon was striker for Eddington's football club and that combined with his father's social stature basically made Devon the drug of choice among the Eddington girls. And damn him if they weren't his kryptonite. *Or they were.*

Things had changed over the summer when Devon's father got sick. He'd been diagnosed with a cancerous brain tumor—the fast growing kind. Not that Devon knew if there were any other kinds, which was surprising, because he knew way more than he'd ever wanted to about cancer. But ultimately, the only important thing to know was that his father's cancer was *incurable.* That one tiny word changed Devon's world.

Now, at seventeen, Devon was being pressured to take over his father's role in the massive tech business he ran with Thomas Connors. Never mind what Devon wanted—*which was go to uni for environmental studies, by-the-by.* Tech was now his future. And everyone was pushing him so hard toward it that Devon hadn't even been able to attend summer football club with his mates. And worse still, he'd been forced to give up his spot on the team a few weeks ago.

It pissed him off. But pretty much everything pissed Devon off these days. He was mad that his father was dying. He was mad that there was nothing he could do to stop it. He was mad that everyone was counting on him. He was mad that no one had ever stopped to ask him what he wanted. Not even his girlfriend, Sophie. *Well, ex-girlfriend, actually.*

Sophie was another thing Devon had lost because of his father's cancer. She wasn't too pleased with the prospects of being attached to a bloke who wouldn't be starring on the football pitch this season. Sophie was a total jersey chaser. *But damn, what a ride.* Sophie was smokin' hot. Devon had felt like a million bucks whenever he had Sophie on his arm. But other than physical chemistry, they didn't really have much in common. So Devon wasn't that broken up about it when she dumped him. Especially when he heard Sam was moving back to Ireland.

Devon felt like fate was finally noticing he'd been dealt a raw hand lately and decided to bring a ray of hope back into his life. When Devon found out Sam was coming home, all those old feelings he had for her returned. And now that Sam was actually here, he didn't know what to do. It was like someone had opened a window in his chest and he couldn't catch his breath.

"Eggsy!" Devon called. "Come on, boy!"

His beloved wolfhound came bounding over. Eggsy was barely two and he was already larger than all the other hounds in the kennel. He had salt and pepper fur with a white chest and belly, and Devon spoiled him rotten. He even let Eggsy sleep in bed with him—something his stepmother hated—which was half the reason Devon did it. The other half was he really did love the lanky mutt. Ever since his step-monster, Cara, and her spawns, had started taking over, Devon felt withdrawn. It was like he wasn't even part of his own family anymore. But Eggsy was his one reprieve.

Devon let the giant dog jump up on him, catching his massive paws on his chest while he ruffled Eggsy's mottled gray fur. "Are you ready to go meet the love of my life?"

CHAPTER
3

Sam

Cara James greeted them warmly after another butler-looking fellow escorted Sam and her father to the *salon*. *Ugh!* Sam forgot how much she hated all the pretentious names for everything in Ireland. Why couldn't they just call it ostentatious room number 1 or 2 or 3? *We get it, you're rich!*

It's not that Sam was poor by any means, but for some reason she always hated it when people flaunted their money. She'd only met Cara for two seconds and Sam could already tell Cara was one of *those* people. Sam was good at spotting pretentiousness. Probably because she'd spent the last few years attending Stanton Prep, Boston's most elite prep school. Everyone who attended basically oozed money. The problem was, there were always the few who didn't, and Sam hated how her classmates ostracized them—not that she ever did anything about it. She wasn't crazy. Sticking up for the less fortunate at Stanton would land her outsider status faster than a faux Prada handbag.

But there was no hiding from the wealth in a place like this. The James's home leaked opulence. It made Rockefeller look like a hack. Sam suddenly wondered if good old Henry was holding out on her father. The thought made her queasy.

"Thomas! It's so good to see you," Cara hailed. "And this must be your lovely daughter, Samantha. Hello, darling."

Darling? Cara wasn't old enough to be calling anyone darling. "Hello," Sam replied, trying to keep her face neutral. She was shocked by how young Cara was. She looked like she was still in her twenties! *Can you say trophy wife?*

A few feet away from Cara, Sam spotted two identical little toe-headed girls playing politely with a tea set—*Tallulah and Isabella.* Next to them, was a baby sleeping in a bassinet—*Charles.*

Sam had been expecting Henry's children to be closer to her own age. Her palms started sweating. She wasn't good with little kids. She didn't really like them. They were always sticky and unpredictable. *Her father better not expect her to babysit while he was meeting with Henry!*

Right then a cheery-faced servant strolled in, silently scooping up the baby and escorting the twins from the room. Of course Sam wouldn't have to babysit. *What was she thinking?* This place probably had enough servants that you didn't even have to wipe your own ass.

For the umpteenth time, Sam found herself wishing Megan was with her. She'd probably be singing *Be Our Guest* from the library ladder by now—*assuming this place had a massive library.* The house looked like it could be the castle from Beauty and the Beast. There were even old china cabinets and tapestries—there had to be a dusty old library hidden somewhere.

"I'm afraid Henry's not well today," Cara started. But just then the doors to the salon opened and a ghostly man wobbled in. "Henry!" Cara cooed, rushing to his side. "What are you doing out of bed, darling?"

"My best mate flies all the way from the states to see me? The least I can do is get my sorry arse outta bed to greet him."

"Henry!" her father boomed, crossing the room to hug the thin man.

If everyone hadn't been saying his name, Sam never would have recognized him as Henry James. The Henry she remembered was built like a rugby player, with a thick head of brown hair and a dark mustache. He had a boisterous laugh, a big belly and wore ridiculously colorful suits. This man was pale and gray. He had no hair and he looked like he weighed as much as his petite twenty-year old wife!

"Henry, I really must insist you lie down. The doctor—"

"Pish! I know what the doctor says, dear. But keeping my spirits up is just as important." Henry gave her father a conspiratorial grin she recognized before turning his attention to her. "No!" Henry squawked. "This can't be little Sam?"

"I'm afraid so," her father confirmed.

"Good Christ! I remember her and Devon in diapers. It seems like yesterday. What did he used to call you?" Henry asked.

Spam! Spam! Spam! "No idea," Sam mused. "But it's good to see you again, Henry."

"Oh, it's Uncle Henry to you," he wheezed pulling Sam into a feeble hug.

"Well, now that we're all acquainted. I really must insist

you lie down, darling," Cara begged.

"Yes, fine dear, but only if I can bring Thomas with me. We have much to discuss."

"Yes, that's fine," Cara conceded. "But please try not to exhaust yourself."

"To the bat cave," Henry proclaimed.

Sam's father smiled and started humming the theme song to Batman. She forgot how silly her father was when he was with Henry. It seemed he'd left that part of himself in Ireland. And now that he'd returned, it was back, like nothing had changed.

But everything had. Seeing Henry made Sam's stomach knot up. *Cancer.* Henry had cancer. She remembered now. *How could she ever forget?* Cancer had stolen her mother too. She had the same gaunt gray skin in the end. And the same sickly sweet smell—like funeral flowers.

What about me? Sam wanted to scream as she watched her father walk away leaving her alone with Cara. But that seemed like such a childish thing to say. Being back in Ireland made her feel so young and uncertain again, and she hated it.

Instead of chasing after her father like she wanted to, Sam turned to Cara and smiled. "Would it be all right to check my email while they catch up?"

"Of course," Cara replied. "Thorton, please take Miss Connors to the study and set her up with Wi-Fi."

"Right away, madam." A third identical butler-looking man had appeared. He seemed to have materialized from thin air, making Sam jump. She would never get used to that. Maybe it was a good thing her father hadn't found them their own little McMansion. It seemed they came with McButlers and Sam hated having people sneak up on her.

Devon

Devon snuck Eggsy in the back entrance to the house after hosing him off in the stables. He hated feeling like he was sneaking about in his own home, but Cara would be murderous if she caught a wet dog inside her house. It was ridiculous how she presided over the place. It was bad enough that she demanded Devon's father buy the palatial home, but she ran it like she thought she was some kind of royalty. They had more staff than occupants. And Devon was always afraid one of them would rat him out for keeping Eggsy in his room. But so far they hadn't. *Maybe they disliked Cara as much as Devon did.*

Cara O'Leary was twenty-four years old. It would be more appropriate for Devon to be dating her than his father. But that hadn't stopped Cara. She had Henry James pegged from the beginning and got herself knocked up with twins before he had a chance to wise up. And now she'd just had his third child—who she grotesquely referred to as his *last* child, since she was just waiting for him to die so she could inherit his fortune.

Devon hated Cara. But mostly, he hated himself. Because it was his fault Cara ever met his father. Devon tried to drive the unsettling thoughts from his mind when he reached his room. He undressed and jumped into the shower. He needed to concentrate on better things, like Sam.

CHAPTER
4

Sam

Sam followed Thorton to the study, which turned out to be a massive Beauty and the Beast-worthy library. She pulled her laptop out of her shoulder bag and connected to the Wi-Fi. As soon as she was online a message pinged. It was Megan.

MEG-lomania: R U IRISH YET?
Sam-I-am: dork
MEG-lomania: WHERE R U?
Sam-I-am: Belle's library
MEG-lomania: FOR REAL?
Sam-I-am: no! But seriously you should see this place. It looks like Hogwarts.

Sam's computer screen was suddenly filled with Megan's goofy face as her video chat request came through. Sam rolled her eyes but accepted the chat.

"You're killing me! You can't say Hogwarts and not show me. And stop mixing fandoms. You know it makes me crazy. Only Emma Watson can pull off Disney and Potter." Megan spoke in rapid-fire like always and Sam's eyes teared up.

"Where are you for real?" Megan asked.

"At my dad's business partner's house."

"Ooo, let me see."

Sam picked up her laptop to give Megan a 360-degree view of the breathtaking library. She could hear Megan squealing a world away.

"Oh my God! I hate you so much right now, Sam. I would kill to be there."

"Calm down. It's just a bunch of dusty old books."

"I'm gonna pretend you didn't say that. Anyway, how's everything else?"

"Fine, I guess."

"Where's Devon?"

"I dunno. Haven't seen him yet."

"I bet he got hot!"

"Give it a rest. We're supposed to be focused on getting me back to Boston, not boys. Besides, if this place is any indication, he's probably an even bigger pain in the ass than I remember."

"Who's a pain in the arse?" a smooth male voice interrupted.

Sam whipped around and her heart fell into her guts as she locked eyes with the most gorgeous human that ever walked the earth.

"Hello, Sam," he purred.

"Devon?" There was no way this gorgeous specimen of

man was Devon. *Right? Right!*

I mean, it was genetically impossible for someone who used to look like a buck-toothed weasel as an eight-year-old to now look like . . . like . . . this. Sam had no words for this level of hotness. But the boy—*no, strike that*—the man in front of her was nodding his head confirming his identity. And even though there was nothing remaining that resembled the Devon she remembered, there was a familiar twinkle in his gray eyes.

Sam blinked waiting for her brain to catch up to the masterpiece she was viewing. The dark-haired boy standing in the library now had to be at least 6'3" and he was easily the most beautiful person Sam had ever laid eyes on. And the way he was smiling at her. *No, smiling was too simple a word.* This boy's smile was scandalous—offensive even. It devoured his face and it was gobbling her up with it. She had to look away.

"Sorry, Meg, gotta go."

"Wait!"

Sam heard Megan's squeals of protest but slammed her laptop shut anyway, turning back to face the Irish god who was striding toward her—still swallowing her whole with his sinful smile. *How was it fair for someone to have a smile like that, when they had everything else too?*

This new and improved Devon had cheekbones that would make a supermodel cry, and the bushy eyebrows she remembered now looked like tailored shutters framing the most beautiful gray eyes she'd ever seen. And that smile . . . *Shit!* She couldn't look directly at it. But even looking near it was dangerous. Devon's smile left ripples of dimples on his flawless skin like it was the surface of a lake, and Sam suddenly couldn't remember how to swim.

Devon took her hand giving it a single shake before pulling Sam into an all-consuming hug. "It's so good to see you again, Sam," he said into her day-old hair making her feel faint.

She couldn't even speak if she wanted to. Her face was mashed into his soft blue sweater that stretched across his broad chest. When he finally released her she stumbled back, acutely aware that she was wearing eight-hour old leggings, Uggs, an oversized t-shirt and a wrinkled gray zip-up hoodie. *Not her best look.* She probably still smelled like the Pringles she ate on the plane, too. And he smelled like . . . like heaven. *Shit!*

Shit, shit, shit! It was the only thought running through Sam's head. This was *not* how she wanted to meet Devon again for the first time. She wanted to dress cute and make him regret ever calling her names. *She* wanted to be the one who looked hot. Sam could be hot when she wanted to. She knew she had a great figure. She played soccer. And when she and Megan got all girl'd up to go out, Sam could really pull off hot. But right now, the only thing Sam was pulling off was *Jersey Shore.*

How embarrassing!

Why the hell hadn't her father told her they were coming to Henry's house straight from the airport? Then, a ghost of a conversation came back to her. He did tell her they were coming here. She just hadn't paid attention. Apparently, she had a mental block for anything pertaining to Ireland. She needed to get it together. Sticking her head in the sand wasn't doing her any favors. All it did was strand her in Uggs.

Devon finally released Sam from his bone-crushing hug and held her out at arms length. "Look at ya!" he exclaimed, squeezing her fit arms. "You're not one of those anorexic American girls at all, eh?"

Yep! Definitely Devon. And apparently, he was still the same jerk she remembered from childhood, but now with a more adult repertoire of insults—*great!*

Sam wriggled out of his grasp, and mumbled. "Thanks, I guess."

"So anyway," Devon continued running his hands through his McDreamy hair. "I hope you don't hold all that childhood rubbish against me. They were only pranks," he said grinning again.

Spam, he'd called me Spam! There, that seemed to work. Sam wasn't blinded by his good looks anymore. Every time she thought *Spam*, she could picture Devon as the eight-year-old who called her that.

"God! Put that thing away, will you? It's blinding," Sam said, shoving her laptop back into her bag.

"Pardon?"

"Your smile! It's ridiculous."

Devon laughed.

His laugh was still the same.

"Good to see you're still as charming as ever, Sam."

"It's Samantha now," she said.

That was a total lie. Her father and Megan still called her Sam. And so did pretty much everyone she'd ever played sports with. But she'd started filling out college applications last year as Samantha and she sort of liked the way it felt—*older and more sophisticated. Exactly the way she wanted Devon to see her.*

Devon shrugged. "I've always liked, Sam. Anyway, my father sent me to see if you wanted company. It looks like they're going to be a while."

"I don't need a babysitter," she replied, laying on the snark.

"I was thinking more of a field trip?" He smiled again, holding up a set of keys.

Damn it! That smile was going to be the death of her. But it could just be her ticket back to Boston if she played her cards right.

"You hungry?" Devon asked.

Sam flashed a grin of her own. "Famished."

Devon

Really? 'Anorexic American girl?' Why the hell had he said that?

Blimey! Devon had basically just called Sam fat, in a total backhanded way. He blamed Sophie. When they were dating Devon spent way too much time watching those mind-rotting gossipy shows with her where the girls were all fake nice to each other and said passive aggressive things. The damn shows must have rubbed off on him. Or maybe it was just that Sam made him so nervous.

Devon should have thought through what he was going to say when he saw her. He basically had. He was going to keep it simple. 'Good to see you.' 'You look grand.' 'I've missed you." That sort of thing. But Devon had been so stunned by how beautiful and real Sam was, that words just sort of fell out of his mouth. *Stupid words.*

Christ. Who waits nine years for another shot at a girl and blows it in one sentence? *This wanker, that's who.*

Everything about Sam was just like he remembered it,

yet better somehow. She wasn't like all the other girls he knew. She didn't hide behind caked makeup or have bottled blonde hair. Sam was raw and refreshing, just like he knew she'd be.

Well there wasn't much to do now but try to move forward. At least she'd agreed to go get something to eat with him. He'd just have to win her over with dinner.

CHAPTER
5

Sam

"So where do ya wanna go?" Devon asked once they were buckled in his shiny black Land Rover Defender.

"How should I know? I haven't been to Ireland in nine years."

"Well, not much has changed," Devon replied.

Yeah, right! Did the boy not own a mirror? "That still doesn't help," she quipped. "Nothing's like I remember it."

He raised his eyebrows like he didn't believe her.

"What?"

"Come on, don't tell me you forgot about me? I never forgot you."

"Oh, spare me. Just take me to get some food, okay?"

Devon laughed. "Yep, that's the attitude I remember."

They drove in awkward silence for about ten minutes or so until they came to the small town of Dalkey. It looked sort of familiar to Sam, but then again, everything in Ireland looked sort of the same—cobblestone streets, window boxes full of petunias and ancient looking buildings. Devon parked outside a sleepy pub called Finnegan's. He came around to open the door for her, but she was already on the street, shooting him a dirty look. "This isn't a date," she said.

"Of course not, but I still have manners."

She snorted. "Then I'd say a lot *has* changed around here."

Devon trailed behind Sam as she pushed her way into the pub. She was momentarily overpowered by its woody-ness. Everything inside seemed to be the same shade of polished wood—the bar, the paneling, the barstools, the floor, even most of the tables. Sam grabbed a small table near the window with a green marble top. She hated dark colors. They made her feel boxed in. Her old house in Boston was modern and all the walls were white. *God, she missed Boston.*

Devon joined her, pulling off his blue sweater before he sat down. The hem of his t-shirt lifted, flashing the bare skin of his perfect abs. Sam bit her lip and stared out the window. *Spam,* she repeated in her head until Devon's eight-year-old image returned. *Why did he have to be so gorgeous now?* It was making it impossible for her to scheme.

Devon finally sat down and handed her a menu. "The cottage pie is amazing. Or if we're lucky they might have Guinness stew."

"How about just Guinness?" She smirked.

Devon's dark eyebrows shot up, followed by a grin. "Two pints it is." Then he disappeared toward the bar.

Sam wasn't a big drinker. Especially beer. Appletini's were her favorite. *Or at least they had been*—for about three hours until they turned on her and decided her stomach wasn't inhabitable. That had been the one and only time Sam ever got wasted. She'd been out with Megan at a party last year and they both drank way too much. Megan ended up having sex with a much older boy, while Sam puked her guts up in the bathroom. Which, thinking about it now, was probably the only reason Sam hadn't given it up to Ryan that night. *Saved by the Appletini.* Both girls did the walk of shame home the next morning. When they got back to Megan's house, they decided to never get that drunk again.

But, in order for Sam's back-to-Boston plan to work she needed to get drunk, or at least make Devon think she was.

Devon

"Who's the lucky lass?" the bartender asked jutting his chin over Devon's shoulder.

Pete was tending bar tonight. He was one of Devon's father's old fishing buddies. Devon tried to shrug off answering, but Pete was like a bloodhound. Plus, it didn't help that Devon's cheeks were probably turning on him. His face always flushed color when he was nervous.

"Oh, come on. She must be somebody," Pete pressed.

Devon slapped a few euros on the counter and grabbed the pints, but Pete didn't let go. "If you don't tell me, I guess I'll just have ta go over and card 'er me self."

Devon paled. "Christ, Pete. If ya must know, it's Sam Connors."

"No! Thomas and Elizabeth's daughter? It's can't be!"

"It is. Now don't make a big deal about this."

Pete gave a raspy laugh. "Yer still in love wit her like the day ya was born."

Devon leveled his eyes with Pete and scowled. Pete got the hint. He was still laughing but he took his hands off the pints and backed away with them in the air.

Devon loosed a breath as he weaved his way slowly to the table trying not to spill the pints. It was nearly sundown and the bar was starting to fill up. He didn't like the idea of his first date with Sam being at Finnegan's. But it was pretty much the only pub worth visiting in Dalkey—*which was half the problem.* He didn't want to run into any of his mates while he was with her just yet. They'd rib him way worse than Ol' Pete. Devon glanced at the clock—*plenty of time.* The boys didn't usually come out until after the dinner crowd left.

He turned his attention back to Sam. She was gazing out the window, the last glow of summer sun casting a golden glow over her. She looked like a painting. And if possible, she was even more beautiful than he remembered. Her clothes were a bit grungy, *but who knew what passed as keen in Boston?* That kind of thing never mattered to Devon anyway. It was Sam's spirit that drew him in. She was always so feisty and sure of herself. None of the girls at Eddington were like that. All they cared about were appearances.

Devon set the pints down on the table. "Guinness for the lady."

"Thanks." Sam offered him a big smile and held up her glass. "Cheers."

"Sláinte," Devon said, clinking glasses.

He watched her take three big gulps. *Shite!* He didn't know it was a chugging contest. He took a few more swigs himself and put the beer down shaking his head.

"What?" Sam scoffed. "Don't Irish women drink?"

"You *are* an Irish woman, ya know?"

She laughed. "Just because I was born here doesn't make me Irish."

"That's exactly what it makes you," Devon argued.

"I barely remember this place."

"Well, it remembers you."

"What's that supposed to mean?"

"Nothing," Devon said taking another swig of his pint.

Sam raised her glass and drained it. "How 'bout another round?"

"Don't you think you should pace yourself? And maybe order some dinner?"

"Look, Devon, I'm not eight-years-old anymore. You can't bully me. If I want another drink, I'll have another drink."

She was on her feet, swiveling her hips toward the bar. He chased after her, touching her elbow when he caught up. "Sam."

She jerked her arm away and signaled to Pete. "I'll have an Irish whiskey, please."

He chuckled. "You're in Ireland lass, we only serve Irish whiskey. Which one do ya want?"

Devon watched Sam's cheeks flush and had the sudden urge to pull her into his arms. *Christ! He needed to get ahold of himself.*

"Oh. Um, I'll have Jameson, please," Sam said, recovering her composure.

"Make that two, Pete," Devon called over Sam's shoulder.

She turned and scowled at him.

"Make mine a double," Sam called. "And I'll have another pint too."

Shite! He couldn't let her drink him under the table. "Me too," Devon added.

Pete just shook his head and served up the drinks. Sam drained her shot without even glancing at Devon. He reached past her to pay and did his shot by himself while Sam marched back to their table.

Devon followed her back and sat down. He took a deep breath and tried to meet Sam's icy glare. "Is that what you think of me?" he asked, his heart in his throat. "Some big bully?"

Sam studied him with her blue-green eyes. Devon felt like an airplane losing cabin pressure when she looked directly at him. Everything he'd tried to keep bottled up just wanted out. "I'm not that guy anymore, Sam. But you're right. I shouldn't pretend to know you. It's been a long time. It's just . . . I thought we used to be friends. And I could really use a friend right now."

Sam

Sam caught her heart skipping a beat as she stared at Devon's beautiful features. His face was crumpling and he seemed genuinely upset that she wasn't all chummy with him. *But what had he expected?* She hadn't seen or heard from him in nine years. Just because he'd turned into the most beautiful man in Ireland didn't excuse his Neanderthal behavior when he was a kid.

But still, it caught her off guard to see that he cared what she thought about him at all. I mean a guy that looked like this in Boston wouldn't give a crap what she said to him in a bar. Scratch that. She couldn't get into any bars in Boston.

One point for Ireland—where the drinking age is eighteen and you never get carded if you look at least sixteen!

"We're friends," she finally said.

"We are?"

Devon's face lit up and she had to fight the urge to cup his chiseled cheeks. *Spam! He called you Spam and stole your first kiss! Do not feel bad for him.* Besides he probably does this with all the girls. *You can do this. Devon is your ticket back to Boston!* Sam cleared her throat. "Yeah. I mean it's not like I know anyone else here. I'm willing to put the past behind us."

"Great!"

"But, we really should remedy the whole not-knowing-each-other thing," she added coyly.

"What do you have in mind?"

"Have you ever played, never-have-I-ever?"

He laughed. "Of course."

"Good." Sam waved to get the bartender's attention. "Another round."

CHAPTER
6

Sam

Maybe Sam's idea to get wasted on her first night out wasn't such a good one. It certainly wasn't going as planned. She was just supposed to *pretend* to be drunk, so when Devon brought her home she could show her father what a bad influence he was.

Look, Dad. First night in Ireland and your bestie's son gets your perfect daughter wasted. This kind of thing would never happen in Boston.

The problem was, Sam *was* a bit drunk. But the bigger problem was that Devon was *way* drunker. He was really bad at never-have-I-ever. Sam had totally been cheating, but still. For looking like an Irish heartthrob, it seemed like Devon really wasn't much of a bad boy. He had the typical drunken teenager stories, but he refused to talk about girlfriends or sex. *What a prude!*

Maybe he was still a virgin? *Nah, no one looks like that and holds onto their v-card this long.*

Maybe he was gay? *Nah, she wasn't getting that vibe from him.*

The drunker he got the more handsy he got. And he kept staring at her like the answer to the universe was hidden just inside her eyes.

Conning Devon was going to be even easier than she thought. She could probably get him to sleep with her and then tell her father he'd forced her. That would get her on the first flight back to Boston! But maybe not tonight. Devon seemed a little too drunk to get the job done. Plus, he was morphing from flirty-drunk to gloomy-drunk.

"Ya know? I'm really glad you're here, Sam. Things with my dad . . . it's not good. I know he doesn't have much time left." Devon sniffled and took another drink. "I don't know how you did it, Sam. Losing your mom . . . how did you survive it?"

Shit. It was time to cut him off.

"I don't think I can survive this," Devon continued, staring into his drink.

"You'd be surprised what you can survive," she said. "But come on. Let's not start mourning anyone just yet," she said taking another sip of her coke.

They'd switched to rum and coke a few rounds ago and Sam kept getting hers sans rum. She expected Devon to notice, but the pub was bonkers. It had turned from a normal restaurant atmosphere to a drunken zoo as soon as it got dark. There were burly men in soccer jerseys chanting fight songs and drunken women, talking and laughing too loudly. It was probably time to go. Sam looked at her phone to check the time. It was dead—but to be fair she hadn't charged it since she left Boston.

Boston. Just thinking the word sent pain lancing through her. She looked over at Devon. He was now back to flirty-drunk, smirking at her adoringly. She'd done enough damage for tonight. "Come on, Casanova. Let's pay our tab."

Devon looked confused. "Who? Why? We're just starting to have fun."

"I think you might have had a bit too much fun," she said helping him up from his chair. She dragged him toward the crowded bar to pay. Devon kept a hold on her hand and when they got close enough to the bar to pay, he was smashed right up behind her.

Sam hated how much she liked the way Devon felt pressed against her. He paid their tab and while they waited for change, he looped a hand possessively around her waist. She nearly had a stroke when he hooked a thumb inside the waistband of her leggings. It was an intimate gesture. Something a boyfriend would do, not a boy you hadn't seen in nine years. *But God, was it hot!*

Devon finally removed his hand when the bartender gave him his change. Sam was already slipping from his grasp, anxious to get out to the street where there was more space and less Devon. He staggered a bit and she had to put her shoulder under his arm to steady him as they moved through the crowd. They were almost to the door, but Devon didn't seem in any rush to leave. He was saying goodbye to everyone they passed and when Sam reached for the door, she let go of him. He almost toppled over and she had to lunge back to grab him, wrapping her arms around his waist to keep him from going down. And of course, Devon took that as an invitation to pull Sam into another bone-crunching hug.

"Christ, I'm so glad you came home, Sam."

"Yep," she said trying to pry herself loose. "Me too." She had experience with drunk people—okay, mostly just drunk Megan—but Sam knew being agreeable was usually the best plan of attack.

Devon loosened his grip so he could look down at her. He really had to look down too because the top of her head only came to his chin. It hurt her neck to look up at him.

"I really missed you, Sam," he said dreamily.

"Yep, I missed you too. Now let's go," she said trying to pull him out the door. But Devon pulled back and before she knew it, she was locked in his arms, her feet dangling inches from the sticky wood floor. She tried to say something in protest, but her face was so incredibly close to his, she worried if she opened her mouth they'd be kissing.

Devon nuzzled her cheek with his nose. He smelled like a distillery.

"I don't think you understand, Sam," he whispered. "I really missed you. Like for the past nine years, missed you."

Her breath caught in her throat again, and all her devious plans vanished. All she knew was that she needed to get out of Devon's arms or soon she *would* be kissing him—and from the looks of his perfect lips—enjoying it. *Down girl!*

God, she'd never wished for a bucket of ice water so badly.

"Devon," she started. But he nuzzled her lips with his nose. And that was dangerous territory, because his lips were right under his nose—his perfect, beautiful, delicious lips. And then, they were on her lips.

Shit! Stop!

No, wait. *Don't stop. Don't ever stop.*

If kissing were an Olympic sport, Devon would be a gold medalist. No, he'd be Michael Phelps. Yes, Devon was definitely the Michael Phelps of kissing. His tongue swept hers slowly at first, but then his strokes increased. Sam wrapped her hands around Devon's strong neck, hanging on for dear life as he swam for the finish line in her mouth.

Good God! No wonder Devon hadn't said anything about his past girlfriends. They were probably all deceased if he could kiss like this. *Died of spontaneous combustion.* Sam was pretty sure her panties were on fire at the moment. She was just waiting for the rest of her to go up in flames as she curled her fingers in his perfect brown hair when a splash of something cold hit her in the face.

Not now!

Of all the times for her stupid wishes to come true . . . Sam and Devon broke apart, which pretty much meant she stumbled to the floor trying to catch her breath and balance all at the same time, while wiping at the contents of whatever beverage had just been dumped on her—*it didn't taste like water . . . more like vodka.*

"Are you fucking kidding me?" a shrill female voice demanded.

Sam regained her composure and followed the voice. It belonged to a petite blonde that looked like she'd just walked out of a Ralph Lauren ad. She was holding an empty glass and glaring at Devon.

"Sophie?" Devon looked like he was just waking up from a nightmare.

"Still snogging anything with tits, I see," she added with a scathing sneer.

"It's not any of your business who I snog. You broke up with me, remember?"

"Best decision of her life," said the handsome thick-necked man that walked up behind Sophie. He put his hands around her waist and promptly shoved his tongue down her throat.

Watching them kiss wasn't pretty, but it must have been offensive to Devon, because he paled three shades and then a red flush crept from the back of his neck to the hollows of his cheeks. His mouth hung open for a moment before he tried to form a sentence. But it just came out as jumbled sounds. He looked like a fish gulping for air. The anguish twisting his perfect features was agonizing to watch. Sam didn't really know what was going on, but she couldn't help but feel bad for Devon, because it seemed to be crippling him. Her instincts told her to pull him away from the couple who were still going at it. *Damn, was kissing an Olympic sport in Ireland?*

Thankfully, Devon followed Sam's gentle tugging and let her lead him out of the bar.

"Good seeing, ya Dev!" the thick-neck boy called after them.

Sam looked back to see the couple had finally stopped kissing. The blonde girl was sneering at Devon and finger-waving patronizingly, while thick-neck laughed. Sam didn't know who the hell they were to Devon, but she instantly knew them. They were the popular kids—*mean girls and jock gods*—and their language was universal. Sam would recognize it anywhere. *How could she not?* She was one of them. Or at least she used to be at her old school. It seemed all bets were off here if that's how they treated a guy that looked like Devon.

Sophie

Sophie McKenna stared after Devon and the scrubby looking brunette she'd caught him snogging. After Sophie watched them get into Devon's car, she whirled on her boyfriend, Zander. "Who the hell was that twit with Devon?"

"Samantha Connors, I think. She's his friend from the states. She'll be joining us at Eddington this year."

"How do you know that?"

"Her father is Henry's business partner. Henry asked him to come help run the company and get Devon up to speed. He's supposed to be brilliant. I'd love to pick his brain about Cor-Tec and—"

"Oh shut up, Zander! I hate when you blither on. I thought we agreed no geek talk. I'm not dating you for your brain."

"Right," Zander grumbled.

"What else do you know about *Samantha?*" Sophie asked, hissing the other girl's name like it was a dirty word.

"Not much. She was born here, but moved to the states, Boston I think, after her mum died. And now she's back."

"How do you know all this?"

Zander laughed. "Devon never shuts up about her. He used to have a crush on her when she lived here. And I'd say he still does."

Sophie felt her temper flaring. *Stupid prat.* Zander should have led with that! It was all she needed to hear to make up her mind. There was no way Sophie was going to let some American twit dressed like a rehab-reality star get in the way of her plan.

She could feel Zander frowning at the back of her head. "What?" Sophie spat, not even turning to look at him.

"Is Samantha a problem for you?"

Sophie laughed. "Girls like *that* are never a problem for me."

Devon

"Friends of yours?" Sam asked when they were outside.

"Used to be," he mumbled.

"Do they go to Eddington?"

He nodded.

"Great." Sam groaned. "Is everyone at Eddington so welcoming?"

Devon scrubbed his face in frustration. Seeing his ex-girlfriend snogging his ex-mate had made him queasy. "I don't wanna talk about it, Sam. Can we just get out of here, please?"

"Sure."

"I don't think I should drive," Devon said, once they'd crossed the street. He stood outside his Defender with his hand on the back of his neck. He felt like a total wanker asking her to drive, but the last thing he wanted to do was endanger her by getting behind the wheel after drinking too much. He'd put her through enough tonight.

Sam looked at him like she was just figuring out he was drunk. He tossed her the keys. "You drive."

"What? No! I can't."

"Sam, I'm not kidding. I'm not gonna drive you home like this."

"Well, I can't either," she said trying to hand the keys back.

Devon refused to take them. "I don't know how you managed, but somehow you seem a lot more sober than me, so just drive, okay? I don't want to be here right now."

"I can't!" she yelled. "Just call a cab or something."

Devon huffed a laugh. "Where do ya think ya are? There's no cabs in Dalkey. This isn't Boston."

"Clearly!" she fumed.

"Christ, Sam, why is everything so difficult with you? Just drive us home."

"I can't!" she yelled. "I can't drive! As in, *at all*. I don't have a license." She crossed her arms angrily. "I don't know how to drive, okay?" she said quietly.

Devon didn't know if it was the booze or the shear insanity of the notion, but it took a while for what Sam was saying to sink in. And when it finally did, for some unknown reason, Devon thought it was hilarious. *Okay, he did know why he found it so funny, it was the booze—he'd always been a giddy drunk.* He started shaking with laughter, which must've been the wrong thing to do, because Sam looked like she was going to punch him. She shoved him instead.

"Jesus, just get in, Devon! I'll drive us," she grumbled angrily.

"No way! I'm not letting a half drunk Yank who doesn't know how to drive touch my baby," he said jokingly as he blocked her from getting into his Defender.

He was only half joking. He really did love his car.

Sam huffed defiantly. "I thought I was Irish? *Ireland remembers*, and all that crap," she said, quoting him.

"Yeah, that was before I knew you were still a child."

Sam's eyes widened and then went twitchy. *Wrong thing to say, mate!*

49

"Oh, *I'm* a child? Do you normally go around kissing children? Is that sort of thing acceptable here in Ireland? Because let me tell you, the rest of the world frowns upon it."

Devon ran his hands through his hair. "No, Sam . . . I didn't mean . . ." he blew out an exasperated breath. *How was he going to talk his way out of this one?* "About that kiss . . ."

"Forget it! I don't want to talk about it. Let's just pretend it never happened and figure out how the hell to get home."

"Fine by me," he said.

"Good. So, which way's home?"

Devon watched Sam spin helplessly around looking up and down the street. *Poor thing didn't even know where she was.* Once again he found himself compelled to wrap her up in his arms and never let her go. She was just so damn cute— *too cute for her own good.* Just like he remembered her. She was still the same willowy girl he memorized, yet not. There was more to her now. And all of it was good. The familiar parts, the new parts, the kissing parts.

Shite! He needed to get his mind out of the gutter. He needed to focus on getting out of here before Sophie and Zander came out for round two of layin' boots to him. Devon still couldn't quite believe they were together. It wasn't so much Sophie, but Zander. They'd been mates forever. And that was their one rule. Put a lass before your mate and end up on your arse. Bro-code and all that. But things had been complicated with Zander ever since Devon's father married Zander's sister, Cara. Technically that made Zander, Devon's uncle. It still grossed him out when he thought about it that way.

"Earth to Devon! How are we getting home?" Sam yelled.

"I guess we'll have to walk," Devon replied.

Walking wouldn't be bad. It wasn't that far. Plus, it meant more time with Sam. *Maybe more time kissing Sam.*

Sam

"Walk?" Sam frowned. "How far is it?"

Devon shrugged. "Not that far. Maybe five . . . six miles."

Sam looked down at her feet, once again regretting her choice of attire. She was still wearing her Uggs—not exactly long distance walking shoes. Plus, she felt dumb in them. They were cool for like a minute. And not even in Sam's lifetime, but she secretly loved them. They were so comfy and warm. They were her official airplane shoes. It's not like she ever dressed up to fly. She wasn't expecting to run into anyone she was trying to impress on an airplane. *Or parade five miles through town in them.* Sam suddenly wished she *was* one of those people who dressed up to fly. She never understood how people wore suits on planes. But now she sorta saw the appeal. Then, at least she wouldn't be in her stupid Uggs.

She scowled at her boots considering her options. *What if she ran into more of Devon's so-called friends?* She didn't want to be cast as a social pariah just because they saw her wearing Uggs.

Sam was popular at her old school in Boston. And Stanton Prep wasn't the easiest place to be part of the in crowd. She wasn't a Golden or anything—those were the crème de la crème at Stanton. You couldn't be a Golden unless you were obscenely rich, famous or blessed by divine birthright. And sometimes that didn't even guarantee you would be a Golden for life. Goldens fell from grace all the time. Sam's mind instantly flashed back to Cody Matthews, a boy a few years older than her at Stanton. He was probably the most famous fallen Golden. She couldn't even imagine dealing with his disaster.

But, anyway, that didn't matter, because Sam wasn't a Golden, she wasn't even at Stanton anymore. But she was still hoping to be popular at her new school, Eddington Academy.

She knew from experience being part of the in crowd made things a lot easier. Sam thought it would be easy to win everyone over at Eddington. She was pretty, played sports, got good grades, and made friends easily. But if the popular crowd at Eddington treated a guy like Devon this bad, Sam was afraid to see what their versions of Goldens were like. With Devon's looks and wealth he would be a reigning monarch at Stanton. Eddington must be a viper's nest if even Devon couldn't survive.

That sealed the deal. She wasn't risking walking through town in her current attire. She didn't want to be referred to as Ugg-girl for the next few months of her miserable life in Ireland. She turned to Devon. "Screw that! It's freezing. I don't want to walk home."

Devon

Sam was right. It was unseasonably cold, but that was pretty much the only temperature Ireland had in the fall—*cold and colder.*

"Here," Devon said shrugging off his sweater and offering it to Sam.

"Thanks."

She stuffed her head through and damn it all to hell if

she didn't look even cuter. Her tiny frame swam in his massive baby blue sweater—*like a kitten wearing clothes or some rubbish.*

"Better?" he asked.

"Yeah, but I'm still not really crazy about walking six miles in these boots."

"Unless you're joking about the whole not-knowing-how-to-drive thing, I don't see what other choice we have."

"I wish I was joking. But, how hard can driving a few miles be? Maybe you could teach me?"

She sounded so optimistic Devon would have said yes to anything. *You'd like a kidney or maybe my liver? Sure thing, kitten. Anything for you.*

⟋♡⟍

Ten minutes later they were both buckled into the Defender and Devon was running through the basics of driving a manual transmission, completely regretting his decision.

"Like this?" Sam asked.

The car lurched forward and stalled.

Shite! This was a bad idea.

She tried again. Grind, lurch, stall. Grind, lurch, stall.

A very bad idea.

People inside the pub were watching and pointing now.

"You're too close to the car in front of you. Put it in reverse," Devon directed.

"Okay." Sam slammed the brakes, grinding to a halt.

Devon winced, putting his arm behind Sam's seat to look over his shoulder so he could guide her. He listened to Sam grinding into reverse and closed his eyes. *His poor baby!*

When Devon opened his eyes he realized entirely too late that they weren't moving backwards—but forward. "Stop!" he bellowed.

Crunch.

"Shite!" Devon yelled, staring at the wreckage in front of them.

"Oh my god!" Sam's hands were covering her face, which was a good thing because half a dozen people came charging out of the bar and they looked murderous.

CHAPTER
7

Sam

It turned out her father had been right to be scared to teach Sam to drive. She was apparently horrible at it. She hadn't even made it out of the parking spot without an accident. The car she hit belonged to one of the bartenders at Finnegan's. She hadn't really hit his little Fiat *that* hard, but the damn thing still folded up like a tin can. And it didn't help that the Defender was basically a tank. It didn't even have a scratch on it. Probably a good thing considering they were stupid expensive.

The bartender—his name was Pete—was actually a pretty good sport about the whole thing once he calmed down. Devon explained it was his fault after basically tossing Sam into the back seat so no one would see it was her who'd been driving. He climbed into the driver's seat and hopped out before she could argue.

"This is all my fault," Devon groaned. "Sam was trying to reason with me, telling me not to drive because I'd had too much to drink. I shoulda listened to her. I'm so sorry, Pete. I'll pay for all the damages. I promise."

Sam didn't know what to say. That clearly wasn't what happened, but she also wasn't eager to pay for the damages to Pete's car. She wanted to be sent back to Boston, but not at the expense of bankrupting her father.

"Shite, Devon. Wait here and I'll drive ya both home."

"No, Pete, you don't have to do that," Devon protested.

"Yes, I do. Or yer Da will have me head. He'll already be mad as a box-a-frogs I let ya get langered in my bar. The least I can do is get ya home safely."

❧

The ride home was awkward and definitely longer than six miles. It made Sam glad she'd vetoed the walking idea— *even though the driving idea had been an epic fail.* The whole uncomfortable car ride back to Devon's was pretty much a nonstop string of Devon apologizing to Pete, who ignored him.

When they finally arrived, Pete dropped them off at the front door, while Devon continued to beg forgiveness.

"Ah, quit yer Olagonin'," Pete yelled. "I remember what it's like to be young. Besides, yer ol' Da and I got into it a lot worse when we was yer age. Henry owes me one. I'll talk to him an' smooth things over for ya, Devon."

"Thanks, Pete. You're a lifesaver."

"Nah," he said waving Devon off. "Just quit being a stook and get yer lass inside before she catches her death."

Sam watched Pete drive off and then followed Devon into the house. To Sam's relief there was no butler to greet them. She glanced at the massive grandfather clock in the foyer—11:30. *Maybe butlers didn't work late?* Speaking of late, her father was going to flip. She'd left with Devon hours ago for a bite to eat. She almost felt a twinge of guilt, but maybe tonight hadn't turned out so bad after all. Returning home late, wearing some drunk guy's sweater after a car accident—her father would have to see that Ireland was already a bad influence on her.

That was if he was even still here. Sam had expected to see her father rush out to greet her, but the house was deadly silent.

"Sam, about tonight," Devon started. "I'm really sorry—"

She cut him off. She wasn't sure if he was going to apologize for the driving, the drinking or the kiss—*most of which had been her fault*—but she wasn't in the mood. She really just wanted to go home, *wherever that was.* "Devon, it's been a long night. Can you just help me find my dad so I can go home?"

He looked at her strangely. "Your father's already asleep."

Sam's eyes widened. "What? He left me here?"

"No, he's asleep here. He sent us both a text. Didn't you get it?"

"No! My phone's been dead since we got to Finnegan's."

Devon fished his phone from his pocket and handed it to her.

Sam's eyes welled as she read through the messages in the group text her father had sent to her and Devon.

Thomas Connors: Don't rush back. Henry and I are on a roll. You kids have fun.

Thomas Connors: Slight complication with our lodging. Standby, Sam.

Thomas Connors: We're going to stay with the James's tonight, Sam. I'll explain in the morning.

Thomas Connors: Off to bed. Cara had the Merlin room made up for you, Sam.

The last text had come through hours ago.

This was unbelievable. Her father just went to bed without even knowing where she was or if she was getting his messages! *How could he do that?* Sam didn't care what he said, the James's weren't *practically* family. They were *practically* strangers! She hadn't seen them in nine years. The least her father could do was have a conversation with her before just putting her up in some stranger's mansion with his handsy son lurking around.

God! Sam wanted to scream. Sometimes her father was so clueless about having a daughter. He didn't know when to worry about things, like leaving her alone with boys. All he worried about was not letting her drive. Her plan to get back to Boston by acting out suddenly seemed hopeless. Sam's father would have to notice her in order for that to work.

She stomped off down the hall, realizing she didn't know where she was going. But she didn't really care. She just wanted to be alone so she could scream and then call Megan and cry about how terrible her life was. She was pretty sure the library was in the direction she was headed and that's where she'd left her laptop.

"Where are you going?" Devon called catching up with her.

"I don't know," she said stopping suddenly and throwing her hands up. "Thanks for telling me about the texts, by the way."

"I thought you got them," Devon said incredulously. "Besides, I didn't see them until the car ride home. I was a little preoccupied at the bar."

"Don't you dare blame tonight on me," she shouted. *Even though it was all her fault.*

"Sam, I'm not. Everything is my fault." He ran his hand through his thick brown hair, pausing at the nape of his neck. "This isn't how I planned for today to go."

"Oh, you had a plan?" she yelled—*not really sure why she was still yelling.* Especially when Devon looked completely defeated. His eyebrows scrunched together in the most adorable way when he was frustrated.

Sam took pity on him. Besides, she was really too exhausted to fight with him right now. All she wanted was a shower and a bed. "Look, can we just forget about tonight. I need to find my laptop and take a shower."

"Yeah, come on. I'll show you to your room."

Devon

Devon led Sam to her bedroom—noting the fact that it was right across the hall from his. He opened the door and turned on the lights for her.

"Shower's in there," he said pointing to the en suite bathroom. "It should be stocked with everything you need."

Sam walked over to the bed, inspecting the shoulder bag that lay on it. She pulled out her laptop, seeming relieved to have located it. Then, she sat down on the bed and kicked off her clunky boots. There was still so much more he wanted to say to her, but everything seemed jumbled in his head. Tonight was already a disaster. He should probably just go to bed and start over in the morning.

"If you need anything, my room's right across the hall," he said turning toward the door.

"Um, wait. What about clothes?" she asked sheepishly. "I have an overnight bag, but I left it in my dad's rental car."

"You'll find everything you need in the dresser," Devon replied robotically.

He wasn't a fan of his stepmother, but he couldn't deny that her hospitality was flawless when it came to entertaining guests.

Sam jumped off the bed and started pulling open drawers like she didn't trust him. She pulled out a pink and white striped silk nightgown—*and not the sexy kind, the old lady kind.*

"I'm not wearing this!"

"Would you rather borrow some of my clothes?" he offered.

She seemed to remember she was wearing his sweater and pulled it off, tossing it back at him. "I want *my* clothes," she whined.

"The staff's all gone home for the evening, Sam. Can't you make that work?" Devon grumbled pointing to the frilly nightgown.

"No. And I don't need staff. I can go get my bag myself if you can just tell me where my dad's car is."

"Good luck getting in without the keys," Devon said, instantly regretting his tone. He hadn't meant to get snippy, but Sam had a way of getting under his skin. *She always had.*

"Great! Well, thanks for a wonderful evening, Devon. It

was a pleasure as always," she said sarcastically. "Goodnight!"

Devon watched Sam march into the bathroom and slam the door. He left when he heard the shower running—slamming the door behind him too.

CHAPTER
8

Sam

The Merlin room wasn't so bad. The shower was amazing. Sam wished she wasn't so tired or she would have stayed under the jet-powered showerhead until the water ran cold. For a place that looked like Beast's castle, it sure had state-of-the-art features. Like plumbing and heated floors. And there were so many buttons on the toilet she didn't know which one to push. *Who has a remote control for a toilet?*

Being clean had lightened Sam's mood so much that she gave in and slipped into the silk nightgown. She looked at herself in the full-length mirror and cringed. The material was soft and luxurious, but she looked like Wendy from Peter Pan. *Screw it.* Half the town had seen her dressed in her nappy travel clothes and Uggs. The nightgown was just the icing on the cake.

Sam decided to pretend she didn't look humiliating and finished getting ready for bed. She found a toothbrush, toothpaste, contact solution and a travel case in the perfectly labeled drawers in the bathroom. *Devon was right, this place was stocked with everything.* She found her glasses in her purse and put them on, before hopping into bed to boot up her laptop. She was about to see if Megan was online when she noticed the low battery light flashing. Sam rifled through the drawers to find a UK adapter for her power cord. No luck. *Guess this place doesn't have everything . . .*

Sam scowled at the door. Devon probably had an adapter, or at least could help her find one. But that meant she'd have to suck up her pride and ask him nicely. And that was the last thing she wanted to do. *At least she thought it was.* She still hated him, but her mind kept wandering back to that kiss. *That Olympic kiss!*

She was seriously confused by Devon. On one hand he was still the same jerk who tormented her when they were kids, but he was also this new jerk, who was ridiculously handsome, opened doors for her, paid for her drinks, gave her his sweater and took the blame for an accident she caused. Not to mention that when she'd gotten him drunk he confided how scared he was about losing his father.

Damn it! Sam was the one who should be apologizing to Devon.

Loosing a parent wasn't something she couldn't exploit. And Devon seemed genuinely worried. He was going to need a friend. Sam knew from experience how bad it hurt to lose a parent to cancer. The least she could do was be there for Devon after what she'd put him through tonight. She'd have to find another way to get back to Boston. Besides, there were probably dozens of bad boys at Eddington who'd help her get the job done. Unfortunately, Devon wasn't one of them.

Devon

Devon's heart leapt when he heard a knock at his bedroom door. He hoped it was Sam. It was torture knowing she was just across the hall from him. He quickly towel dried his hair, then wrapped the towel around his waist.

When he opened the door he couldn't help but smirk. Sam was standing there wearing the ridiculous grandma nightgown. It made her look like a little kid again, and all his boyhood feelings came rushing to the surface.

"Hey," she said. "Sorry to bother you, but I was wondering if you had a power adapter I can borrow so I can charge my laptop and phone?"

"Yeah, one second," he said slipping back into the room and closing the door. He dug around in his desk drawer and found an adapter, then slipped back into the hall. "Sorry," he said, noticing the strange look Sam was giving him. "I'd invite you in, but my dog's in there and he's not good with strangers. He'd probably wake up the whole house and Cara already hates him as it is."

"Okay," Sam said, still studying him.

"Here." Devon offered her the adapter.

"Thanks." Sam closed her fingers around it.

Their hands brushed for a moment and Devon felt every cell she touched ignite.

They both stood there silently, lingering outside his door. Sam looked like she wanted to say something, but she didn't. She just stood there, gazing at him like she'd forgotten what she'd been about to say. Devon didn't trust himself to ask her what she was thinking. Besides, his mind was so clouded with thoughts of kissing her that he could scarcely think himself.

He was suddenly aware that he was standing inches away from Sam in nothing but a towel. Not a good choice, considering the way his body reacted to her. But if he didn't know better, he could swear Sam liked what she saw. Her eyes roved to his chest, then lower. It might be wishful thinking . . . but then again . . .

Devon took a risk—*tonight couldn't get any worse.* He reached up and brushed a stray hair from Sam's face. Her dark hair was still damp and it slipped through his fingers like ribbons of chocolate. The sensation made her shiver.

"Sam," he said softly. "About tonight . . ." He moved his hand to gently cup her cheek and her breath caught. "Kissing you was . . . really nice."

She brought her hand up to his, laying her fingers over his. For a moment he thought she was leaning into his touch, but then she pulled his hand away from her face. "It was," she said giving him a half smile, while she continued to hold his hand. "But it can't happen again."

"Why?"

"Devon, it's late. And we've both been drinking." She let go of his hand and tried to turn back toward her room.

He grabbed her hands, gently pulling her back to him. "Drinking or no, there's some things I need to say to you, Sam."

"Devon," she warned trying to pull her hands free. "Please don't."

"I have to, Sam. Ever since I found out you were coming back, I've been thinking about all the things I want to say to you."

"You don't have to say anything, Devon."

But I do! I have to tell you that I've never stopped thinking about you and I'm fucking in love with you!

Christ! He wished he could just get those words out of his mouth. They were expanding in his chest like they might explode if he didn't say them. But he wasn't good with words. He was good with his tongue and his hands, and he really just wanted to skip to that part.

"Honestly, Devon. You don't owe me anything. I don't even know you."

Her words hit him like a slap in the face. "But, don't you want to?"

"What I really want is to go to bed and pretend that tonight never happened. Can we please just start over tomorrow, Devon?"

It felt like that window in his chest, the one that let in all the air and light when he first saw her, was closing. And taking everything that mattered with it.

"Sure, Sam. If that's what you want."

"It is."

"Okay," he conceded.

"Goodnight, Devon."

"Goodnight, Sam."

CHAPTER
9

Sam

Sam was sitting in the ridiculously ornate four-poster bed video chatting with Megan on her laptop. She didn't know what time it was in Boston, but she knew Megan would be wide awake. Sam was convinced her best friend never slept. Megan practically mainlined double espressos. According to her, all film students did. And since Megan planned to major in film writing, she'd been getting a jump on her vampire lifestyle since sophomore year.

"What are you wearing?" Megan asked, wrinkling her nose in distain.

Sam had already given Megan a tour of the ostentatious bedroom in hopes she'd be too distracted to notice the frilly nightgown. *No such luck.*

"Some ugly pajamas I found in the guest drawer. My dad fell asleep and didn't even bother to bring my bag in from the car. Which is apparently locked up until morning when the valet staff comes back."

"Oh poor princess, locked in a castle. I feel so bad for you, Sam."

"Shut up, Meg! You're supposed to be making me feel better."

"What do you have to feel crappy about? You're staying in a castle . . . in Ireland! I would kill to be you right now."

Sam snorted.

"Is super hot Devon there?"

"Yes," she groaned.

"Oh my god! Like in the same castle as you? Why aren't you jumping his bones right now?"

"Ew, Meg! Who says that? And it's not an actual castle, by the way. It just kinda looks like one."

"Who cares? Tell me more about hot Devon. What happened after you slammed your laptop closed in my face?"

"Not much, we went out to a pub."

"And?"

"And nothing."

"Oh, give it up, Sam. I can see it all over you face. Something happened."

"We *may* have sorta kissed."

"Eeeeeeeeeeeeeeee!!!!" Megan shrieked so loud Sam had to hit the mute button on her laptop. Sometimes being friends with Megan was exhausting. The girl had more energy than a Chihuahua on Red Bull.

"Will you calm down?" Sam squawked once Megan stopped screeching.

"I knew it! I can always tell when you're hiding something. You can't look me in the eyes! And NO! I will *not* calm down. You just made out with the hottest man in Ireland. I want details."

"He's not *that* hot," Sam lied, trying not to think about the Olympic kiss.

"Are you kidding? He looks like James Franco, Rob Pattinson and Ian Somerhalder had a love child. He's genetic perfection!"

"You only saw him for like ten seconds," Sam argued.

"That's all I need. I can spot flawlessness."

Sam rolled her eyes instantly wishing she hadn't told Megan about the kiss. This was the kind of thing she wouldn't let go. Sam flopped onto her stomach and got comfy, preparing for Megan's speech about fate and star-crossed lovers.

Devon

Devon lay in bed, fuming. He kept replaying his conversation with Sam over in his head.

Start over?

What the hell was she talking about?

Devon didn't want to start over. And he certainly couldn't pretend that kiss didn't happen. *It was still wreaking havoc on his body.* That kiss was the best thing that had happened to him in a while. No way in hell was he going to forget about it.

Sam could stand there and say she didn't know him as much as she wanted, but he knew it was a load of bollocks. *How could he remember everything about her and she remember nothing?* This thing between them couldn't be one-sided. *Could it?*

Even if it was, it didn't change the facts. Devon was in love with Sam. He'd always thought maybe it was just some weird childhood crush—*lingering first love or something like that.* But now that Sam was actually here and he'd kissed her, he knew it was real.

Devon had never felt anything so consuming in all his life. He'd kissed dozens of girls—hell more like hundreds. But nothing compared to kissing Sam. And he didn't know what it was if it wasn't love. He tried to remember what it was like kissing those other girls, but it was all one big blur—*a white noise of lips.*

Then, he tried to remember kissing Sam. It was more like trying *not* to remember. That kiss stormed his memory like an electrical current. It'd always been like that with Sam. He didn't have to try with her. She consumed him effortlessly.

He tried to remember how it happened—what pivotal moment turned her from childhood crush to heart wrenching love interest. But he couldn't put his finger on it. All he knew was that Sam Connors was the only thing that mattered to him. And perhaps it had always been that way.

That settled it. Devon wasn't going to give up that easily. He pulled on his favorite jumper and slipped into the hall. In four quick strides he was standing in front of Sam's door. He took a deep breath and psyched himself up to knock. *Do or die, Devon*—it was something he said to himself before every football match, and it had inadvertently become his mantra for focus and success.

Devon was about to knock on the door when he heard Sam's voice coming from within. He leaned closer to listen. She was talking to someone. *Maybe on the phone?* Devon felt creepy eavesdropping and was about to knock before he overheard something he shouldn't—his name. His hand stopped midair.

"God, I can't believe you kissed Devon!" a shrill female voice said. "I seriously hate you so much right now."

"Well don't," Sam answered and Devon's heart jumped into his throat. *Sam was talking about their kiss!* It must have meant something to her too if she was talking about it.

"Why? Is he a bad kisser?" the other voice asked.

"No, but I'm not interested in Devon. I told you, he made my life hell when I lived here. He's half the reason I didn't want to come back to Ireland. I honestly wish he'd just back off. The only thing I want right now is a ticket back to Boston."

Devon's heart thudded to his feet and his resolve crumbled. He never knew words could hurt so badly. He quickly retreated to his room before he overheard more soul-crushing words from Sam.

Once inside, Devon shut his door and leaned against it trying to catch his breath. *How could this be happening? Were he and Sam really over before they even started?*

He slid to the floor and hung his head between his knees. He felt woozy. *How the hell had his life gotten so messed up?* In one year, he'd gone from having it all—a girlfriend, friends, football, his father, a future full of opportunities. And now . . . well now it just felt like everything was slipping away.

Eggsy hopped off the bed and came over to console Devon. The massive dog flopped down at his feet. Devon pulled Eggsy's head into his lap, burying his face in his thick coat, wishing he could go back to the life he'd taken for granted.

CHAPTER
10

Sam

The next morning, Sam was rousted from sleep way too early by a stern-looking servant. The woman drew the curtains and placed a pair of slippers and a robe next to Sam's bed. "Breakfast is being served in the parlor, Madame."

Sam wasn't a morning person. And she'd barely slept last night. Plus, being woken up by a stranger that looked like an extra from the cast of Downton Abbey was too much to handle. Sam grumbled around the room sleepily trying to find something more her style in the guest drawers, but she was met with more lace and ruffles and finally gave up and settled for the robe.

By the time Sam found her way to the parlor, it looked like breakfast was finishing up. Cara was sipping tea with Sam's father while more servants cleared their plates.

"Sam!" her father exclaimed as she dropped into the

open chair across from him. "Good morning, honey. I was almost ready to send the search party out," he joked.

She scowled at him. *Almost?* She grabbed the cloth napkin one of the servants placed in her lap and twisted it, imagining all the ways she could use it to choke her father.

"Anyway, I'm glad you're here. I have some news."

Cara stood up and smiled sweetly. "I'll give you two some privacy to discuss things."

Sam frowned. *That wasn't a good sign.*

Before she could question her father, another servant came in and placed a plate in front of her—greasy hash, baked tomatoes, poached eggs, ham, beans, burnt toast and blood sausage—a traditional Irish breakfast. *God, she missed Boston.*

All Sam wanted was a strawberry Pop-Tart and black coffee in her favorite Red Sox mug.

"So," her father said once they were alone. "I have good news and bad news."

"Bad news first," Sam said reaching for the toast.

"Our storage container isn't going to be arriving for another few weeks."

"What? My whole life is in there, Dad!"

"I know, honey. And it will all get here safe and sound. It's just been delayed."

"I start school next week! What am I supposed to do without my clothes and everything? Dad, this is a nightmare!"

"Well, that brings me to the good news. Henry and Cara have invited us to stay with them until our things arrive."

Sam dropped her toast. "What?"

"Well, we can't very well move into the house I rented. It's unfurnished. But, Henry overheard my conversation with the shipping company and offered to let us stay. Isn't that great?"

Sam felt like her world was circling the drain. *Stay here? With Devon? With the creepy twins and that baby? With Cara? With servants she didn't know? With another person dying of cancer?* No! This was too much, even for her father to ask.

"No way, Dad!"

"Honey . . ."

Sam got to her feet. "I said no. I am *not* staying here!"

"Samantha!" Her father never used her full name unless he was really pissed. His voice was low and rushed. "I will not have you treating my dearest friends poorly. They've been nothing but kind to us, and this is not negotiable." He recovered his composure and pointed to her plate. "Sit down and finish your breakfast."

Sam sat, her temper barely leashed. And, as if her morning wasn't already bad enough, Devon chose that moment to waltz into the parlor looking like a million bucks. He stopped short when he saw the scowl on Sam's face. She was sure the tension in the room was palpable, but her father tried to smooth it over. "Good morning, Devon," he greeted.

"Uh, hi," Devon said looking uncomfortable. "I didn't mean to interrupt."

"Nonsense," her father replied. "Please, join us. Actually, you might be able to help. Sam and I were just discussing how she'll be staying here for the next few weeks."

Devon's eyebrows knitted together in confusion. "She is?"

"Well, we both are. As, long as it's not a problem for you, of course?" her father added.

What? Devon has a choice?

So not fair.

Sam tried her best telepathy powers on him. *Please say no! Please say no!* But Devon only stared at her with his pretty gray eyes and shook his head. "Of course not, Mr. Connors. I'm glad for the company."

"Great! Then it's settled," her father said. "I think it'll be great. That way I'll be nearby to work with Henry when he feels up to it. And you and I can work together when you're free, Devon."

"Sounds grand," Devon said.

"Grand!" her father echoed. *God, she hated when he tried to sound Irish.* He smiled at Sam and she gave him a patronizing smirk.

"So, what's on the agenda for today, kids?" her father asked.

"I don't know, Dad. Seeing I don't have any clothes or belongings, I guess I'll just lock myself in my room. That's what you want, isn't it?" She stood abruptly and stormed out of the parlor, marching back to her bedroom.

Devon

"I'm sorry about that, Devon. Sam's not really a morning person," Mr. Connors said, sounding a tad embarrassed.

"She's a bit feistier than I remember," Devon ventured.

Mr. Connors chuckled. "Yeah. But, I may have thrown a bit too much on her plate at this hour. I usually wait until she's had at least one cup of coffee."

"I'll have to remember that," Devon replied, offering Mr. Connors a smile. "Anything else I should know?"

Mr. Connors shook his head and shrugged. "I wish I knew. Honestly, I'm probably the last person to give advice about Sam. She doesn't really talk to me, no matter how hard I try. I guess it's my fault for dragging her back to Ireland. I was really hoping she'd see what a great opportunity this was for us to spend time together before she goes off to college."

Devon felt bad for the man. He was visibly upset that his daughter was unhappy. And Devon couldn't help but think Sam was being a spoiled brat. Here her father was, a kind, healthy parent, wanting to spend time with her and she was treating him like rubbish. Devon would kill for that.

"Maybe I could talk to her for you. Help make it easier for her to adjust."

"You would do that?" Mr. Connors asked.

"Yeah, I'd be happy to. I could take her to campus and show her around. Maybe that would help her shake out her nerves."

"Shoot! I almost forgot I was supposed to bring Sam by Eddington today to pick up her books and uniform before classes start next week." He glanced at his phone and frowned. "I told Henry I'd meet him to go over the flaws in the new BETA at noon. Do you think I can get to Eddington and back by then?"

Devon shook his head. "Maybe my father can reschedule?"

Mr. Connors frowned again.

An idea sparked in the part of Devon's mind that he thought had been mortally wounded by Sam's words last night. "Or, if it would help you out, I could take Sam to Eddington?"

"Devon! You're a lifesaver! Here," Mr. Connors pulled a black credit card out of his wallet. "Please, get her anything she wants. And even the stuff she doesn't want. I just want her to be happy here."

Devon took the card and shook Mr. Connors' hand. "You got it."

~♡~

Devon walked down the hall to Sam's room. Finding out she was going to be living with him had given him a whole new outlook. It was like a sign from above that he wasn't supposed to give up. Maybe things would work out after all. Devon hadn't met a girl yet that he couldn't win over. Besides, after the moody way she was treating her father, Devon was thinking he might need to reconsider if he even wanted to date Sam.

This time when Devon reached her door, he knocked immediately, not wanting to overhear her saying something else degrading about him. Sam answered wearing her clothes from the day before. Her eyes were dewy, like she'd been crying and her lips looked like they'd been formed from two perfect rose petals as she crossed her arms and pouted at him. *Yep, he definitely still wanted to date her. And kiss her. And other things . . .* Devon mentally scolded himself, *Get it together, mate!*

"What do you want?" Sam asked.

"I come in peace," Devon said, handing Sam a mug of black coffee. *Just how she liked it, according to her father.* "Your father asked me to take you to Eddington today to get your books and uniform."

"Great," she muttered. "He's passing me off already."

"You should try being nicer to him, Sam. He cares about you."

"Yeah, so much that he's sending you to take me school

shopping. Something *he* promised to do."

"I'm sure he's doing the best he can."

She snorted. "Not likely. The only thing he really cares about is his stupid company."

"That may be, but he's the only parent you've got left."

Sam's face fell and Devon instantly regretted his words. It was insensitive being that Sam had already lost her mother. But lately, Devon had been saying stupid things like that because of his own fears over losing his father.

"Shite, I didn't mean it like that, Sam, I—"

"It's fine," Sam interrupted. "Let's just go to Eddington, okay?" she grabbed her purse and tried to push past him.

"Wait." Devon grabbed her arm. "Last night—"

"Oh my God! I thought we agreed to forget last night!"

"Christ, we did! But this is what I mean."

"What?"

"You said you wanted to start over."

"So?" Sam retorted sharply.

"Well, I was hoping we could start over as friends."

Sam eyed him suspiciously.

"I mean it. My life's a mess. I could really use a friend right now, and I think you could too."

"I don't need a friend," she scoffed.

"I can tell. I mean that winning attitude of yours is probably going to get you all kinds of friends at Eddington," he teased.

Sam rolled her eyes. "Fine, we can be friends. But *just* friends."

Devon smiled and stuck out his hand to Sam.

She took it and added, "Friends don't kiss, you know?" A hint of a smile cracked her delicate features. She was even prettier when she was trying to look mad.

Devon couldn't help himself. "Sometimes they do," he said squeezing her tiny, warm hand.

"Then we're the kind of friends that don't kiss."

We'll see, Devon thought as he shook Sam's hand while trying to contain the hope that fizzed in his chest. It felt like someone had cracked the window again—just enough for him to breathe.

CHAPTER
11

Sam

Despite yesterday being a total disaster and this morning starting out even worse, Sam found herself enjoying the drive to Eddington with Devon. At least she was out of that stuffy mansion.

Who would have thought you could feel so claustrophobic in such a large house?

Devon had stopped at a petrol station and came out with two Styrofoam cups of hot coffee and a bag of pastries.

"I noticed you didn't eat anything at breakfast," he said handing her the coffee and putting the bag in her lap.

She couldn't protest. Her stomach had been growling since last night so she sucked up her pride and thanked him before stuffing her face. The food really did improve her mood. And with the sun shining while they drove the rolling green hills, Sam found it hard to be so angry. Plus, she reminded herself that she and Devon had just called a truce. She might as well give this friends thing a chance, because he was right, since she was fighting with her dad, Devon was really the only other person she had left to talk to.

"So, tell me about Eddington," she said.

"What do you want to know?"

"Everything. The good, the bad and the ugly. Like who do I avoid? Where do I sit at lunch? What are the mating rituals?"

Devon laughed. "It's just school, Sam. We don't sacrifice a virgin at the beginning of term."

"That's a relief," she said laughing. "I'd be safe even if you did," she added, instantly regretting it.

It was a total lie. Sam was still a virgin, but that was just the kind of thing she was used to saying. At her old school being a virgin was worse than having leprosy. Freshman year she and her friend Toby made a pact to say they had sex with each other at their co-ed soccer camp that summer. *It was better to lie than risk going to Stanton with their v-cards.*

Sam had done other stuff with boys. She wasn't a total prude. But she had never really found anyone she liked enough to have sex with. Megan said that was because Sam was too in love with soccer to have time for boys. *Megan was probably right.*

Devon seemed uncomfortable when he glanced over at Sam. His full lips were pressed together like he was concentrating and his brow was furrowed again. She couldn't see his eye behind his sunglasses, but the sun was kissing his golden skin and Sam turned away. It physically hurt to look at someone that perfect.

"So, there's about sixty or so students in our year," Devon ventured. "Which we call sixth year, by the way. First term is kind of intense. Eddington makes us cram all of our core lessons in so we can take our leaving certificate exams before break. That way if anyone fails they can make up the lessons and retake exams second term. That's how Eddington keeps their perfect graduation record."

Sam groaned.

"It's not all bad. There's a big party at the end of first term. We call it the Grad Ball. It's like your prom in the states. Everyone gets flashy and goes out on the lash."

She gave him a questioning look.

"It means we dress up and go drinking."

"Got it."

"Then, second term is a breeze. It's mostly just internships and electives. Which basically means coasting to the finish line and partying."

Not that I'll even be here then, Sam thought.

"And as far as where to sit at lunch, your guess is as good as mine."

"What do you mean?"

"Well, I used to sit with my mates from football club. But—"

"You play soccer?"

"Football," he corrected. "I used to."

"You quit?" Sam scoffed, appalled that anyone would ever give up the beloved sport. She planned to try out for Eddington's team right away.

"Not by choice, but things with my dad . . ." Devon sighed. "It's complicated."

"I'm no stranger to complicated father relationships," Sam offered.

Devon ran his hand through his hair twice before resting it back on the stick shift. Sam was starting to notice he messed with his hair when he was nervous. She smirked, because it was a girly thing to do. She tried to straighten out her face. She really did want to try to be friends with Devon. Especially when it came to dealing with his father's illness. She knew what he was going through. And as much as Devon had been an eight-year-old jerk most of the time she knew him, he was also the boy who held her hand at her mother's funeral, as if he'd known how empty Sam's hand felt without her mother to hold it. *She owed him.*

"I know I can come off kinda harsh . . ." she started.

"Oh, so you're aware of it?" Devon mocked.

Sam ignored him. "You don't have to talk about it. But I'm here for you if you want to."

Devon ran his hand through his dark hair again. After an awkward silence, he spoke. "My dad made me quit the team. Said the time for boyhood games are over. It's time I step up and take his place in the business."

"But it's your last year to play," Sam argued, incredulous. *She'd do more than mentally strangle her father if he ever tried to take soccer away from her.*

Devon just shrugged. "He's right though. It's not like I'm good enough to play professionally."

"So. That's not the point. It's your life and this is your last year to be young and stupid. It's the last year we get to make mistakes and have fun without consequences."

"Yeah," Devon said quietly. "But I guess my timeline has been shortened."

"Your dad . . . how bad is he?" Sam asked.

"He has grade four Glioblastoma. It should have killed

him already. The tumor's inoperable. Radiation and chemo don't seem to do anything but make him weaker. His doctors gave him twelve months to live. But that was fifteen months ago. This is all just borrowed time."

Sam didn't know what to say. She let the heaviness of the situation settle over her while Devon silently clenched his jaw and ran his hand through his hair again. When he put his hand back on the stick shift, Sam placed her hand on top of his. She laced her fingers with his. They were warm and dry—like a big baseball mitt.

"Maybe we can sit together at lunch," she said.

Devon grinned and squeezed her fingers. "I'd like that."

The rest of the drive went by rather quickly. Sam had started asking Devon questions about soccer. It turned out they both played offense. Devon was a striker and Sam played forward. They immediately filled the rest of the trip debating strategy. It was awesome having someone to talk soccer with. Her father wasn't interested in sports. And Megan came to some of Sam's games, but the only sport she really understood was Quidditch.

Sam was enjoying chatting about her favorite pastime with Devon and was actually disappointed when he pulled up to Eddington. The school reminded Sam so much of Stanton Prep that an eerie wave of déjà vu fell over her as they drove under the stone archway onto campus. It was stone rather than brick, but everything else was the same as Stanton—arches, pillars, perfectly manicured grounds, expensive cars. Eddington had a bit more of the old-world, Irish flare, with stone crosses adorning the towers and porticos, but otherwise, Sam felt pretty much at home. *Maybe a few months here wouldn't be too bad?*

"So," Devon said, "How 'bout we divide and conquer? I'll take your class schedule and pick up your books, you go to the school tailor and get fit for your uniform. That way I'll have time to show you the sports complex."

"Sounds good to me."

"If we're lucky Coach Tomlin will be in and I can introduce you," Devon offered.

"That'd be great!"

"Grand."

Sam smirked. *Okay, Megan was right. The whole Irish accent thing was sorta cute.* At least when it was Devon speaking and not her father's lame attempts.

Devon pointed her in the direction of the school tailor. She found it easily and a sweet old woman, named Tara, helped her gather everything she needed to be a proper Eddington lady. It seemed it would be another semester of plaid skirts and blazers. The Eddington uniforms even looked like Stanton's. The blazers at Eddington were heather gray instead of Stanton blue, but the plaid skirt was nearly identical. Sam wished she could use that as an argument for sending her back to Boston. *Dad, these schools are identical. Why not let me stay at the one I'm happy at?*

But she could already hear his response. *If they're the same, it shouldn't matter that you'll be going to Eddington.*

Sam waited patiently while the woman folded all her new clothes and put them in crisp white shopping bags with the Eddington crest on them. Tara informed her that everything would be charged to her school account, so Sam grabbed her bags and headed back out to find Devon.

She spotted him striding toward his Defender with his arms full of books. Sam trotted over to help him with the door. "You weren't kidding about first term being hard," she retorted eyeing the pile of thick textbooks.

He laughed. "Are you mad? They're not *all* yours. I grabbed mine too."

"Oh, thank God," Sam replied, relieved.

"Looks like we have some classes together too," he said handing her schedule back. He'd circled Honors English and Physics. "Ready to check out the sports complex?"

Sam paused. "Are there going to be any students there?"

"Yeah, I'm sure some of the teams have started practice already."

Sam cringed as she glanced down at her stretched out leggings and grubby Uggs. "Would you mind if we skipped it?"

"Why? I thought you wanted to meet Coach?"

"I do, but . . . I'm wearing two day old airplane clothes and I was sorta hoping to put my best face forward, ya know?"

"You look fine," Devon replied staring at her like he thought she always dressed like pop star going through a re-hab phase.

"Well, I'm sorta going for more than fine."

He shrugged. "Okay. So, what do ya wanna do?"

"Is there anywhere I could do some shopping? My dad said the rest of my clothes won't be here for a few weeks and I really don't want to wear that frilly nightgown again."

"It was cute," Devon replied, trying not to laugh.

"Yeah, if you're into *Little House on the Prairie*. Besides, I need other stuff. So far all I have are school uniforms. I need normal clothes, and shoes and soccer gear."

"Well, your dad said to make ya happy," Devon replied pulling a black credit card from his pocket and handing it to Sam. She grinned like she'd just won the lottery! Devon smiled back. "Come on, I know just the place."

Devon

Devon took Sam to his favorite sports outfitter in Dublin and actually had a great time helping her pick out cleats and gear. He normally hated shopping and thought it would kill him to walk into the sports store knowing he wouldn't be playing this season. But he and Sam talked non-stop so he hardly even noticed that he was picking out gear for someone else. Sam went crazy over the selection of balls, saying they didn't have such variety in the states. She picked out a white ball with big blue stars on it.

It wasn't until they went to pay that reality came rushing back. Sean Dougherty, one of Devon's mates from the team, was manning the cash register. He gave Devon a smug look as he rang up Sam's gear. He held up a pink sports bra and grinned. "Ah, this explains why you quit on us. I always knew you were a fag, James."

"Buggar off, Dougherty," Devon growled.

Sam looked between them trying to figure out what was going on.

"And who's this?" Dougherty asked looking at Sam. "I know you're not with a stook like him, are ya sweetheart? He doesn't wear a jersey anymore if that's what you're chasing."

"I'll be wearing my own jersey, thank you very much," Sam said shoving three more sports bras across the counter. "And I'm only using him for his fine ass," she said giving

Devon's backside a fierce squeeze. Devon coughed roughly, trying to disguise his surprise. "Isn't that right, baby cakes?" Sam asked, apparently continuing her charade.

"Uh, yeah. And I love your sweet arse too, kitten," he said cupping Sam's perfectly toned backside with one hand.

Devon tried to keep the color from creeping to his cheeks, but he was enjoying this game way too much. Dougherty's face was priceless. He seemed like he wasn't sure what to say, and honestly Devon didn't give a damn about his ex-mate right now. Sam had Devon's undivided attention. Finally running his hands over Sam's tight little leggings was a wet dream come true. *Christ, her ass was divine!* It was a work of art. Devon wanted to hang a private property sign on it. *This stretch of perfection hereby belongs to Devon James.*

Perhaps this whole friends thing was going to work out after all.

Dougherty kept his mouth shut and rang Sam up quickly. She kept her hand in Devon's back pocket the whole time. It wasn't until they were back outside that she pulled away.

"Kitten?" she gawfed. "Really?"

"I don't know? You said you liked me for my arse! And you called be baby cakes! I had to think fast."

Sam laughed. "Sorry about that. But at least we shut him up."

"Yeah, thanks for that."

"What's his problem anyway?"

"His name's Sean Dougherty. He's in Eddington's football club. He's pissed at me for quittin'. The whole team actin' a maggot over it."

"I'm assuming that means they're mad?"

Devon nodded.

"Didn't you tell them about your dad?"

"Yeah, but they're a bunch of wankers. They think I'm a traitor for abandoning them. They don't care that I didn't have a choice in the matter, or that it's killing me."

"Is that why that couple at Finnegan's was so rude to you?"

"Those two are their own special case."

"Why's that?"

"Well, the girl, Sophie, she was my girlfriend up until this summer," Devon shook his head in disgust. "She dropped me when she heard I wouldn't be on the pitch this season. And Zander, we used to be best mates. We were always sorta rivals, trying out for the same position and that kinda thing. But, when his sister married my father, he started getting all high and mighty. Just giving me shite for no reason."

"Wait, so your dad married your best friend's sister?"

"It sounds bad when ya say it like that."

"It *is* bad, Devon. Your ex-best friend is your uncle, and I'm guessing, from the way they were sucking face, that he's now dating your ex-girlfriend. That's Shakespearean!"

Devon sighed. "I told you my life was a mess."

"That's the understatement of the year!" Sam replied. "Do you know what this calls for?"

"What?"

"Drinks!"

"Oh no, we've already established you can drink me under the table, Boston."

"As any good Boston girl should," she replied grinning at him.

Christ, he loved it when she smiled. It was like each one caught in his chest and filled him with too much air.

"Seriously though. I'm starving. Let's go get lunch and a pint and you can tell me all about your fucked up life so I feel better about mine."

CHAPTER
12

Sam

One pint turned into three as Devon filled Sam in on everything she'd missed in the past nine years. It turned out they had a lot in common. Soccer, no mothers (apparently Devon's left when he was eleven. She now lived in England and had a new family), work-obsessed fathers, and an obsession with sliders. They'd each polished off five of the delicious mini cheeseburgers and fries while they tried to out do each other in a game of my-life-sucks-worse-than-yours. *Devon won hands down.* And Sam couldn't stop staring at the wave of dimples that rippled through his face every time he laughed at one of her sarcastic jokes.

"No! You don't get any points in the ex-girlfriend column," Sam argued. "She left you for your uncle! That goes in the family drama column."

"Alright, but you don't know how to drive and you've

been wearing the same clothes for two days."

"Hey!" she argued. "Neither of those are my fault. Which by the way, you're supposed to take me shopping for real clothes."

"I will, just as soon as you wipe the ketchup off your face."

"Oh my God! How long have I had food on my face, you jerk?" Sam self-consciously wiped her face with a napkin.

"You missed a spot." Devon swiped the corner of her mouth with his thumb, then licked his finger clean.

Sam felt her mouth go dry watching him. "Foul!" she cried when she found her voice.

"What's wrong now?"

"Friends don't lick food off each other."

Devon glowed with laughter. "I didn't think they called each other baby cakes and kitten while playing grab ass either, but I'm game if you are."

"That was a special circumstance. It falls under, friends have each other's backs."

"There sure are a lot of rules to this friendship," Devon teased.

"Yeah, just remember the first one and we'll be okay."

"Friends don't kiss friends, I got it."

"Good, now take me shopping."

"Anything for you, kitten."

⁓♀⁓

Sam dragged Devon up and down the multiple floors of Brown Thomas, her favorite department store in Dublin. She was grabbing everything from makeup to socks. She had a wardrobe to replace and was all-too-happy to put it on her father's bill. *It was the least he could do after uprooting her entire life.*

Devon was being a pretty good sport. He actually seemed to be having a great time picking on her fashion choices.

"Blimey, could you look more American?" he teased when Sam picked out a pair of converse.

"What's wrong with these?"

"Maybe nothing in Boston."

"Alright, Tim Gunn. What kind of shoes do the fairest Irish lasses wear?"

"Try these," he said pointing to a pair of uncomfortable-looking brown oxford loafers.

"Ew! They're hideous."

"They're European."

"They look like boy shoes."

"No, they look posh. Unlike whatever these travesties are," he said scuffing the toe of her Uggs with his own sophisticated oxford loafers. *They did look really classy on him, actually.*

"Fine, but I don't want plain brown ones."

"How about these?" Devon offered, pulling down a pair of blue suede oxfords with tiny silver studs all over them.

"Oh! They look like stars," she exclaimed running her fingers over the studs.

"You have a thing for stars, huh?"

"Who doesn't love stars?" she asked gazing at the display shoes. They were her size! She sat down and slipped them on. The soft leather was surprisingly comfortable and the studs caught the light, making the shoes remind Sam of the night sky, alive with stars. *She loved them.* "Okay, these will do."

Devon smirked, triumphantly. "Now you're a proper posh Dubliner."

"Come on, we're not done," she said, unwilling to let him win that easily.

⁓

Sam dragged Devon to the lingerie department and went to work tormenting him. *They were friends, but that didn't mean they couldn't have fun, right?*

"Here, hold these," she said handing him an armful of lacey bras.

"This is cruel and unusual punishment," Devon whined.

"What? I need underwear," she replied coyly.

"I know, but do I really have to help you with the girly stuff?"

"Well, I *am* a girl, you know? This is what happens when you're friends with a girl. The girly stuff comes with it."

"I know you're a girl, but you can't buy girly stuff like this in front of me," he said holding up a see-through bra.

"Why not?"

"Because, that's something you do with your boyfriend. Not your friend. And you clearly stated we're just friends."

"That's right, but I said we're friends that don't kiss, not friends that don't help each other shop for underwear."

"Studies show underwear shopping leads to kissing," Devon said in his most proper warning label voice.

Sam snorted. "Have you conducted these studies yourself?"

"I may have," he replied, giving Sam a wolfish grin.

Damn! That was the kind of grin that could start forest fires—if forests were made of panties.

Get it together, Sam. You're teasing him, not the other way around. "Well, I think you're wrong," she mused.

94

"Trust me on this, Sam. I'm not wrong. You'll see."

"What if you were my gay best friend? Then this wouldn't lead to kissing."

"I think we've established I'm not gay."

"You're right, you don't dress sharp enough."

"I do so! You're the one dressed like an American."

"Oh, overly sensitive about fashion critiques . . . maybe it's too soon to rule out the gay best friend thing."

"You're impossible," Devon muttered. "I'm beginning to see why you didn't have any points in the boyfriend column."

"Oh, shut up and hold these," Sam said piling under-wear into Devon's arms. "And if you don't behave I'll model them for you."

Devon looked like he was about to make a witty come-back when a girl called his name.

"Devon James?"

Sam and Devon turned their attention to a sales girl slinking toward them. She was about their age with a perfect figure and blonde hair in a pixie cut. *Was every girl in Ireland adorable and blonde?*

"A new girlfriend so soon?" blondie asked Devon.

"Hello, Tess," Devon said politely. "This is my *friend,* Sam Connors."

"Samantha," Sam corrected.

"Right, sorry," he added. "Samantha, this is Tess Jenkins. She's in our year at Eddington."

Tess gave Sam an unimpressed once over. "*You're* going to Eddington?" she asked raising a perfectly sculpted eyebrow.

Sam wished she'd changed into something cute she'd bought, but she was still in her stupid old clothes.

"Yep. Nice to meet you." Sam held her hand out and

Tess took a step back with a huff, like the thought of shaking Sam's hand was offensive.

Tess shook her head at them and gave them a sour look, as if she and Devon were ruining the pristine atmosphere of the department store. Without another word she turned and sashayed away.

"Wow! Eddington is seeming more and more like Stanton everyday." Except Sam feared she was on the wrong side of the popular line here.

"Don't worry about Tess. She's Sophie's best friend. She doesn't have an original thought in her head."

"Great, so now your ex's fem-bot is going to report back that we were underwear shopping together! I don't need to make enemies before I even start school, Devon."

He laughed. "Too late for that. If you're friends with me, you won't be making any friends. But don't worry. I'm just as untouchable as I am hated."

Sam wasn't comforted by that thought as she headed into the dressing room.

Devon

Devon tried to distract himself while he waited for Sam in the humiliating pink and gold chair outside the dressing room. But he was failing miserably. He was surrounded by women's lingerie, and he knew at that very moment, Sam was trying on bits of lace and satin. It was making him sweat. He'd already stripped down to his t-shirt, but that didn't seem to help, because his mind was still stripping Sam completely naked. *The little minx! She knew exactly what she was doing to him.*

He tried to keep his mind elsewhere, but Devon knew nothing short of seeing Sam in her knickers would stop the intoxicating visions that kept erupting in his mind like erotic fireworks. *Sam in lace. Sam in silk. Sam in his arms.* It was torture.

But he couldn't leave. He was guarding her army of shopping bags. It baffled him how many things girls managed to need. If it were up to Devon, he'd live in his favorite red and white Arsenal jersey and a pair of faded jeans.

Sam finally emerged and paid for her unmentionables. Devon gave a sigh of relief when they were finally back in his Defender driving home. Shopping had worn him out. *Okay, maybe it was all the fantasizing about Sam in lingerie that wore him out.* He needed to think about something else. Anything else. Because in Devon's mind, he and Sam were still rolling around in the sheets as he tore off the layers of skimpy underthings she'd bought.

"So," he said. "I was thinking I could talk to Coach Tomlin for you. Maybe get a try out set up?"

"You would do that for me?" Sam asked, a hopeful grin illuminating her face.

"Yeah, sure."

"Oh my God, Devon, I'd love that! Thank you," she squealed and leaned over planting a light kiss on his cheek.

Shite! All the work he'd just done to stop thinking about sex had been instantly undone with a brush of Sam's perfect lips. The inside of the car suddenly felt like the sun and Devon couldn't contain his smile. "I told you underwear shopping leads to kissing."

"What? That wasn't a kiss."

"A kiss is a kiss, Sam. You just broke friend rule number one."

"That rule refers to kissing on the mouth."

"There sure are a lot of specifics to your rules. Perhaps you should write them down for me."

Sam whipped out her cell phone. "What's your number?"

"First kissing, now asking for my number? I knew I'd like being friends with you."

"Do you always have to be so narcissistic?"

"Do you always have to be so flirtatious?"

She rolled her eyes. "Number?"

"Fine." Devon rattled off his phone number and Sam put it in her phone. She continued typing furiously.

"What are you doing?"

"Texting you."

"Texting me what?"

"You'll see."

His phone buzzed with a message and he glanced at it while keeping one eye on the road.

SAM: Rule #1: Friends don't kiss.
Rule #2: Friends don't lick each other.
Rule #3: Friends don't shop for underwear together.

Devon laughed and tossed his phone into the backseat. "That's what I think of your rules.

Sophie

"What do you mean they were underwear shopping together?" Sophie practically shrieked into her cell phone.

"I'm sorry, Sophie," Tess said. "I know it's not what you want to hear, but I thought you should know."

Sophie took a deep breath to steady herself. "Maybe it wasn't what it looked like."

"Soph! He was following her around like a lap dog carrying her bras and knickers!"

"Well then, you know what this means," Sophie growled into the phone. "Can I count on you?"

"Always," Tess replied.

Sophie could practically hear Tess smirking through the phone. She smiled back. "See you at school, Tess."

"Looking forward to it," Tess replied.

Sophie hung up and threw her cell phone across the room.

CHAPTER
13

Sam

Sam was in much better spirits after her shopping trip with Devon. He helped her bring all her bags in and promised he'd call Coach Tomlin right away before he left to go join her father in Henry's office. They apparently had been texting Devon about urgent business matters while he was chauffeuring Sam around Dublin. She apologized for keeping him, but he said she was currently his favorite brand of procrastination.

She busied herself setting up her new room. Just because she had to live in a dusty old castle didn't mean it had to feel like one. Cara had expressly told her to make herself at home that night at dinner—which ended up being just the two of them—*awkward*.

Sam didn't waste any time settling in. She switched out the heavy red and gold embroidered comforter for the fluffy white one she bought at Brown Thomas, and replaced the millions of ornate pillows with some new simple ones that she wasn't afraid to lay on. They were all various shades of white or off-white. She bought a couple of those faux white fur rugs too and laid them around the room. Then, she strung the curtain of fairy lights she'd bought on the underside of the canopy above the bed. She lay on her back admiring them— her very own starry night sky. It really helped brighten the place up. She'd done the same thing in her old room in Boston, and it made her homesick.

She sighed and decided to keep going until the transformation from castle to teen suite was complete. Sam set up her new Keurig coffee maker so she could at least enjoy coffee in the mornings. She'd been unable to find Pop-Tarts while shopping, but Devon had turned her on to his favorite breakfast bars, so she'd loaded up on them in the strawberry variety. After Sam finished setting up her vanity and desk she sat back on her bed to survey her work. It wasn't home, but it was getting better. The walls were still bare, but Sam liked the soft stone gray color. And adding the new white bedding she'd bought made the bedroom feel more familiar.

It was late by the time Sam finished sorting her new wardrobe. She collapsed onto her inviting bed to call Megan and fill her in on her day. But to her dismay, Megan didn't answer. Sam glanced at the time. It wasn't late in Boston. Maybe Megan was eating dinner? Or still at drama club? Sam couldn't keep track. *Damn time zones.* She checked her emails, then Snapchat and Instagram. After exhausting all her options, she shut her laptop and lay back on her bed. She was tired, but her mind was still buzzing for some reason. It was probably jetlag or something.

She found her mind wandering to Devon. She wondered what he was doing right now? She was strangely disappointed that he hadn't shown up for dinner. *Her father had probably dragged him into his computer geek vortex—a place where time didn't exist.*

Sam actually felt bad for Devon. He didn't look like the stereotypical nerds her father normally worked with. She snorted. Devon probably couldn't be further from computer geek if he tried. He oozed European soccer-god—a fact that Sam sort of hated. Soccer boys were her weakness. *Especially cute soccer boys.*

She picked up her phone, thinking about texting him. But when she saw the text she sent him earlier glaring back at her—the one with all the friend rules—she thought texting your friend in the middle of the night probably wasn't a good idea. She hopped in the shower instead, eager to try out her new hair products. But even the scent of grapefruit couldn't wash Devon from her thoughts. *Damn him and his sexy soccer-god body.*

Sam slipped into her new pajamas—a stretchy white tank top and gray drawstring bottoms. *Goodbye ugly nightgown!* She was plugging her cell phone in when a text came through. Her heart skipped when she realized it was from Devon.

DEVON: Hey Sam, what's the rule on friends visiting each other's bedrooms at night?

Sam's face flushed scarlet and she felt her blood rush to embarrassing places. Devon was right across the hall. If she said yes, he could be in her room in six seconds. Maybe less—

his soccer-god body looked like it could move fast. Shit! Now she was thinking about his body again. This definitely was a bad idea. Today had been fun. Like, real, actual fun. She hated admitting that Devon was right—she did need a friend. And she hated admitting Megan was right—Devon was sexy and charming. But most of all she hated how scared she was of screwing everything up. *How had this happened?* She was losing focus already. Getting back to Boston was the only thing that mattered, and now because she was being a stupid girl and having stupid feelings, she was risking screwing it all up. She couldn't let herself get attached to Devon. Inviting him to her room would only complicate things.

Sam grabbed her phone and tapped out a reply.

SAM: Rule #4: Friends definitely don't booty call.
DEVON: Rules were meant to be broken.

A tingle of fear jolted Sam to her feet. She ran to her bedroom door and locked it. Then, she shut off her lights and hopped into bed, like a little kid afraid of the man in the moon. *In Sam's case, the man was Devon, and the moon was her big fat beating heart.*

Devon

Devon sat in his room staring at his cell phone, but Sam didn't respond. *Damn him for getting his hopes up.*

What did he expect? Sam to run into his room and jump into his open arms?

He'd dreamed it enough times that he could imagine exactly what it would be like. And thanks to her little shopping spree, he now knew exactly what lingerie she'd be wearing. And he couldn't stop imagining all the ways he'd take it off of her.

Awake or in dreams, Devon's mind drifted back to Sam. In his dreams, he told her he loved her and she said she'd never leave him. Then, they fell into his bed together.

"Get a grip," Devon scolded himself.

He paced his room while Eggsy stared at him lazily from bed. "Don't look at me like that," Devon berated the dog.

Eggsy was giving him that, *You're not going to do anything about it, look.*

"Maybe I will," Devon retorted, realizing he sounded daft, carrying on a one-sided conversation with his dog.

He opened his door and peered into the hallway. There was Sam's door, taunting him. He could do it. Just a few short steps across the hall and knock on her door. Screw knocking. Maybe he'd just go in and surprise her. *Christ, he could imagine her lying in her bed waiting for him in a pair of those lacey knickers she'd bought.*

Fuck! She'd scrambled his brain. He was thinking with the wrong head. He couldn't just go charging into her room. She didn't want him to come or she would have said so. Her text was a hard no. And it was driving Devon mad, because the more she said no, the more he wanted her. But deep down, he knew he needed to wait until he could win her over. He'd never force himself on her. He wasn't the aggressive type, unlike half the blokes on his team.

The other thing eating at Devon was that today had been the best day he'd had in a year. He couldn't remember the last time he'd smiled or laughed so much. Just being near Sam made everything better. And the last thing Devon wanted to do was muck it up because he couldn't keep it in his pants. He needed to play it cool. He'd rather be Sam's friend, than nothing at all.

CHAPTER
14

Sam

The rest of the week passed by in hours of boring monotony. Sam hadn't seen much of Devon except for at breakfasts. He was always working with his father or hers. She spent her days reading through her course work and taking practice exams. When she wasn't cramming for school, she was video chatting with Megan.

School had already started at Stanton and Megan was making Sam homesick with all the gossip.

"Guess who your Ryan is dating?" Megan squealed.

"He's not *my* Ryan," Sam corrected, while her heart plummeted. He *wasn't* hers, nonetheless it hurt to hear he hadn't even waited a week to move on.

"Okay, if you don't care, I won't tell you," Megan quipped indignantly.

"Fine, just tell me."

And so opened the floodgates. Megan filled Sam's head with news about Stanton. Apparently, Ryan was officially dating Terese Byers, a pretty underclassman. Hearing he'd landed a girlfriend in the first week of school made Sam feel like she'd been holding Ryan back all this time with her non-committal dating style. She thought he felt the same way about not seriously dating, but apparently not.

She listened to Megan's gossip, but it all felt useless. Sam had been sequestered at the James's estate for almost a week and already everyone was moving on without her. And to make matters worse, she was no closer to finding a way back to Boston. After spending time with Devon, she didn't have the heart to exploit him in her back-to-Boston scheme. And without him, she didn't see any other options, and resigned herself to start at Eddington.

After Sam hung up with Megan, she wallowed around her room feeling sorry for herself. But that wasn't getting her anywhere. Her shiny new soccer ball caught her eye and Sam's heart lightened a little. *Soccer was just the thing to cheer her up.* Playing solo wasn't much fun, but she could use the practice. Especially if Devon came through with Coach Tomlin.

Sam changed into her new workout gear and grabbed her star spangled ball, ready to head out and find somewhere to kick it around. *Shouldn't be hard on the immaculate mansion grounds.* She opened the door and ran smack into Devon's broad chest.

"Hey Sam!" he said cheerfully. "I was just coming to find you."

"You were?"

"Yeah and from the looks of it, you're about to be very happy about my news."

"You talked to the coach?" she asked.

"Yes. He's agreed to let you try out in two weeks."

"Omigod!" Sam dropped the ball and threw her arms around Devon's neck, bouncing on her toes. "Thank you, thank you, thank you! I owe you big time, Devon!"

He laughed and hugged her back. "I was hoping you'd say that," Devon murmured.

Sam let go and looked up at him. He was smirking at her. "What do you mean?"

"Well, I kinda already have a favor to ask."

"What is it?"

"I need a date."

"What?"

Devon ran his hands through his hair. "I wouldn't ask, but my father's being an absolute buggar about it."

"So your dad wants you to ask me out?"

Devon loosed a frustrated breath and continued to run his hands through his hair. "Well, it's sorta turned into that. The short version is, there's this wedding, and it's important for a member of our family to attend. Of course my father can't, so he's sending me instead, as I RSVP'd with a plus one a while ago. That was when I was still with Sophie, so he's forcing me to bring a date, because apparently, it's rude not to."

"And I'm your only option?"

Devon stuffed his hands in his pockets. "Your father overheard me arguing with my dad and sorta volunteered you."

"Great, so you're really not asking me."

"No! I absolutely am. But I'd never force you to come with me."

"What about our dads?"

"They can piss off. If you don't want to be my date, I'll find someone else. I just thought since we had so much fun the other day . . . I dunno, it might be fun to dress up and drink other people's booze."

Sam smiled. "That does sound kinda fun."

"So you'll be my date?" Devon's grin blinded her.

"Yes, but this isn't a real date. We're just going as friends."

"Of course. I'm sure you have a rule about not dating friends."

Sam rolled her eyes. "I'm pretty sure that's the principal rule of friendship."

"I thought no kissing was the most important rule?" he teased. "Make up your mind, woman."

She couldn't help but grin at Devon. It was impossible not to smile when he was smiling at her with his stupid ripply-dimples dancing on his face.

"I'm just making sure we're clear. When is this wedding anyway?" she asked.

His hands were in his hair again. "About that . . ."

"Tonight! He invited you to a wedding tonight? Omigod, Sam! You're going on a date with Prince Charming," Megan squawked.

Sam knew her best friend would overreact. But Megan was always the one Sam turned to when she needed fashion advice. Or makeup advice. Or anything girly-advice, for that matter. She tried to curb her eye-rolling and get Megan to focus. "It's not a date! We're going as friends. And stop calling him Prince Charming. His ego is big enough. Can you just help me pick out a dress to wear?"

"Okay fine, hold them up."

Megan helped Sam pick out a dress and sent her a few YouTube tutorials about how to apply an elegant smoky eye. *It was a total fail.* Sam ended up washing her face and just going with her normal routine. She showed Megan her finished look and she demanded Sam apply more than just mascara and lip-gloss. After following Megan's makeup instructions word-for-word, Sam felt pretty confident with her look. She still resembled herself, just kicked up a notch.

She was wearing a wine colored off-the-shoulder dress that fit her perfectly. It was a total impulse buy, and she'd pretty much been trying to punish her father with her outrageous shopping spree at Brown Thomas when she'd bought it. But Devon told her it looked *posh,* so she *had* to have it. Sam never thought she'd actually have an occasion to wear the dress. But now that she had it on, she sort of loved it. She added black strappy heels that tied around her ankles with a velvet bow. She'd even curled her hair, pinning it to one side so it fell over her shoulder in soft waves.

"Très magnifique!" Megan exclaimed. "Now have fun at the ball, Cinderella."

"Thanks," Sam replied blowing her best friend a kiss before signing off.

Sam hadn't even flinched at Megan's exuberance, because if she was honest, she was kind of excited for her non-date date with Devon too.

Devon

"Do or die, mate." Devon reminded himself to breathe as he walked across the hall to Sam's room. He couldn't believe she'd actually agreed to go with him. He felt like he'd won the lottery, and that was before Sam answered her door looking like a bombshell. *Shite, his girl was a beauty!*

His girl. Devon really did think of Sam as his girl. And maybe after tonight she would be.

"Wow," he said when he finally picked his jaw up off the floor. "You clean up nice, kitten."

"You look pretty too, baby cakes," she said not trying to hide her smile for a change. "And you know you own me, right? I never get all girl'd up."

"That's a shame. You're kinda sexy when you try."

"Keep it in your pants, baby cakes."

Devon grinned and offered Sam his arm. "Shall we?"

She took his arm and Devon was gripped by a dizzy rush of happiness. His chest felt tight. Everything felt tight. *How was it possible that Sam made it both harder and easier for him to breathe?*

Luckily the wedding ceremony was short and sweet, because Devon was dying to get to the reception so he could whisk Sam onto the dance floor and finally have an excuse to put his arms around her. So far, she'd vetoed hand holding, but looping her arm through his was okay.

This meant Devon had spent the entire evening with his elbows resembling arm rails in the hopes that Sam would touch him again. She was unsteady on her sexy stilettos and Devon thanked whatever masochist had designed them, because it meant Sam had to lean on him whenever they walked anywhere. *Christ, he would scoop her up and carry her wherever she wanted to go if she'd only say the word.* But she was still clinging to her damn rules.

No kissing. No hand-holding. No whispering. *No fun.*

The no whispering bothered him, because he was really enjoying having his mouth so close to her ear while he explained his relationship to the people they met. Perhaps he was letting his mouth linger too long. *Christ, he couldn't keep his mind from lingering on all the other places he wanted to put his mouth on Sam's body.*

At least she hadn't said no to dancing. *Not yet, anyway.*

Finally, it was time for dancing. And as much as Devon was looking forward to having Sam in his arms, it may have been a mistake. Devon had made it through the wedding reception without incident, but that was mostly due to the fact that he and Sam weren't touching. The stupid old biddy sitting next to Sam was bending her ear the whole time. Devon couldn't get a word in, so he kept knocking back glasses of champagne and making small talk waiting for the meal to be over.

The bride and groom eventually cut the cake and it was time to dance. Devon didn't waste any time tearing Sam away from the blabbermouth at their table. "Kitten, it's our song!" he exclaimed.

"Thank you," Sam whispered when they were away from the table. "That woman wouldn't shut up. I don't think I got two words in. All I could do was drink my champagne and nod. Did you know she thinks you're my brother?"

"Well, we'll have to set the record straight on the dance floor, won't we?" Devon said taking Sam's hand and twirling her away from him.

The twirling wasn't the problem. Everything was going really well until he pulled Sam back in from the spin and she landed against him—*everywhere*.

It was ridiculous. Devon couldn't think with every bit of Sam's front touching every bit of his. And then there were his hands. He didn't know where to put them, or not to put them. They seemed to be moving of their own accord, seeking out the most appealing places to hold her. *And the thing was, she didn't stop him.* She only moved her own hands over his body and swayed with the music.

And good Christ! The way she swayed those hips made him want to howl at the moon like some old-timey cartoon. He didn't know how he was going to survive the night feeling like this. Having Sam's body pressed against his shook something loose in his brain. Everything was in overdrive. His heart was pounding and his nerves were live wires, snapping and hissing everywhere she touched. His body was going haywire. Especially the parts of him he didn't want Sam to notice. *Not in a room full of people anyway.*

Devon needed to get some air and settle down or he was going to give Sam an advanced show. Devon wasn't shy about his manhood. But there was a time and place for such things, and a wedding dance floor wasn't one of them.

He used the break in the next song as his opportunity. "I've gotta take this jacket off," he said motioning back to their table. "Can I get you anything?"

"How about another glass of champagne?"

"Sure thing, kitten."

"I'm gonna use the ladies," Sam said, blowing Devon a kiss before she wobbled off the dance floor.

He watched her until she was out of the room. He couldn't help it, his eyes were just drawn to her. He noticed her cheeks were flushed and she had a brightness in her eyes that he hadn't seen yet. Maybe it was the champagne, or maybe she was having as much fun as he was.

Sam

Sam splashed water on her face in the bathroom. She'd used waterproof mascara so she didn't have too much of a mess on her hands. But the rest of her makeup was running anyway since she'd danced up a storm with Devon. It was seriously getting steamy out there. Devon could *dance*! And she couldn't help but notice how well they fit together. With her heels on they were perfectly compatible. *Too bad the stupid things were killing her feet.*

She dabbed her face with a paper towel and then reapplied some makeup from the emergency touch up kit Megan had demanded she put in her purse. Sam smiled at her reflection. She felt strangely light and happy tonight. Maybe it was all Megan's talk about living a fairytale, or maybe Ireland really wasn't that bad. Devon was certainly making the transition easier.

Speaking of Devon, she'd better get back out there before some bridesmaid tried to steal her date. He was easily the most eligible bachelor on the dance floor.

Sam found Devon standing by their table holding two glasses of champagne while chatting with some wedding guests. He'd taken his blazer off, loosened his tie and rolled up the sleeves of his blue dress shirt.

Good God, he was handsome.

Sam preferred his more casual look. *She'd actually prefer to take his tie off and unbutton his shirt all the way.*

Shit! She needed to get ahold of herself. Maybe another glass of champagne wasn't a good idea. But Devon had spotted her and his face lit up. She was starting to recognize it was a special smile he reserved just for her. *He didn't pull out those dimples for just anyone.*

Christ, if he did there'd be panty-less women all over the place.

He excused himself from the conversation and moved toward her. Once Sam was back in his arms she couldn't remember what was a good idea or not and she drained her glass of champagne.

⚬

They danced until Sam's feet were screaming. She finally gave in and took off her shoes when the music turned into slow songs. Devon led her back to their table so she could rest her feet. The guests were starting to thin out and they had the table to themselves.

Sam took a sip of water and put her feet up on the chair, groaning. Devon smiled at her and lifted her feet so he could slide into the chair under them. He pulled her feet into his lap and Sam tried to pull them away. "I don't think friends give each other foot massages," she warned. But when Devon started kneading the arch of her foot she nearly moaned. She was putty in his hands. "I take that back. Friends definitely give foot massages."

Devon laughed. *She loved his laugh.*

"Thanks for coming with me, Sam," he murmured. "I needed a night like this. Something to keep me from thinking about my dad."

She looked up at him and smiled. "A happy distraction?"

"Exactly."

Sam knew all about happy distractions. She was practically the master of them. She perfected the art on her father. She used the technique on days when he was struck with missing her mother so badly that he didn't get out of bed. Or he forgot to change his clothes. Or eat. It broke Sam's heart knowing Devon was going to have to go through days like that. She remembered how bad she'd missed her mother in the beginning. How she'd cried and felt like she would break apart from missing her.

Sam wished there was a way to spare Devon that misery. But then, she thought about how she could barely feel the pain of missing her mother anymore. Time had dulled it, along with her memories. Sam looked at Devon, who gave her a kind smile, and decided maybe the best thing she could do for him was to let him hang onto the pain of missing his father. To let it fill him up and wash over his bones, so that he'd know it was real and he'd have something to hang onto when time slipped in to steal pieces of the pain away.

Yes, the best she could do was be his friend and offer a few happy distractions. Sam regretfully pulled her feet from Devon's lap and took his hands. "Come on. I think I got a few dances left in me."

Even though her feet were throbbing, it wasn't hard for Sam to drag herself back to the dance floor. Dancing with Devon was like running downhill, and she never wanted to stop—even barefoot.

Devon let her stand on his shoes and it made her giggle. The emcee came on the mic announcing the last dance. Devon scooped Sam up and twirled her around as, *I had the Time of My Life*, blared through the speakers.

She cracked up as he sang all the words.

"I didn't know you were a *Dirty Dancing* fan?"

"There's a lot of things you don't know about me, Sam."

"I'm sure there are."

"Wanna know what I'm thinking right now?" he asked wiggling his eyebrows impishly.

She grinned. "I'm not sure."

"I'm thinking about kissing you, Sam."

"Devon! Friends don't kiss. Remember? And stop saying my name so much. It's weird."

"I like saying your name, *Sam*. And your rules are rubbish!"

"No, they're not!"

Devon shrugged and they kept dancing.

"Wanna know something else, Sam?" he asked.

"No!"

"But it's something about you," he taunted.

"I don't want to know!"

"Yes you do. It's a secret."

"Fine. What is it?"

"I think you almost had fun tonight, Sam."

She rolled her eyes, but she couldn't hide her grin. "Almost."

"I knew it!"

"Don't go getting a big head. I just like weddings. And can you please stop calling me Sam? It's Samantha."

"But I like Sam. It's a grand name."

"It's a boy's name."

"I like Sam," he said firmly, like the discussion was over. Then, he spun her and started singing the lyrics again. When she was back in his arms, he looked down at her with a more serious expression on his face. "I know this isn't Boston," Devon said. "But is it really so bad?"

Ugh, why did he have to bring up Boston? Not now. Not when she was almost having fun!

But now that he *had* brought up Boston, Sam felt like she wasn't allowed to have fun. Like she was betraying her home if she enjoyed herself somewhere else. She knew it was stupid, but it was Boston pride. Anyone who considered themselves a good Bostonian thought this way.

"Boston's my home, Devon. It's where I grew up. I had all my firsts there and I really thought I'd get to finish my journey there. I'm not going to get to graduate with my friends or finish out my soccer career with my team. It sucks."

"I'm sorry," he said quietly. "But, I'd kill to be you, starting over somewhere new. Getting to be anyone you want. I'm going to be stuck here managing my father's company forever. I feel like my life's over before it even started."

They weren't dancing anymore. Sam was looking at the sadness held between Devon's furrowed brows. He already had lines there, like he'd spent entirely too much time worrying for someone who was only seventeen. *Maybe being seventeen just sucked for everyone.*

"Have you told your father how you feel?" she asked.

"He doesn't care. Cor-Tec is his dying wish for me. I can't let his half of the company go to the highest bidder. Your father would be ruined too if I did that."

"I'm sorry, Devon. I didn't know . . . "

"No, *I'm* sorry. I didn't mean to crap on your problems with mine. I just mean to say that I know this isn't Boston, but things might not be as bad at they seem. If you're open to it, you could have some pretty grand firsts here."

Staring up at Devon made her think of some pretty grand firsts, indeed.

She nodded at him, not sure what to say. Devon's problems were much bigger than hers. She could go back to Boston next year, or anywhere she wanted. And she still had her father, even if he was a pain in her ass half the time.

"You ready to go home?" he asked.

"Sure."

CHAPTER
15

Devon

Devon was quiet on the drive home. He felt like a wall had gone up between him and Sam all of a sudden. He was cursing himself for ruining their perfect night by bringing up Boston and his father. Sam was right; she was his happy distraction. He just wanted to bury himself in her and the magnificent way she made him feel. But that wouldn't solve his problems. *He was beginning to realize nothing would.*

He walked Sam to her door and they both stood awkwardly in the hall looking down at their feet. *Sam was still barefoot, and Devon wished he still had her feet in his lap.*

"Thanks again for tonight," Devon said, finally looking at Sam.

"It was fun."

"It was. And I'm sorry about what I said."

She looked at him like she didn't know what he was apologizing for.

"The wanting to kiss you thing," he clarified.

"Oh."

"You were right," he continued.

"I was?"

"Yeah. We need rules if we're going to be friends. Crossing the line would just muck things up. And I really don't want to muck it up with you, Sam."

She looked up at him, her face a sea of turmoil. "You're not going to mess things up, Devon. I know how hard losing a parent can be. I'm always going to be here for you if you need me."

"What about Boston?"

"Who knows? But whether I end up in Boston or China, I'm only ever a phone call or text message away."

"Good, because I think I need you." Devon could feel his face breaking. "I know I do."

He watched his reflection twist in Sam's eyes. He hated acting like a sniveling fool around her. *He must have drunk too much champagne.* But Sam didn't seem put off by his sudden rush of emotions. She reached her hand up and gently cupped his face. "You have me, Devon." And then she kissed his cheek.

Devon pulled her to him trying to hide his tears. *He knew she didn't mean it the way he wanted her to. But it was good enough for now.*

They stood in the hallway holding each other tightly. Sam stayed patiently in his arms, rubbing her hands in soothing circles on his back until Devon could collect himself. When he finally felt like he could take a shaky breath without breaking down, he pulled away from her.

"Thank you," Devon said taking both of her hands.

Sam stood on her tiptoes and kissed his cheek again. "Goodnight, Devon."

"Goodnight, Sam."

Sam

Sam felt like she was dragging her heart behind her as she shuffled into her bedroom. It had been a traumatic night as far as her heart was concerned. She went from being all fluttery dancing with Devon, to shredded, after she tried to comfort him from the impossible loss he was facing. She was exhausted, and she wished there was more she could do for Devon. But all she could offer was to be there for him—whether he needed a shoulder to cry on or a happy distraction.

She and her father had been that for each other after Sam's mother died. And that was really the only thing that got them through it. The casseroles helped, but there's no recipe to heal a broken heart.

Sam forced herself to take a quick shower and then slipped into her new comfy pajamas before climbing into bed. She had just turned off the bedside lamp when she heard her phone ping with a text message. She rolled over and grabbed it off the nightstand.

DEVON: Just checking out your theory.

SAM: I'm still here.

DEVON: Good.

SAM: You know I'm only across the hall if you need me.

DEVON: I know.

DEVON: Thanks again for tonight.

SAM: Stop thanking me. I already told you I had fun.

DEVON: It was fun, wasn't it? Maybe we should do it again?

SAM: Are you asking me out, friend?

DEVON: No. That would be against the rules.

SAM: Good. Besides you still owe me for this non-date.

DEVON: What do you have in mind?

She thought for a moment. There was something she'd been dying to ask Devon for help with . . . She bit her lip and contemplated a bit longer before quickly typing a response.

SAM: Soccer practice? Tomorrow morning?

DEVON: Only if you call it football.

SAM: Deal.

DEVON: What time?

SAM: 7 am. See you bright and early.

DEVON: Perfect it's a date ;-)

SAM: It's NOT a date! See you in the morning.

Sam was grinning. Tomorrow was going to be a good day.

Sophie

Sophie rolled over trying to read the caller ID on her cell phone. *Who on earth was calling her at this hour?* It was the middle of the night.

"Hello?" Sophie said groggily.

"Soph? It's Molly."

"Mol! It's 1 am!"

"I know but this is important."

"It better be."

"You'll never guess who I saw at my cousin's wedding!"

"I'm not playing guessing games with you, Mol."

"Devon!"

Sophie sat up.

"And guess who he was with?" Molly asked.

"Don't tell me, that drab looking American, Samantha?"

"How'd you know?"

"I know everything, Molly."

"So you don't care that Devon's dating someone?"

"Of course not. *I* broke up with *him*! But that doesn't mean we're going to let that little slut go unchecked. She needs to learn the order around here."

"I was hoping you'd say that. So what's the plan?"

"You'll see."

CHAPTER
16

Sam

Sam was up at the crack of dawn. She was so excited to have an opportunity to get some soccer practice in that she couldn't sleep. She dressed in her new pink sports bra and matching shorts, before pulling on a gray long-sleeved shirt that said, *What's Life Without Goals?—she loved puns, especially soccer puns.* Sam quickly braided her hair and then searched for her phone to text Devon to see if he was ready.

She found it in her bed. It was dead. *Damn it.* She forgot to plug it in. *That's what happens when you fall asleep texting, Sam!* Oh well, Devon was only across the hall. She'd just go knock on his door. Sam shoved her ball and some gear into her athletic bag and headed across the hall.

She knocked on Devon's door.

No response.

She knocked louder.

Still nothing.

He better not have forgotten about her.

Sam knocked again, her temper rising. If Devon thought he was going to stand her up after she'd gotten all dolled up for him last night he had another thing coming. She'd march right in there and kick him out of bed.

She twisted the knob and the door swung open. It was dark inside his room. And loud. What was that noise? It sounded like rushing water. *Oh shit!* It was the shower! Devon was in the shower! *Naked.* She was in Devon's naked room. Naked Devon's room. *Devon was naked!*

Sam's brain seemed to be malfunctioning as the word *naked* lit up like neon lights in her head blinding out rational thought. She tried to escape from his room, but she kept trying to push his door open instead of pull. She heard the water squeak off and then the bathroom door opened.

Shit!

"Sam?"

Don't turn, Sam. She turned.

He was frozen in the bathroom doorway, completely naked, holding a dark towel at his side. The lights were glowing behind him and Sam swore she heard angels singing as she drooled over his perfect glistening body. He quickly covered himself with the towel and took a step toward her. He was starting to say something when a giant beast skirted around him from somewhere in the bathroom.

All Sam could do was shriek and cover her face as the massive wolf-like creature leapt for her.

Devon

Devon was so shocked to see Sam standing in his room, for a moment he thought he was imagining it. *It wouldn't have been the first time he'd dreamt she was in his bedroom.* But when Eggsy charged out of the bathroom behind him he knew it was real. And his dog was about to tackle the girl he loved.

"Eggsy! No!" Devon hollered, but the dog had already launched himself at Sam.

She screamed and crumpled to the floor as Eggsy stood over her growling.

"Eggsy! Heel!"

The dog immediately backed down, but the damage was done. Sam was on his bedroom floor shaking as tears streaked down her face.

"Shite, Sam. I'm sorry. Are you okay?" Devon asked kneeling down to inspect her.

"No!" she yelled. "What the hell is that thing?" she gasped glaring wide-eyed at Eggsy, who was now obediently sitting at the foot of his bed.

"My dog. I'm sorry. He's not used to people sneaking into my room."

"I wasn't sneaking," she said indignantly. "I knocked."

"I'm sorry. I didn't hear you. I was in the shower."

"Clearly," Sam said, averting her eyes as her face reddened.

Devon looked down and suddenly realized he was crouching in a towel that left him entirely too exposed in the front. He abruptly stood, adjusting the towel before offering Sam a hand up."

"I'm really sorry, Sam. Eggsy doesn't mean any harm. He's just protective."

"Tell that to my arm," she whimpered, gingerly touching the gaping hole in her new shirt.

"Let me see." Devon moved closer to Sam and Eggsy growled.

"Um, I think I'm fine. I'm just going to go back to my room now."

"Sam . . ." But she was out the door before he could protest.

Devon shot Eggsy a dirty look. "Some wingman you are!"

The dog cocked his head like he didn't understand. And clearly he didn't, because now Sam was probably terrified of Eggsy. And rightly so.

Devon dressed quickly and left Eggsy in his room before dashing across the hall to check on Sam. She answered the door in her sports bra and his words evaporated. Then he saw the bright red mark on her arm.

"Shite," Devon murmured. "That looks bad."

"I'll live," Sam replied. "But my shirt . . . might not recover." She nodded to the torn gray shirt on the floor.

"I'm so sorry," Devon said again. "Here, I brought you some first aid cream. You should disinfect before applying it though."

"Why? Does your hell hound have rabies?"

"He's not a hell hound!" Devon argued, genuinely hurt that Sam didn't like Eggsy. "Until you came along he's pretty much the only one I had to talk to around here."

Sam crossed her arms and gave Devon an unsympathetic look. "He may be a good listener but he murdered my shirt."

"Go tend to your arm, I'll fix your shirt."

Sam stomped into her bathroom and shut the door. Devon found a pair of scissors on her desk and cut the sleeves off her gray shirt, turning it into a tank. It's something he used to do to all his shirts during summer club, when it was too hot for sleeves. He wasn't sure if Sam would like it, but at least the shirt was salvageable this way. Now, if only repairing her opinion of Eggsy were so easy.

Sam came out of the bathroom with a smear of first aid cream on her arm. Devon shook his head. She was helpless. "It'll scar if you don't protect it from the sun."

She only shrugged.

Devon frowned. "You shouldn't take skin cancer so lightly."

Her eyes flicked up to his and they held each other's gaze for a long moment, each thinking the same unspeakable truth—cancer was a likely possibility for their futures based on their parents' history.

"Here," Devon said softly. He held up a spare strip of sleeve as he moved toward Sam. She let him tie it gently around her arm.

Devon tried not to let his hands linger on her soft skin too long. It was bad enough he let his dog harm her. He didn't need to accost her too. When the makeshift bandage was in place, Devon held out the rest of Sam's shirt. "It's the best I could do."

"It's great. Thanks."

"Still up for football?" he asked, awkwardly.

"Absolutely!"

"Grand. Let's hit the pitch?" he asked.

"You have an actual soccer pitch?" Sam asked, her eyes widening.

"Football," he corrected. "And of course."

She grinned.

"Come on."

⁓

Devon led Sam and Eggsy through the gardens toward the football pitch he and his father had built when they first moved in. They'd always shared an admiration for the sport. And Devon had fond memories of kicking the ball around with his old man. He hated that soon that's all they would be—*memories*. His father's sporting days were over. *Actually all his days would be over soon.*

Devon tried not to let the heaviness settle in his heart. Today was for the living. And Devon intended to live. *How could he not when he was spending the morning playing his favorite sport with his favorite girl?* He looked over at Sam. She was keeping one eye suspiciously fixed on his dog.

"Did he have to come with us?" Sam asked shooting Eggsy a dirty look.

"Yes. I can't keep him cooped up in my room. Which reminds me. Would you mind not mentioning what happened this morning? Cara hates Eggsy already."

"Can't imagine why," Sam quipped.

"He's a great dog. Please give him another chance," Devon begged.

Sam huffed as she glared at Eggsy, who barked at her.

"He can tell you don't like him," Devon added.

"The feeling's mutual."

"Can't you try to get along? I can't have my two favorites fighting." Devon knelt down next to Eggsy and whispered loud enough for Sam to hear. "We like this one, boy. She's almost my girlfriend."

"Don't fill his head with lies!"

"Go give her a kiss, boy."

Eggsy trotted over and started licking Sam's arms. She rolled her eyes but Devon caught her slight smirk.

Sam

The rest of Sam's morning went infinitely better than how it had begun. She and Devon played soccer for hours. They ran drill and scrimmaged, and even Eggsy got in on the action. He was a great out of bounds retriever. And he hadn't displayed any more hell hound attributes. *Maybe he wasn't so bad.* Sam actually loved dogs even though her father never let her have one. It's just that Eggsy was the size of a small horse and he was kind of intimidating when he came bounding toward you— even if his tongue was lolling about like he just wanted to lick you to death.

Devon finally called quits, claiming he needed to get Eggsy some water. But secretly Sam thought it was Devon who needed the break.

"Tired?" she asked.

"Yes!" he admitted. "Missing camp this summer has set me back."

"Yeah, me too."

"Doesn't look like it. You're really good, Sam."

"Thanks."

"I mean it. You play like a guy."

Sam glowed. That was probably the best compliment she'd ever gotten.

"You'll have no problem making the team," he continued.

"I hope so. It's seriously the only thing I've been looking

forward to about Eddington. Do you think we could keep practicing?

"I'd love to, but I don't know how much time I'll have once school starts up."

"Well, we still have two days before school starts. Let's make the most of them."

"You don't have to twist my arm. But let's clear it with your father. He's put a lot on my plate."

"You let me handle my father."

CHAPTER

17

Sam

Unfortunately, Sam didn't get a chance to test her powers of persuasion. She found out at lunch that day, her father was whisking Devon away to some software conference in London and they wouldn't be back until school started. That pretty much left Sam stranded at the James's Estate for the next two days. She hated not having a car—not that she'd even know where to go or have anyone to visit. She tried calling Megan, but she was already swamped with schoolwork. The only friend Sam had left to talk to was Eggsy.

Devon had asked her to take care of him while he was out of town. She'd agreed to feed him, but said there was no way she was going to let him sleep in her room. But, the first night Devon was gone, Eggsy howled so much that Sam ended up letting the stupid dog in her room. She told him he had to sleep on the floor, but when she woke up in the morning, Eggsy was sprawled out next to her. *Damn dog.*

It *was* surprisingly nice to have a companion though. Eggsy definitely wasn't a hell hound. By the second day, he was following Sam around like it was completely natural. She even found herself talking to him.

"So what should I wear to school tomorrow, Eggsy?" she asked while surveying her closet. Eggsy was lying upside down on her bed looking more like a bearskin rug than a dog.

"Fine, be that way, but if I don't wear the right thing I'm blaming you."

Sam heard laughter behind her and whirled around to see Devon standing in her room trying to cover his huge grin.

"Devon!" she yelled.

Eggsy leapt off the bed and tackled Devon.

After he escaped the dog's incessant licking, Devon greeted Sam. "Well, it looks like you two have been getting on."

"He's alright," she muttered unable to hide her smile.

"Do you want help picking out your school clothes, or does Eggsy have it covered?" he teased.

"Shut up."

Devon burst out laughing. "That was the cutest thing I've ever seen."

"Oh, whatever! Take your mangy mutt so I can have my bed back."

Devon ignored Sam's protests, and gave her a big hug. "I knew you'd grow to love him. He's just like me. Irresistible."

Sam rolled her eyes as she tried to push Devon away, but secretly she was happy to have him back. *And being in his arms wasn't so bad either.*

Devon

Not seeing Sam for two days had just about driven Devon crazy, not to mention that every hour he'd spent in London was filled with mind-numbing software lectures. He'd wanted to text Sam, but he felt funny about it with her father always around. They'd even shared a hotel room so Mr. Connors could spend his down time working with Devon on Cor-Tec.

The weekend was an utter nightmare. It was a glimpse into Devon's future—or lack of one—and it made him want to stab his eyes out. Devon was an outdoorsman. He wanted to major in environmental studies. So being locked in a building staring at a computer screen for two days straight made him want to scream. And that was only a weekend. Soon he would be spending every day like that.

That thought brought the old suffocating feeling back to his chest. But when Devon came home to find Sam chatting with his dog, his heart nearly melted. His stress instantly vanished and he could breathe again.

Devon was so happy to see Sam that he had to remind himself that she wasn't actually his girlfriend when he crushed her in a massive hug. He'd wanted to kiss her. He wanted to do so many things. *Stupid rules.*

Instead he spent all night hanging out in Sam's room with Eggsy. He loved what she'd done with the place. It was so bright and airy. It kind of reminded him of being in the clouds—*which was ironically how he felt when he was with her.* Devon especially loved the white twinkling lights Sam hung above her bed. She said it was so she could pretend she was sleeping under the stars and he felt his heart swell too big for his chest. *A girl that liked to sleep under the stars? Could she be any more perfect for him?*

They lay under her starry sky for hours while he filled her in about his dreadful trip to London and answered her first day of school questions. The poor thing had the jitters and it just made him want to hug her.

"There's no need to be nervous, Sam."

"Easy for you to say. You've gone to Eddington all your life. And you're a boy."

"What's that got to do with anything?"

"Being the new girl sucks. Girls are evil. Haven't you ever seen *Mean Girls*?"

"No, but being the new girl, means all the blokes will be keen for ya."

"Yes, which is exactly why all the girls are going to hate me."

"You know, I think they'd hate you less if you have a boyfriend," he suggested.

"That's not true."

"Think about it. If you have a boyfriend, you're not a threat to steal their blokes."

"And I suppose you're *volunteering as tribute?*"

Devon laughed. Sometimes he didn't understand half the weird American slangs she used. "Yeah, why not. It's almost like I'm your boyfriend anyway."

"An *almost boyfriend* sounds complicated."

"Good thing we have all your rules."

Sam threw a pillow at him and dramatically flopped back on her bed. "This sucks! I wish I was just going back to Stanton tomorrow. And that I had a pizza."

"Pizza?"

"Yes, it's my back to school tradition. Or at least it was. Megan and I would stay up late and eat a whole pizza and write down goals for the year."

Devon felt that fizzy feeling in his chest again. Sam was giving him one of those wistful smiles that made him want to lasso the moon for her.

"Well, we can't break tradition, now can we?" Devon said taking Sam by the hand and pulling her out of bed.

"Where are we going to get a pizza at this hour in the-middle-of-nowhere-Ireland?"

"We're not, but that doesn't mean we can't make one."

Sam

Sam was sitting on the metal counter of the industrial kitchen that she hadn't even known existed until a few minutes ago. This house really was ridiculous. *How did you hide a kitchen this big?* Although, Sam supposed it was meant to be hidden. Devon told her it was where the chef and staff prepared all the family's meals and they hated when he snuck in and raided it. *Which apparently, he did often, because he certainly knew his way around.*

Devon looted the pantry, while Sam looked up a pizza recipe. Then they created their masterpiece.

"It looks like a pizza," Sam said optimistically.

"Hopefully it tastes like one," Devon said after placing it in the oven.

He had flour on his forehead and Sam desperately wanted to wipe it off, but she didn't trust herself. She'd already felt butterflies every time their hands touched while arguing over where to put the toppings. And now he was smiling at her—*one of his just for her smiles*—and whenever he did that she just wanted to grab him by the dimples and kiss him. *No, the flour stays.* She didn't want to risk turning her almost boyfriend into the real thing the night before school started. She had enough to worry about.

Devon took a swig from a bottle of red wine and handed it to her.

She looked at him feigning horror. "Drinking on a school night?"

"I know we have school tomorrow, but what's pizza without red wine."

"That face was because I don't drink wine with pizza," she teased. "I'm more of a pizza and beer kinda girl."

"Grand, pizza and beer it is," Devon sang.

He returned from the massive walk-in refrigerator with a cold bottle of beer for Sam, which she happily drank.

~♡~

They took the pizza and a few more beers back to her room and ate it in her bed. The pizza actually turned out well. "You know, this almost feels normal," Sam said, finishing off the last slice.

"You say almost a lot," Devon replied. "What's with that?"

"You sound like Megan. She thinks it's because I'm afraid of commitment."

"Are you?"

"God, I don't know? Aren't we all?"

"No. I'm not."

Sam didn't like the way Devon was looking at her

now—*all hopeful gray eyes and perfect mouth.* That was the kind of look that precedes a declaration.

"Thanks for tonight, Devon. It's late. We should get some sleep. Tomorrow's gonna be a long day."

Disappointment flickered across his face, but he converted it to a polite smile.

"Right. Goodnight, Sam."

"Goodnight, Devon."

Eggsy groaned when Devon tried ousting him from Sam's bed. "Come on, ya traitor."

Sam watched them leave her room. And once the door was shut, she felt a crushing loneliness. Maybe Devon and Megan were right. Maybe she was afraid of commitment and this was her future—endless hours of being alone because she could never get past almost. She wished she could talk to Megan. But for tonight, she was alone with her thoughts.

CHAPTER
18

Devon

Devon groaned. "Stop worrying about things before they happen."

He was driving Sam to Eddington and so far she'd spent the whole trip spewing enough worry to shake even *his* confidence. "I've already promised to walk you to your first class. We have the next one together, and then lunch. It'll be fine."

"But—"

"But nothing. You look grand. You sound grand. Everything's going to be grand!"

"Fine!" she huffed.

They drove the last few miles in silence.

When Devon pulled into the lot at Eddington, he headed straight to his designated spot. All the students who drove on campus had special permits and got their own personal parking spots. The athletes always decorated theirs with their jersey numbers and such. Devon hadn't had time to paint over his spot. He wondered bitterly if someone else wore his jersey number now. But before Devon even got to his spot he could tell something was wrong. *Maybe everything wasn't going to be grand.*

"What's that?" Sam asked as they pulled up to his spot.

There were a bunch of students gathered around his parking spot and at first he couldn't tell what they were pointing at. But when they got closer his mouth fell open. Someone had spray painted all manner of foul words across his spot. His name was crossed out and an effigy wearing his old jersey was sitting in a chair with a noose around its neck.

Devon choked on his anger, the muscles in his jaw bulging as he silently drove past the crowd.

"Was that supposed to be you?" Sam asked, sounding appalled.

"I imagine so," he grumbled.

"What the hell? I know you quit the team, but this is ridiculous."

"It's just a first day prank."

"What happened to *everything will be grand*?" she asked.

"It will be, for you."

"Maybe you should tell the administration about this."

"Let it go, Sam. It's just a bunch of blokes blowing off steam."

"But they *hung* a mannequin that was supposed to be you. That's some messed up voodoo shit, Devon!"

"I let them down. I get it. If the shoe were on the other foot I'd have been helping them degrade some other poor bloke's space."

She just stared at him open-mouthed while he drove

to the back of the lot to find an empty parking space. Devon parked and opened the back hatch so they could grab their books.

"Look," he said gently putting a hand on Sam to stop her from walking toward the school. "Maybe it's not such a good idea for us to walk up together."

"What? Because of that?" she asked gesturing in the direction of his old parking space.

Devon nodded. "I know you're already worried about starting at a new school. I don't want to make things harder for you."

"Fuck 'em," she said taking Devon's hand and lifting her chin a little higher. "Friend rule number one. Friends always have each other's backs."

Devon squeezed her hand and felt his chest open a little further. He laced his fingers with hers and they strode up to Eddington together.

Maybe things were going to be just grand after all.

Sam

Things were not grand.

All during Sam's first period class she felt like she was in a bad dream. The kind where you're giving a speech in your underwear and everyone is pointing and laughing. She may not have been in her underwear, but everyone was definitely laughing at her expense.

They were all whispering about her. Saying her name just loud enough for her to overhear. She knew that game. She'd participated in it. But she'd never been on the receiving end. *It sucked.* She kept hearing words like slut and bitch. And she heard Devon's name mentioned with hers a lot. Everyone definitely thought they were dating, or at least a packaged deal. There went Devon's boyfriend theory. Almost boyfriend or not, Sam knew she had a target on her back.

She excused herself to the girls' lavatory halfway through class and hid in a bathroom stall trying not to cry. She just needed to get it out. *God, she hated this.* She was every typical teen movie right now. She could see the credits—*Samantha Conners as, girl crying in bathroom.* Sam dabbed away the few tears that slipped out and texted Megan.

SAM: Today blows.

Megan instantly Facetimed her. "Are you in a bathroom?"

"Yes," Sam hiccupped. "Keep your voice down."

"Okay, Moaning Myrtle."

"Could you just *not* right now? I'm having a really shitty day."

"What's wrong?"

"I feel like I'm on the set of *Mean Girls*! Every person in my first period class has literally been whispering about me and saying I'm a slut. I'm just waiting for someone to say *On Wednesdays We Wear Pink*. At least then I'll know I'm stuck in a nightmare. This can't be my life now, Meg!"

"Is it really that bad?"

"I'm calling you from a bathroom stall!" Sam hissed.

"Okay! Okay! Just calm down. I'm so sorry, Sam. I wish there was something I could do."

"Me too."

"Maybe if you tell your dad about it he'll let you come home?"

"Doubtful. He'll just say something lame like *give it time*, or *hang in there*."

"He *does* love those motivational posters."

"Ugh! What am I gonna do, Meg?"

"Just ignore them. If they don't see how awesome you are, they're blind. And you'll be back in Boston in no time. So who cares what they think, right?"

"You're right."

"I'm always right." Megan smiled.

"I miss you, Meg."

"I miss you too! Call me if the natives get restless."

By the time Sam made it to lunch she was checking her back for *kick me* signs. Thank God she had Devon, because she didn't think she could face the lunchroom alone. It was like walking into the belly of the beast. Sam knew the students weren't audibly booing her, but it kinda felt like they were as she and Devon walked through the rows of tables. She felt hundreds of eyes swivel, watching them until they found a seat.

"This is not grand," Sam whispered once they were seated.

"I know. I'm sorry," Devon replied. "I have a feeling it's all my fault."

"Are you sure this is just about you quitting the soccer team? Did you maybe murder someone and forget to mention it?"

Devon smirked. "Sadly, no. I have a feeling this is So-phie's doing."

"Why?" Sam asked while tearing her sandwich into tiny pieces for no reason other than that she needed something to do with her hands.

"Sophie made a couple rude comments about you being my girlfriend in first period."

"And did you correct her?"

"Yes, of course. But I don't think she believes me."

Sam sighed and shoved a straw in her can of soda, taking long slurps. "I mean why does she care anyway? You said *she* broke up with *you.*"

"I don't know. But maybe we shouldn't spend a lot of time together while we're on campus. Seeing us together will only piss her off and feed the rumors."

"You heard the rumors too? Everyone definitely thinks were dating!" Sam was still nervously slurping her soda, when Devon gently pulled it from her hands.

"Sam, you're shaking. I don't think you need the extra caffeine right now."

"It has nothing to do with caffeine! You can't abandon me, Devon! They'll eat me alive!"

"No one's going to hurt you, Sam. It's all just talk. You said your old school was kinda like this, no?"

"Not this bad. And I was never the one being picked on."

"The first day is always the worst. They'll find someone new to pick on soon enough. But for now let's lay low."

Sam had calculus after lunch. And of course, Sophie and Tess were in her class. Sam already hated math. *Why not make the nightmare complete and throw in a few of Satan's blonde Barbie spawns?*

Things just kept getting worse. Sam was late to class, so the only seat available was right in front of Sophie and Tess, and apparently a third one, named Molly, who had matching perfect blonde hair. *God! Maybe Sam could just dye her hair blonde and they'd think she was one of them.*

Halfway through class, Sophie leaned forward and poked Sam with a sharp pencil. "Psst."

Sam tried to ignore her.

"Psst! It's Samantha, right?"

Sam peeked over her shoulder.

"I'm not gonna bite you," Sophie whispered after a dramatic eye-roll.

"What do you want?" Sam asked.

"Are you *really* dating Devon James?"

"No!" Sam said a little too loudly. A few other students looked at her.

"Good. Because that would be a bad idea. Devon's not a good guy. And you're new here. I wouldn't want to see you get hurt."

Jesus! Was Sophie threatening her? Wasn't that the kind of thing people said on the *Sopranos?* Then Sam's defenses kicked in. *Who was Sophie to talk shit about Devon?* Devon was the only good person Sam had met so far—although saying so seemed like suicide at the moment. She wussed out and instead muttered, "Well, there's nothing to worry about because we're not dating."

"It's just that it seems you two spend a lot of time together," Sophie added a few minutes later.

Really? Sam thought their conversation was over.

"I sorta have to. I'm staying at his family's house. Our parents are friends. It's a long story."

"So you're not dating him?" Sophie asked again.

"No!"

Tess chimed in. "Then why did I see you two shopping for lingerie?"

"It was just a joke."

"And I saw you dancing with him at my cousin's wedding," Molly added.

"We went as friends," Sam replied.

"But my boyfriend said you told him you were dating Devon," Tess continued.

Sam scoffed. "Who's your boyfriend?"

"Sean Dougherty," she said proudly.

"Oh." *The prick from the sports shop. What are the chances?*

"Listen, Samantha," Sophie purred. "It seems you're confused about what's going on between you and Devon, so let me help you figure it out. Stay away from him or you're not going to like it here."

"What are you talking about? And didn't you break up with Devon for his best friend?"

Sophie laughed. "If you think Zander and Devon are friends you're even dumber than you look."

Then the bell rang, and the three evil blondes flounced out of class, like they hadn't just been spouting death threats.

～♡～

Sam really didn't think things could get worse after

calculus. But she was wrong. All through her Poly-Sci class a steady stream of boys walked past her desk laying panties with their phone numbers scrolled on them on top of her books. Her face was burning with shame. And the stupid teacher was either too old or too blind to notice what was happening. *Or maybe panty-grams were a normal first day greeting at Eddington.* Either way, all Sam could do was stuff them in her backpack and try not to cry.

One of the girls sitting behind Sam snickered. "I heard all it takes to get her in bed is a new pair of panties."

"That's because she goes through them so quickly," another one added.

Sam closed her eyes and prayed to just make it through the day. *Twenty more minutes. You can do this.*

When the bell finally rang Sam gathered her things and bolted from the classroom. When she got to the portico she realized it was pouring. She grabbed her umbrella—*the one Devon told her she'd need that morning*—thankful for at least one mercy in this hellish first day. She unsnapped the umbrella and started opening it above her as she rushed down the steps to the parking lot. She was midstride when a colorful storm of lace rained down around her from inside the umbrella. She looked at her feet and saw soggy pairs of panties strewn over the parking lot. Then, she looked up to see one more pair dangling from the umbrella, caught in the wires. She yanked it free and froze as she stared up at the words someone had written inside the umbrella. *Last chance . . .*

A burst of laughter nearby caught Sam's attention and she looked over to see a group of blondes giggling wildly. One of them held a cell phone, steadily aimed at Sam, recording her mortifying moment, while Sophie smiled and waved.

Devon

"I swear to God, Devon. They're threatening me. We have to go to the principal."

"Headmaster."

"Whatever. We need to tell an adult. Those bitches are crazy. And they're planning something."

"That's just how they are. They always try to stir up trouble, but they're all talk. It's nothing to worry about."

"How can you say that? This morning you were all, *everything's going to be grand, Sam*. Does *grand* mean *psychotic* in Ireland? How did you deal with Eddington all these years?"

"It wasn't always like this. Or maybe it was, but I dunno . . . I was never targeted."

"So you're saying you used to be popular and now just because you quit the soccer team everyone hates you?"

"Football! And yes, basically."

Sam frowned.

"What's wrong?"

"Nothing. Something similar happened at Stanton a few years ago, and it didn't end well. I really think we need to tell the administration what's going on."

"Listen, I'm not going to stop you if you really want to talk to the Headmaster," Devon said. "But there's nothing he can do. Going to Eddington is a privilege. Parents pay a lot of money so their kids can go here. Which basically means the students get away with murder because no one wants to piss off the people footing the bills. He'll most likely say if Eddington isn't to your liking, find a different school."

Sam looked like she was going to cry and it was breaking

Devon's heart. He knew all of this was his fault. And he had a plan to fix it, but it would depend on Zander's cooperation. Until Devon could smooth things over and get the target off Sam, the best thing he could do was to distance himself from her—*even if that was the last thing he wanted to do.*

"I know you don't want to hear this, but maybe tomorrow we shouldn't drive to school together."

"What? How am I supposed to get to school?"

"We have a car service. I'll ask Thorton to drive you."

"So that's it? You're ditching me already? Some almost boyfriend you are."

"Sam, come on. It's not like that. We're still friends."

"Don't, Devon. Don't you dare give me the, *I like you, but only when no one else is around,* bullshit. I'm not an idiot. I used to be popular too."

Devon forced his mouth shut and ground his teeth to stop himself from objecting. He wanted to scream. *Sam couldn't actually think that's what he thought of her, could see?* He fucking loved her. He wanted to shout it from the rooftops. But not if it meant hurting her. Not when it was his fault school was a nightmare for her. He could take it if she was angry with him, as long as it would protect her. *What were a few more days of Sam not knowing he was in love with her?* He'd waited this long. A little bit longer wouldn't kill him.

CHAPTER
19

Devon

A few more days turned into a few more weeks. And Devon was no closer to talking to Zander. They didn't have any classes together and Zander refused to talk to Devon when he waited for him after practices.

Zander finally acknowledged Devon, after he cornered him in the parking lot after school. "It's too late to come crawling back, mate," Zander warned.

"That's not why I'm here."

"Then I have nothing to say to you," Zander replied strolling to Sophie's car.

It seemed all Devon's old teammates were determined to shut him out and Zander wasn't going to cross that line. *Hell, he'd probably been the one to draw it.* And Devon couldn't even blame him. He knew he'd behave the same if it had been Zander to ditch the team while Devon still played.

Devon stood in the parking lot at a loss. He watched Sophie and Zander make out before pulling away. And then he watched Sam slink into a sleek black town car without so much as glancing in his direction. Misery settled into Devon's chest. He didn't know what to do. Things with Sam had gone wrong so quickly. She wasn't speaking to him. She took the car service to and from school and didn't even come to the lunchroom. He had no idea where she was hiding.

They saw each other at home, but mostly at dinner, and he couldn't really talk to her in front of her father, Cara and the kids. And every time Devon went to Sam's door, she refused to answer it.

It was probably just as well. *What would he even say? How's school? Sorry you think I'm avoiding you, but I'm actually trying to protect you?*

Devon knew he was running out of options, so he gave up his pride and begged Cara for a favor. She was his last hope.

Sam

Sam's phone was dead—again. It was dead a lot these days. It didn't charge right with the stupid UK adapter. And she'd spent all day texting Megan while she was at school so she could pretend she was at Stanton instead of in hell—*otherwise known as Eddington.*

It'd been two weeks since her first day. Things weren't any worse, but they weren't better either. Sophie and her minions were leaving Sam alone now that she wasn't talking to Devon. *But she wasn't talking to Devon.* And that pretty much left no one for Sam to talk to, making her desperately lonely.

After radio silence for two weeks—*which was her doing*—Sam realized how much she missed Devon. He kept trying to talk to her at home, but her pride got in the way. She hated feeling used. If he wasn't brave enough to be her friend at school, she wasn't going to be his friend at home. She knew he was trying to help her, but it still stung.

Sam plugged her useless phone into the charger and decided to video chat with Megan before it got too late. Sam practically lit up when she saw Megan's face pop onto her laptop screen. "Hey, Meg!"

"Hey, kiddo!" Megan greeted.

"Kiddo?"

"Yeah, I'm trying it out. I need a thing. All great film writers have a thing."

"Well, it's not kiddo," Sam said crinkling her nose.

"What about tootsie? Hey there, toots?" Megan said in a ragtime voice.

Sam giggled and shook her head. "No. Definitely not toots."

"It worked."

"What?"

"You laughed! I haven't heard that sound in ages."

Sam hadn't either. She smiled back at her best friend, wishing she could reach through the phone and hug her. "Thanks, Meg. I needed that."

"So how goes Camp Half-Blood?" Megan asked. That was her code word for Eddington since it referred to a school full of demons and demi-gods.

Sam sighed. "Same, it still sucks."

"And Devon?"

"He still sucks too."

"Are you still not talking to him?"

"Yeah. But it's probably for the best. He's basically Eddington's Cody Matthews."

"Well, maybe you could be his Hannah Stark!" Megan mused, referring to Stanton's legendary wunderkind who somehow cracked the Goldens and rescued Cody from social exile and jail time.

"I don't want to be his anything. I just want to come home."

"What about your dad? Still won't budge on Boston?"

"Nope." Sam had told her father how much she hated Eddington and that kids were teasing her, but as suspected, he pulled his usual *give it time* speech.

"Well, I may have some good news for you," Megan offered.

"You chartered a helicopter to break me out of this prison world?"

"No, but what would you say to having another inmate join you for a bit?"

"What? You're coming to Ireland?"

"If you're still there by winter break, my mom said she'd buy me a ticket to come visit."

Sam started to tear up, both from happiness and dread. The thought of getting to see Megan made her giddy, but that meant she'd have to survive Eddington all the way till break.

"Is that okay?" Megan asked when Sam didn't respond.

"Oh my God, yes! That's amazing, Meg. I think I'm just in shock."

Sam opened another window on her laptop and started counting.

"What are you doing?" Megan asked.

"Counting the weeks until you get here."

Megan laughed. "I already did that. There's eighteen."

Sam closed her eyes. That seemed like a lifetime away.

"Hey! None of that. You've got this, Sam. Are you doing what I told you and going to the library during lunch?"

"Yes."

"And?"

"And you were right."

"I knew the nerds would take pity on you."

"They haven't befriended me."

"But they don't give you shit either, right?"

"Right. But I hate it. I feel like a coward hiding in the library. I could totally take those stupid Irish Barbie dolls."

"Easy, killer," Megan said. "Channel that energy into your soccer tryouts tomorrow."

"I will." That was pretty much the only light at the end of the tunnel for Sam. Soccer was her solace. Soccer didn't play favorites. Soccer let you prove yourself and leave everything on the pitch. Plus, Sam couldn't wait to lay some blonde bitches out.

"Okay," Megan said. "I gotta get some studying done. Kick ass tomorrow." She blew Sam a kiss.

"Bye." Sam waited for the screen to go blank, then she balled herself up on her bed and cried.

How had this happened to her? Her life sucked. Her classes were hard. She had no friends. And she missed Boston so bad she feared she might have actually left her heart there. Plus, her father didn't even care. Megan was the only one who did, but their friendship was contained to a laptop or cell phone for the next eighteen weeks.

Having no one to interact with face-to-face was starting

to depress Sam. She stared at her bedroom door. She almost wanted to go across the hall and sit on Devon's bed so she could pet Eggsy and maybe convince Devon to bake another pizza. *Almost.* But almost wasn't enough.

CHAPTER
20

Sam

The next day Sam had a text from Devon when she woke up.

DEVON: Good luck at tryouts today.

She ignored it.

Sam went through the school day on autopilot—keeping her head down, eating in the library, and focusing on assignments. As hard as her classes were, she was actually staying on top of them since she had nothing better to do. She'd been a mediocre student at Stanton—mostly B's, maybe C's in math. But when Sam got her first Eddington Calculus quiz back with a giant red A on it she did a fist pump. Sophie and Tess snickered, but Sam didn't even care. Nothing was going to get her down today. Today was soccer day.

When the last bell sounded, Sam practically sprinted to the sports complex. She'd already met with Coach Tomlin the first week of school to confirm her tryout. He was holding a special one just for her since the rest of the girls' team had been selected during summer club. Sam changed quickly and reported to the soccer pitch expecting to see Coach Tomlin waiting for her. But when Sam walked through the bleachers to see the boys' team on the field she stopped dead. She glanced at her watch. She was right on time. *And there was no way she'd gotten the day wrong. She'd been living for this moment.*

Coach Tomlin blew his whistle when he saw Sam. "Boys, I'll need this half of the pitch," he called while motioning Sam over. "Apologies," Coach said. "First day of practice. The blokes were early. Guess everyone's eager to get this season started. Are you ready?"

Sam glanced over her shoulder. She hated having to try out with the boys watching. But she wasn't going to let that stop her. "Ready, Coach."

"Good lass," he said patting her on the back.

Coach Tomlin put her through all the standard drills— speed, agility, passing, throw-ins, headers, goal accuracy— and Sam nailed them all. *Even with the boys cat-calling behind her.*

"You're good, Connors," Coach Tomlin praised when she'd scored her tenth goal in a row. *Of course there hadn't been a goalie, but she hit her target every time.* "Do you mind running a few drills with defenders? The girls' team is in the weight room. I can pull a few of them out to—"

"I'll run drills with her," called a voice behind Sam.

She turned to see Zander O'Leary grinning at her. She

recognized him from Finnegan's and from seeing him attached to Sophie in the halls at Eddington.

"O'Leary!" Coach growled. "Why don't you return to drills with your *own* team." He turned back to Sam. "Grab a drink and take ten. I'll be back with McVickers and O'Toole."

"Yeah, you're right, Coach. I didn't think the little American princess could handle real football anyway."

Sam was halfway to the sideline when she heard Zander's taunt. She rolled her shoulders. *Keep walking,* her voice of reason muttered. And she almost did—*almost.*

"I can play as well as any guy on your team," Sam boasted.

"Wanna put money where your mouth is, Boston?" Zander goaded.

"O'Leary!" Coach shouted. "Sideline now!"

Zander laughed. "I told you she was all talk," he called to his team as he turned toward the sideline.

"I'll run drills with O'Leary," Sam called after Coach Tomlin, but he was already striding toward the sports complex. He just waved her off and kept walking.

"Sorry, princess," Zander jeered. "It's just as well. I wouldn't want to embarrass you."

"You wouldn't. I've been practicing with Devon. I can keep up."

Zander laughed. "Anyone can keep up with that wanker."

Sam's temper snapped and she kicked the ball that had been resting at her feet directly at Zander. It hit her target squarely and Zander crumpled to his knees, covering his balls and gasping for air. She couldn't help but curtsy before she walked away. She knew she shouldn't have done it, but she couldn't help herself. She was sick of taking shit from these over-privileged Micks. She took a seat on the sidelines, grinning as Zander rolled back and forth in pain.

Of course Zander couldn't let it go. Once he'd recovered from having his balls knocked back to pre-puberty, he found Sam on the sideline. He kicked a ball in her direction taunting her with vile hand gestures. She should have stayed seated. That would have been the smart thing to do. But for a smart girl, sometimes Sam was pretty stupid.

~♡~

By the time Coach Tomlin came back to the pitch, Zander and Sam were locked in a full on scrimmage. The two of them jostled for the ball, spinning and faking equally. They were a good match. Even though Zander outsized her, Sam made up for it with speed and agility. Zander had taken a few cheap shots that would have definitely earned him at least a yellow card, but Sam wasn't backing down. She was playing for more than herself. She was playing for Devon, too. All Sam wanted was to score on Zander once so she could shut him up. And she was close. So close.

If Sam had realized Coach Tomlin was back she would have stopped, but she didn't even notice him amongst the roar from the rest of the boys' team. She was too focused on the goal looming in front of her. Just a few more yards and she'd be in range. She felt Zander shift his weight. She was starting to know his tells. He was going to strike. Sam quickly feigned right and broke away with the ball. She had a clean shot at the goal and let it rip, falling to her knees in victory when the ball sailed into the net!

Half of Zander's team were calling foul, the other half

were cheering wildly for Sam and teasing Zander, who was looking at her in disbelief. His face twisted into a cocky smile and he trotted over to her. She had the sudden urge to run, but when Zander approached, he offered her a hand and shook it once she was on her feet.

"You're not bad, Boston," he admitted with half a smile.

"You too."

Coach Tomlin appeared and the ruckus from the boys died down immediately. "Now, if you're quite done showing off, Connors . . ." *Shit, Coach had seen?* "Why don't you join the girls in the weight room?"

"Yes, Coach." She paused. "Does that mean . . ."

"Welcome to the team, Connors."

Sam's heart soared.

"But lets try to avoid any more co-ed scrimmaging, shall we?"

"You got it, Coach."

Sam practically skipped to the bleachers where two girls from her team were waiting to take her to the weight room. From the way they were grinning they must've seen her score on Zander. She was almost to them when she saw two blonde girls sitting high in the bleachers. It was Sophie and Tess, and they were glaring at her.

Sophie

"Molly's on the girls' football team, right?" Tess asked.

"Yes," Sophie replied, stony.

"So are we gonna use her to show that Yank slut our boys are off limits, or what?"

Sophie's eyes followed Samantha as she walked to the

sports complex, burning holes in her back. "What do you think?" Sophie muttered.

Devon

Devon wished he could watch Sam's tryout. He was disappointed she hadn't even texted him back after he wished her good luck this morning. But he couldn't really blame her. As far as she knew, Devon had ditched her to save face at school. She didn't seem to believe he was only doing it for her own good, no matter what he said. Devon sighed and rubbed his temples. All he could do now was wait, and hope Cara could come through with Zander tonight.

Devon was still sitting in the parking lot catching up on his English homework when students slowly started to trickle out of the sports complex. His chest swelled when he spotted Sam among them. She was twirling her starry ball and grinning from ear-to-ear as she waved goodbye to a few of the girls. *She made the team!* He knew she would. Devon couldn't wait to hug her and celebrate. And if tonight went according to plan, he'd be able to.

He didn't wait for Sam to get into the town car with her driver. Devon had parked close to the exit so he could make a quick escape. He eased the Defender onto the road and set off to prepare for tonight.

CHAPTER
21

Devon

Zander arrived right on schedule—one hour before dinner. *Thank you, Cara!*

Devon had begged his stepmother to invite Zander to dinner. He hadn't told her the real reason, of course; only that he wanted to have the family together as much as possible while his father was well enough to enjoy it. It was no secret that Zander and Devon's father didn't get along. When Henry and Cara first announced their engagement, Zander had spouted off that his sister was only marrying Henry for his money. But yesterday, Devon told Cara that in light of Henry's diminishing health, perhaps it was time for everyone to make peace.

Cara had reluctantly agreed to invite Zander to dinner, but Devon had feared he wouldn't show up. Zander hadn't been to Devon's house since Cara married his father—Cara marrying Henry was another thing Devon routinely blamed himself for. If Zander and Devon weren't friends, Cara never would have met his father. In grammar school, Devon and Zander used to hide when Cara came to pick Zander up. It was only because Devon was such a lonely child and never wanted his friends to leave, but that loneliness had brought Cara into his life—permanently. Henry spent hours entertaining her until Devon and Zander finally got bored of their games. It was right after Henry had divorced Devon's mother and apparently he was lonely too. *Lonely enough to fall for a nineteen-year-old, more than twenty years his junior.*

Devon tried to shake the bitter memories from his head as he led Zander to the library. Zander was following him, smugly admiring the excessive wealth that lined the hallways.

"All of this will be mine someday," Zander mused.

Devon knew Zander was trying to get under his skin, but he held his tongue. Devon was going to have to hold everything back if he was going to have a chance of succeeding. Zander was like a piranha—he could smell even the tiniest hint of blood.

When they were finally in the library, Devon shut the doors and locked them.

"How very cloak and dagger, Dev. What are you plotting?"

"I have an offer for you," Devon said.

"What could you possibly have that I'd want?" Zander scoffed. "You're off the team, I'm captain now, and I even have your girl. Sophie is quite a ride," he sneered.

"I'm not talking about any of that boyhood shite, Zander. I'm talking about Cor-Tec."

Zander's eyebrows narrowed. "I'm listening."

"If you're still interested in Cor-Tec, I can put you on the board."

After Cara married Devon's father, Zander started sniffing around about the business. He was surprisingly techy and actually interested in the operation, but Devon's father was good at holding grudges. He told Zander that he'd never touch Cor-Tec after the way he disgraced Cara and himself, saying his sister was only after Henry's money. *Gold-digging whore, were Zander's exact words.* Zander wasn't the only one who thought that, of course, but he was apparently the only one stupid enough to say it straight to Henry's face. *Devon could hardly blame his father for shunning Zander after that.*

"What do you say?" Devon asked, anxious to bait Zander.

"And what do you get out of it?" Zander asked.

"You call Sophie and her hens off Sam."

"Connors? What's she got to do with this?"

"She's a guest here. And my friend. She doesn't deserve to be treated rudely at Eddington because she's associated with me. Get everyone to leave her alone, including if I'm around her or not, and I'll put you on the board at Cor-Tec."

Zander smirked. "How touching. You must really care for her, but I'm afraid you don't have anything left to bargain with. Everyone knows it's only a matter of time before your father dies. And when he does, my sister will inherit everything. So you see, I don't need you, James. I never have." Zander gave Devon a cunning grin and walked away.

"My father is leaving the company to me," Devon called after Zander. "That's why I quit the team. He's grooming me to take over. So unless you take this deal you'll never touch a piece of Cor-Tec."

Zander was at the library doors. He turned and gave Devon a smooth smile. "We'll see." And then, he left.

❧

Devon's conversation with Zander hadn't gone as planned and dinner wasn't any better. At first, Sam seemed surprised to see Zander in the dining room along with the entire family, including Henry. It was rare that everyone made an appearance at dinner these days. Sam had taken to eating in her room, Henry was too ill to eat much and Mr. Connors usually worked through dinner—*the man was a workaholic.* But tonight, everyone was in attendance. And to Devon's dismay, Cara had seated Sam right next to Zander, while Devon was seated across from them. There was only a table between them, but Devon felt like he was a million miles away as he watched Sam and Zander carry on a pleasant conversation— something to do with tryouts.

"How *were* tryouts today?" Devon asked, trying to steal Sam's attention.

"Good," she said nonchalantly. "I made the team."

"I knew you would," Devon replied giving her a smile, even though she missed it.

"You should've seen her," Zander bragged, putting his arm on the back of Sam's chair. *Devon wanted to smack it off.* "The girl can play. She even scored on me. We're still on for club this weekend, right?" Zander asked Sam.

"You're playing weekend club together?" Devon asked nearly dropping his fork.

Sam shrugged. "I could use the extra practice. And you're never available."

Devon caught Sam's eye, unable to hide his hurt. Sam only held his gaze for a moment before looking away.

When Devon recovered his hurt expression he caught Zander smirking at him. *The bastard didn't miss a thing.*

"I'm afraid that's my fault," Mr. Connors said. "I've been keeping poor Devon busy with Cor-Tec. I'm sorry, Devon. It's just that you're such a valuable asset. And I'd say you're really starting to get the hang of the new platform."

"New platform?" Zander asked.

"Let's not bore them with business," Henry interrupted before Mr. Connors could reply. "Tonight, I'd like to enjoy a meal with my family and friends."

After dinner, Devon was feeling dejected. His plan to win Zander over had backfired, and now Sam seemed farther away than ever. He excused himself and retreated to his room. He planned to take Eggsy for a walk to clear his head, because if he had to sit around listening to Zander flirt with Sam for another second he was liable to smash Zander's face into a wall.

Devon was just leashing Eggsy when he heard a knock at his door. Zander stood in the hall and Eggsy growled.

"Heel," Devon commanded.

"I've reconsidered," Zander said, eyeing the wolfhound. "I'll talk to Sophie and see what I can do."

"Really? What do you want for it?"

Zander shrugged. "Nothing."

Zander never did something for nothing. The whole time he and Devon had been friends Zander had made it clear that he'd come from nothing and clawed his way to the top. *So why this sudden change of heart? What was his angle?* "I don't get it," Devon said.

"Let's just say our interests have aligned. Sam's a special girl. I can see why you spend so much time with her."

Devon's hair rose on the back of his neck. *He didn't like this at all.* He'd seen that look in Zander's eyes before. He was on the chase, and Sam was in his sights. But there was no way in hell Devon was going to let that happen. Steal his team, steal Sophie, steal his God damned inheritance for all he cared, but not Sam. Sam was not negotiable.

But fine, if Zander wanted to think he had a chance with Sam, Devon would let him. He wasn't worried. Sam wasn't a game to him. He had real feelings for her and even Zander couldn't challenge that. All Devon needed was assurance that Zander would call Sophie off.

"So you'll tell Sophie to leave Sam alone. And that she doesn't have to stay away from me?"

Zander nodded.

"Why?"

"So when I take everything you've ever wanted, I'll have the satisfaction of knowing I beat you on my own. Just like everything else I've accomplished."

Another pair of footsteps echoed down the hall. Both boys looked to see Sam approaching. Zander grinned and waved at her. Before he went to meet her, Zander turned back to Devon. "All is fair in love and war, mate."

Devon scowled. *War it would be.*

It was well after dark by the time Zander finally left. He and Sam had been in the library for hours, their laughter wafting back to Devon from where he was spying in the drawing room. He didn't even wait a heartbeat to knock on Sam's door once Zander was gone.

Sam was smiling when she opened the door, but it faded when she saw it was Devon. *Had she been hoping it was Zander knocking?*

"Yes?" Sam said crossly.

Devon squashed his disappointment. "Hi," he said nervously. "I was wondering if you wanted to go for a walk?"

"Now?"

"I know it's late, but I really need to talk to you and it can't wait."

"Okay, but I don't want to go for a walk. It's cold out. Can we talk here?"

"Are you sure you're from, Boston?"

"It's colder here. And you don't get to tease me. We're not friends, remember?"

Devon bowed his head in shame. "About that, I was hoping I could make it up to you?"

"How?"

"Come with me."

She rolled her eyes—*Christ, he even missed her eye rolling*. She followed him across the hall to his room. Eggsy was lying on the bed sniffing a pile of pizza boxes with two six-packs of beer on top. Once his dog saw Sam, he bounded off the bed and leapt up on her so she had to hug him to avoid being toppled over.

"Don't use Eggsy to win me over," Sam reprimanded after she'd ruffled the dog's fur.

"That's why I got beer and pizza too," Devon replied trying not to grin too wide.

Sam wasn't buying it. Her face was set to perma-scowl—*which was quite adorable, actually.* She looked like an angry kitten. But Devon knew under that adorable exterior was the spirit of a lion, so he needed to tread lightly.

"Look, Sam. I'm sorry. I was wrong. You were right. I just want to go back to being friends with you."

"Oh, so now you want to be my friend? Now that I'm not a social pariah and I've managed to actually have a good day at Eddington?"

"No, that's not what it's about. I told you from the beginning I was just trying to protect you by keeping my distance. I knew things would calm down and you'd win everyone over. And you have. So we don't have to pretend anymore."

"Oh, I'm not pretending, Devon. I'm actually mad at you."

"Sam, please. I miss you. You said you'd always be there for me. This is me, saying I need you."

"That's not fair, Devon. You can't just turn friendship on and off like that. That's not how it works."

"Sam, you're the only thing that matters to me. And you were right from day one. It doesn't matter what we do. People are gonna believe what they want to. So who cares?"

"You do! You obviously care what people think or you wouldn't have ditched me."

"I didn't ditch you at home."

"That makes it worse, Devon!"

Devon loosed a frustrated breath and ran his hands through his hair. He'd been pacing his room and finally gave up. He sank onto his bed. Nothing was going as planned. *How could he care so much for Sam, but never find a way to express it with words?* Words just screwed everything up. What he really wanted to do was kiss her. But the way things were going she'd probably punch him.

He rubbed his eyes with the heels of his hands until he saw stars. *Fuck! Even stars made him think of Sam.* When his vision cleared he looked at Sam, his heart heavy. She was frowning at him from the doorway. Her arms were folded and she looked like she already had one foot out the door. Eggsy was sitting at her feet. *Traitor.* Even he was against Devon.

Devon stood up and tried again. This time he tugged one of Sam's hands loose so he could hold it while he talked to her. Touching her seemed to help loosen his heart. "I'm sorry, Sam. I'm an idiot. I'm no good at being friends with you. But I don't know how to stop."

Her frown vanished. "That's the first thing you've said that doesn't make me want to kick you."

He smiled. "That's something, no?"

She didn't answer.

"I swear my intentions were never to hurt you, but obviously I suck at being friends with a girl. Can you just be in charge from now on?"

She smiled—*an actual smile.* "You don't *totally* suck. You knew to get beer and pizza."

"Want to give me some more pointers on not sucking while we have said pizza and beer?" he asked with mild hope.

"Come on, you big idiot. But this is your last chance, so don't blow it."

Sam

Sam sat in Devon's room all night, eating pizza, drinking beer and catching up on what they'd missed in each other's lives over that past few weeks. She told him everything about soccer tryouts. And he actually cheered when she told him about scoring on Zander. He ran around the room screaming GOOAAALLLL like a proper Premier League fanatic. Eggsy had gone insane and overturned her can of beer trying to tackle Devon. The beer casualty was totally worth it to be laughing with Devon again.

In just that one night, Sam learned more about Devon than she had in nearly a month. His favorite soccer—*sorry, football*—team was Arsenal. Which was apparently disgraceful because Arsenal was an English team. He had to hide all his Arsenal jerseys because his father was a diehard Galway United fan. Growing up they used to steal each other's jerseys and tear them to pieces. To Sam, it sounded horrendous, but Devon seemed to think it was the best thing ever. He recounted endless stories of shenanigans, as he called it, with his father and jersey pranks.

Six beers and too many slices of pizza later, she and Devon were right back where they started before that awful first day at Eddington. Maybe they were even closer. When Sam thought about it, fighting and making up only made friendships stronger. She and Megan used to fight all the time growing up. Every time had seemed like the end of the world, and she'd vowed she would never forgive Megan for whatever it was they were fighting about. But they would always end up patching things up over ice cream. Sam secretly wondered if she should share her weakness for chocolate chip mint—

the white kind with candy cane chips—but she figured Devon would use it against her in their next fight. *He already knew about the pizza and beer.*

Regardless, Sam was glad to have Devon back in her life.

CHAPTER

22

Sam

If anyone had told Sam that she would be enjoying the next six weeks at Eddington, she would have called them crazy. But here it was, eight weeks into the first term and Sam was starting to feel at home. No one at school was picking on her. Even Sophie and her minions left her alone. They still glared at her, but glaring was harmless. Zander continued to flirt with her. But flirting was harmless, too. And Sam actually liked hanging out with Zander at his Saturday football club. A few of the other girls on Sam's team played too. She won her team over instantly because she was by far the best player. And due to Sam's superior offensive moves, the Lady Eddi's, were currently undefeated.

But by far, the thing that made Sam happiest, was Devon. *And Eggsy.* Okay, mostly Devon, but she'd grown to love the lanky mutt, who much to Devon's dismay, slept in Sam's bed now.

"You're a traitor!" Devon called across the hall at Eggsy on Thursday night.

"No, he's just smart," Sam called back.

At some point, Sam and Devon had started leaving their bedroom doors open so they could talk continually. That's how Eggsy ended up in Sam's bed. That's where the huge dog currently was, with Sam's feet propped on his furry back as she tried to concentrate on her homework.

"It's not fair. I'm lonely over here," Devon called.

"Well, no one said you had to stay over there all alone."

"It's the principle of the thing," Devon pouted. "He's *my* dog. He should hang out in *my* room."

"Maybe if your room was more fun . . ." Sam teased.

"My room is fun!"

Sam was about to yell a witty comeback about his room being dark and boyish, when her laptop screen chimed and Megan's face flashed on the screen. "Hey, Meg!"

"Hey, doll face!" *Megan had settled on doll face as her thing.*

"Is that Megan?" Devon called from across the hall.

In two seconds he was crowding onto Sam's bed to talk to Megan with her. *This had become their thing*—talking to Megan, and volleying for her attention. Megan loved it. She made Devon say all sorts of random words that she thought would sound funny in his accent.

Today she greeted Devon with her best Irish accent. "-Ello, 'ansome!" *It was terrible.*

"Have I taught you nothing, lass? You sound bloody British!" Devon teased.

Megan giggled. "So, what's my favorite duo up to tonight?"

"You're looking at it," Sam said holding up her homework.

"Blimey! You should be out drinking pints or playing the fiddle!" Megan retorted.

Sam rolled her eyes. *Megan thought all Irish people played the fiddle.* "I think you're gonna be sorely disappointed when you come to visit, Meg."

"It's under twelve weeks now!" Megan squealed.

"Seventy-nine days!" Devon added.

"How do *you* know that?" Megan asked.

"Sam made a calendar," he said grabbing her laptop and swiveling it so Megan could see the corny poster board hanging over Sam's desk.

"Correction! You helped me make it," Sam said grabbing her laptop back from Devon.

"You guys are disgusting!" Megan yelled. "Can you just get married and have babies already!"

Sam hated when Megan said stuff like that. It made her face hot, but Devon just took it all in stride. He'd say things like, *not without you*, or *so, we have some news . . .*

Today he said, "Didn't she tell you, we're going away together!"

"You are?" Megan asked, her eyes as big as saucers.

"Not like that," Sam corrected before her best friend exploded. "Just camping, and I haven't even agreed yet, Devon."

"Why not? Are you scared?" Megan teased.

"Yeah, why not, Sam?" Devon pestered. "Even Eggsy's going."

Devon had invited Sam on his annual camping trip. They both had Monday off from school for some random Irish holiday, and Devon apparently always spent the holiday weekend camping with his father. But this year, Henry obviously couldn't go, so Devon invited Sam instead.

Sam wanted to go to be a good friend, but if she was honest, she was nervous to be alone in the wilderness with Devon. Sleeping in the same tent with him was a temptation she didn't need. Lately, she'd caught herself staring at him, in a more-than-friends kind of way. And last week, she had a dream about him that broke every friends rule there was. *So yeah, camping with Devon sounded dangerous.*

Megan was still carrying on about Sam being a scaredy cat. "Why don't you want to go?"

"Because. I've never been camping," Sam said hoping to skirt the real issue.

"You'll love it," Devon said.

"Yeah, Sam, you'll love it," Megan echoed. "Don't be scared."

Ugh, they always ganged up on her.

"What's not to love?" Devon continued. "Wilderness and stars and fresh air."

"Bugs, dirt, sleeping on the ground," Sam added. "Plus, I'm a girl. Peeing in the woods doesn't excite me."

Devon laughed. "Come on, it'll be grand."

"Come on, Sam!" Megan begged. "I want to go camping in Ireland. Do it for me!"

Sam contemplated her options. A weekend home alone, or a weekend sleeping under the stars? "I do like stars . . ." she said tentatively.

Devon and Megan both started chanting her name. "Sam! Sam! Sam!"

"Oh my God! Fine! But if I die in the woods I'm going to haunt you both."

~~

When they finally disconnected with Megan, Devon took both of Sam's hands excitedly. "Are you really gonna come camping with me?"

The enthusiasm in his voice was intoxicating. *How could she say no when he was so happy?* Besides, she couldn't make him go by himself. One, she would be worried about him. Two, he'd be all alone and thinking about a lifetime of lonely camping trips without his father. She had to go. It's what a good friend would do. She'd just stuff her feelings down. They probably weren't even real anyway. It was just hormones. Being constantly surrounded by hot Irish guys that looked like they'd just gotten off a yachting photo shoot was making her boy-crazy. *But she could do this. She would conquer her hormones and be a good friend.*

Sam sighed and nodded her head. "Yeah. Why not?"

"Ah! Grand! This is going to be brilliant! I'm gonna go grab my map so I can show you where we're going. Ah! Grand!" He said again, practically skipping out of the room.

Sam flopped onto her back, hoping she hadn't just made a huge mistake.

CHAPTER
23

Sam

The next day was the Lady Eddi's biggest soccer match of the year. And it seemed like the whole school showed up to cheer them on. It was probably because everyone was excited about the long weekend, but Sam pretended it was because of her team's undefeated record.

Devon sat in his usual spot—front row on the bleachers—with Eggsy. Sam loved when Devon brought Eggsy to her matches. The massive dog always growled at the girls that tried to talk to Devon. Sam ran over to say hello to them both before the game started. After chatting for a quick moment, Coach blew the whistle calling her in.

"Knock 'em dead, kitten," Devon cheered as Sam jogged away.

She blew him a kiss over her shoulder. "Thanks, baby cakes."

They talked like that a lot, and pretty much the whole school thought they were dating. But Sam didn't care anymore. Things were going well. People could think what they wanted. She had Devon and Eggsy and soccer. *Nothing could bring her down.*

Sam joined her team on the pitch and got ready to do their token huddle before they kicked ass and took names.

Devon

Devon cheered like a wild man when Sam scored her third goal off a free kick.

"Hat trick!" he hollered while Eggsy barked.

Sophie and Tess had showed up after the game started and stood next to the section where Devon was sitting. They looked pissed that they had to stand, but there were no seats left. Devon's manners got the best of him and he offered the girls his seat. He was on his feet cheering most of the time anyway. Plus, it would be half time soon and he wanted to run over and high-five Sam for that awesome goal. She was an absolutely brilliant player. And if he weren't already in love with her, he surely would be after watching her play.

By the time Devon let Eggsy do his business and made it to the other sideline where the players were, there was only five minutes of halftime left. He went to find Sam, but someone had beat him to it—Zander. He was chatting with Sam with his arm draped around her sweaty shoulders. Devon growled. *Those are my sweaty shoulders!* Sam was laughing. *How could she not see Zander for what he was? A womanizing sycophant!*

Devon wanted to scream. But then Sam saw him and shirked Zander's arm off her shoulders so she could run to Devon. She practically leapt into his arms.

"Did you see my free kick?" she squealed.

"And that header! You're on fire out there!"

"We're killing them!" She turned to Eggsy scratching him behind the ears. "Thanks for cheering, boy. I can hear ya out there."

"Is he distracting?" Devon asked.

"No, I love having my boys here." Her coach blew his whistle. "Gotta go," Sam said, giving Devon and Eggsy each a quick hug.

My boys . . . the words made Devon's heart swell. His jealousy had almost subsided, as Sam jogged back to join her team. *Almost*—until he saw Zander glaring at him threateningly. *He was up to something.*

Devon returned to his spot by the bleachers trying to shake the foreboding feeling he got from Zander. Luckily Zander remained on the other side of the field with the boys' team so Devon could keep an eye on him. Only the girls' team and coaching staff were technically supposed to be on the sidelines during games, but Coach never reprimanded his players. That was half the problem. All the blokes on the team thought they were untouchable—Zander most of all.

Devon leaned up against the bleacher railing as the game got back under way. He noticed Sophie and Tess arguing. They were too engrossed to notice he'd returned.

"I can't believe you're not going to do anything about Zander," Tess was saying. "He's been blatantly flirting with that Samantha girl for weeks! Are you guys over or something?"

"We are definitely *not* over!" Sophie huffed.

"Then, I don't get it. Why don't you do something?" Tess continued.

"I am, Tess. It's all part of the plan. Just wait and see."

Devon gritted his teeth. He'd heard enough. He was going to keep his mouth shut about Zander until after their camping trip so he didn't ruin the weekend he planned, but this couldn't wait. If Sophie was involved in whatever Zander was up to, it wasn't good. Zander was a prick, but Sophie's wrath knew no boundaries—a dangerous combination.

~❧~

Devon waited for Sam after the game. He had the Defender packed with all their gear so they could leave from Eddington to make camp before dark. Sam came bounding over to the car, freshly showered and grinning from ear-to-ear.

She greeted Devon and Eggsy as she climbed in. "There's my favorite fan club!"

Sam seemed on cloud-nine, so Devon had to broach the subject delicately. He waited until they'd driven off campus to say anything. "So, I saw you talking to Zander at halftime . . ."

"Oh, Devon, can we not? We're on our way to have an amazing weekend. I don't want to argue with you about this again. Zander isn't some maniacal villain. He's just a flirt."

"You're not . . . into him . . . are you?" Devon asked awkwardly.

"God, no!"

"Good. Grand!" Devon's chest flooded with relief. It was the first time he'd come right out and asked her. "I mean it's not like I'm telling you who to date or anything. It's just . . .

I don't trust him."

"I know, Devon. You've made that perfectly clear. And I'm not an idiot. Zander's pretty transparent."

"He is?"

"Yeah. He's just flirting with me because he knows it bothers you."

"You think?"

"It's obvious."

"Oh. Well, that's good."

"Hey!" Sam yelled smacking Devon's arm.

"What?"

"It's not good. You're not supposed to want guys fake flirting with me to make you jealous."

"That's not what I meant. It's just good that you can see through his bollocks, because I overheard something unsettling at the game today."

"What?"

"Sophie and Tess were talking. They saw Zander flirting with you and Sophie said it was all part of some plan."

Devon glanced over at Sam in the passenger seat. She was frowning.

"I'm telling you the truth," he argued.

"I know."

"Then why do you look mad?"

"After the game, Trista, one of the girls on my team, got in a big fight in the locker room with Molly. Trista accused Molly of putting hair remover in her shampoo."

"What?"

"Yeah, I guess big clumps of her hair came out in the shower. And I didn't think anything of it until you said you heard Sophie plotting.

"What are you thinking?" Devon asked.

"Trista and I share a locker." Sam shook her head and then looked at Devon. "Sophie and Molly are pretty tight. Do you think Sophie would put Molly up to spiking my shampoo?"

Devon ground his teeth. "There's not much I would put past Sophie."

Sam looked rattled. "That means it should've been me with bald spots, not poor Trista."

"Perhaps your flirting with Zander isn't so harmless."

Sam's face fell. "Can we please press pause on this argument. I really don't want to spend our weekend arguing about Sophie and Zander. I want to go camping!"

Devon couldn't help grinning despite his concerns. "I never thought I'd hear you say those words."

"I might just surprise you yet," she said raising her chin.

Sam was in such a good mood before he'd brought up Zander and Sophie that Devon hated to waste it. Besides, it's not like they could do anything to them while they were camping. "Alright, Boston. You're right. Let's go celebrate your victory in the woods!"

Sam giggled. "I like when you call me Boston."

"I like when you call me baby cakes."

Sophie

"Are you kidding me, Molly? How could you screw this up?"

Sophie was fuming. She was sitting in her BMW with a tearful Molly and a cranky Tess. Her plan to Nair-poo Samantha had royally backfired.

"I didn't realize she was sharing a locker with, Trista! And now Trista wants to kill me."

"That's not my problem," Sophie snapped. "Someone come up with a plan to fix this! Now! I will not have that skank going to the Grad Ball with Devon!"

"Don't you mean Zander?" Tess asked.

Sophie glared at her useless friends. She couldn't believe her plan had failed. *Samantha was supposed to be bald right now!* Sophie could picture it. Samantha would look so hideous without hair that she would never show herself at the dance. Better yet, maybe she'd drop out of Eddington. But no! Molly had fucked it up. Now, Trista, who could actually pull-off a bald head because she was butch as hell, was going to kill Sophie if she ever found out she'd been behind the Nair-poo. *Trista was definitely going to kill Molly.*

"I have an idea," Tess said pulling a vial from her purse and handing it to Sophie.

Sophie read the label and frowned. "I thought I told you to get rid of this last summer?"

"You did, but I don't always do what you say," Tess challenged.

Sophie smirked. *Maybe one of her friends was useful after all.* "Does anyone know you have this?"

"No," Tess replied.

"Good. Let's keep it that way."

CHAPTER
24

Devon

By the time they approached camp, Zander and Sophie were the last things on Devon's mind. Sam was in such a good mood she practically skipped the two-mile hike to their campsite. Devon couldn't stop smiling either. Taking Sam on this trip had been a brilliant idea. He was going to get two whole days with her completely to himself. And she was out of her element, so when she wasn't bouncing and reliving the football match, she was clinging to Devon's hand because every little noise in the woods frightened her. *It was rather adorable.* She'd bound ahead with Eggsy and they'd both come bolting back whenever something spooked them. It was mostly birds. Sam was being too loud for anything larger to still be around.

"You know, if you keep your voice down we might see some red deer," Devon said.

"Really? I've never seen a wild deer."

"That's not true. They used to graze in my mother's garden all the time. Don't you remember? We used to try to sneak up on them?"

Sam shook her head and something sullen reflected in her eyes. It was fast, like sunlight on water.

"What's wrong?" Devon asked.

"Nothing. I just wished I remembered more of those days," she said softly.

"It's alright. I remember enough for both of us," Devon said taking her hand and pulling her to a stop. "Like for instance. I remember how much you hate the idea of sleeping on the ground."

Sam wrinkled her nose. "That's because I told you that last week when you were trying to convince me to come camping."

"You hated it when you were a little girl, too. You used to hide from me under my mother's giant rhubarb bushes, but you always gave up after five minutes. You'd come out crying because you were terrified of all the creepy crawlies on the ground."

"Whatever! That's only because you used to put spiders in my hair and every little brush I felt made me think there was one on me."

Devon smirked.

"You better not get any ideas, Devon James! I know how to defend myself now," she said nudging him with her elbow.

"I actually have a surprise for you."

"I'm not a fan of surprises," Sam muttered.

"I think you'll like this one," he said leading her out of the copse of trees they'd been strolling under to a rolling meadow of purple heather.

Sam gasped when she took in the stunning landscape. Devon watched her take in the beautiful pink sunset reflecting off the peaceful lake at the bottom of the valley. "This is where we're camping?" she asked in a whisper.

Devon moved in close and bent down. His mouth was level with Sam's ear as he pointed to a canvas tent near the lake. "*That's* where we're camping."

"There's already a tent?" She looked bewildered as she glanced at the compact two-man tent strapped to Devon's pack. "What's this one for?"

"Decoy." He smirked. "I wanted you to be surprised."

"Devon! Why didn't you tell me we had awesome accommodations? It would have been way easier to convince me to go camping," she teased.

"I had to make sure you were committed. Come on."

Devon took Sam's hand and squeezed it, trying to hide his nervousness. *Come on, Devon. Do or die, mate.*

Sam

Sam followed Devon to the large canvas tent, while Eggsy raced ahead of them to the lake. Sam could scarcely take it all in. She'd never seen something so beautiful. The fields of heather looked like purple waves crashing down the hills, spilling into the serene lake. The view from the lake was amazing. In the fading daylight, Sam could just make out the silhouette of the mountains in the background. "So this is your secret spot, huh?" she asked in awe as they approached the tent. The sun was burning the sky red as it sunk behind the mountains. "It's beautiful."

"I'm glad you like it."

"Is this where you bring all your almost girlfriends?" she teased.

"Just you," he said quietly.

Sam swallowed. She didn't like when Devon looked at her like he was now—*all shy and vulnerable, no hint of playfulness.* It made her feelings for him rush to the surface. *Stupid, misguided hormones!*

"I have one more surprise," Devon said. "Close your eyes for a second, okay?"

"Why?"

"Can you just trust me, Sam?" he huffed.

"Fine." She put her hand over her eyes.

"Okay, stay there and no peeking," Devon called.

Sam couldn't help peeking. *She wasn't falling for spiders in her hair again.* She peeked through her fingers and watched Devon vanish through the tent flaps. *What was he up to?* She kept peeking until she heard him come out. He seemed empty handed so she closed her eyes as he approached.

"Okay," he said gently putting his hand on the small of her back. "Keep 'em closed and walk forward."

She shuffled forward awkwardly and heard a whoosh of fabric.

"Open!" Devon said.

Sam stood dumbfounded in front of the open tent flaps. What she was seeing couldn't be real. It was like something out of a fairytale. The inside of the tent was fit for a princess. It had a raised wooden floor with a pale yellow rug, and resting on top of it were two mattresses covered in fluffy white blankets and pillows. And everywhere she looked, Sam saw strings of glowing white lights.

"Do you like it?" Devon asked.

"Devon," she whispered. "You did all of this? For me?"

He shrugged. "I wanted you to like camping."

She turned her eyes away from the fairy lights to look at him. He was grinning sheepishly. "How did you do this?"

"It really wasn't too hard. I already had the tent company reserved. I was still hoping my dad might be well enough to come, so I found this company that sets up luxury tents so he'd have all the amenities he'd need. There's even a bathroom! Then, when you agreed to come, I called the company to ask them for something special."

This was something special all right. Megan would literally have a stroke if she saw this. She'd never stop calling him Prince Charming now.

"Do you like it?" he asked again.

"It's . . . I don't even have words for it, Devon. I feel like I'm in a dream."

"A good dream, right?"

She laughed. "So far."

"Grand." A huge, dimpled smile lit his face. "Oh, and look," he said flopping down onto one of the beds in the center of the tent. He stared up at the ceiling and patted the bed next to him. Sam sat on it, noticing how close they were. *The beds were barely separated by a foot!* She clamped down on her raging hormones as she lay back on the bed. She looked up and her breath caught in her throat as she stared through the opening above her that gave way to the sky. A cerulean blanket of stars was just beginning to wink to life.

A tear slid slowly down Sam's cheek. She'd never seen something so lovely.

"I wanted you to be able to see the stars," Devon murmured. "You said you like them, remember?"

Sam turned to look at him. He was already gazing at her, in that tender way that made her feel hot all over. "How do you remember the things I say better than I do?" she whispered.

Devon turned on his side reaching over to tuck a stray strand of Sam's dark hair behind her ear. His fingers lingered on her cheek, leaving a trail of fire wherever he touched. He lightly cupped her jaw and whispered, "I remember everything about you, Sam."

Her lips parted, and Devon's gray eyes noticed. His thumb brushed her bottom lip and she exhaled her nerves. "Devon," she murmured, not sure if it was a warning or a plea. He pulled himself closer. Their lips were a breath apart.

Oh, God! Oh, God! Oh, God! Stop this, Sam! Do not kiss him. She repeated her mantra. *You are the empress of your hormones! They do not control you.* But she knew that was a lie. Her whole body had been hijacked with the sudden desire to kiss every part of Devon.

Devon leaned closer. Sam held her breath. But before their lips could meet, a shaggy giant pounced between them. Eggsy showered them with sloppy kisses ruining the moment.

"Eggsy!" Devon roared, trying to push the giant dog off of them.

Sam sat up, grateful the spell had been broken. She stood and backed away from the beds, fearing they might actually have magical powers, because for a moment there, she almost thought she wanted to kiss Devon—*almost*.

Thanks to Eggsy, the rest of the night was more lighthearted. Sam helped Devon build a fire and they ate their dinner of hand pies and stew huddled around it. The moon was nearly full and the crisp night air was freezing. Sam grabbed a heavy plaid blanket from the tent to wrap around her shoulders while Devon broke out the S'mores supplies. He passed her a flask of whiskey and she raised her eyebrows.

"My father's favorite part of camping," he said. "Keeps away the chill."

She smirked and took a swig, before passing it back to him.

"I can't believe you've never made S'mores!" Devon muttered, while stabbing a pile of defenseless marshmallows. "It's a travesty."

"It's not like I've never heard of them. I've tried the S'more Pop-Tarts."

"You and your Pop-Tarts."

"Hey! Don't knock Pop-Tarts 'til you've tried them."

"Fine, but S'more Pop-Tarts are not gonna hold up to the real thing. You can't manufacture this level of perfection." Devon shook his head, still muttering. "Never had a real S'more."

"Give me a break. Downtown Boston kinda has a zero tolerance for bonfires. The city has a sorted history with fires."

"Well, you're gonna thank me," Devon said feeding Sam a gooey bite of the S'more he'd just constructed.

She bit into it and groaned as the bubbly marshmallow and warm chocolate melted in her mouth. "Oh my God," she mumbled trying to catch the crumbling graham crackers. "Okay, you're right, this is heaven!"

Devon laughed. "Grand, right?" He popped the rest in his own mouth and licked his sticky fingers. "I knew you'd love it," he said, skewering more marshmallows.

"Uh, that's the understatement of the year. Do you think we can get Cara to add these to the menu at home?"

"Believe me, we've already tried. They're my dad's favorite."

"Really? I never would have guessed."

Devon shrugged. "Yeah. He's a different person lately."

Sam noticed a stillness settle over Devon. It happened a lot when he talked about his father. She hated seeing him hurt. "Is it the cancer or Cara?" she asked quietly, hoping she wasn't prying.

"A little of both I guess," was all Devon offered.

"Cancer can change a person. Especially near the end. But he still loves you, you know?"

"I know . . . it's just . . ." Devon sighed.

"What?" Sam asked after he was quiet for a while.

"It's just, everything feels like . . . like I can't hold on to it. Like my dad's slipping away, and my future, and . . . I don't have any control over it." Devon put the stick of marshmallows down and took a swig from his flask. He shook his head and slumped forward to rest his elbows on his knees. "Sometimes I just want to go back, ya know? To before everything got so messed up."

He shivered and Sam wasn't sure if it was from the cold or the conversation. She didn't know what to say, so she adjusted her blanket to drape over Devon's shoulders too. He leaned into her and smiled, passing her the flask. She took a sip and felt the liquor warm her chest on the way down.

"It isn't all bad, is it?" she asked passing the flask back.

"No," he grunted taking a swig. "And I know change is inevitable, but I just want to hold on to all the good things I have right now. My dad . . . you . . ."

"I'm not going anywhere."

"What about Boston?"

"I don't know. Ireland's sorta growing on me."

"Really?"

The hope in his voice tore at her chest. She nodded.

"Well, shite! I should've taken ya camping months ago."

They both laughed.

"Seriously though, Sam. Thanks for doing this. The thought of having to come out here without my dad . . ." he shook his head again. "Well, it's just easier when I'm with you." He took another long drink from the flask. "Everything's easier with you, Sam."

She nudged her shoulder into his, echoing his sentiments. He was staring at her.

"What?" she asked, wondering if she still had marshmallow on her face.

"Sam?" Devon turned so he was fully facing her. He ran his hand through his hair before taking her hands. "I think . . . I mean, I know . . . that I'm falling for you."

Her heart sputtered and a smile snuck out of Sam's mouth before she could catch it. *How much whiskey had he drank? How much had she drank?*

"What's in that flask?" she asked trying to brush off his comment. Because she didn't want it to be true. She didn't think she could handle it, if it were true. Because that would mean she was alone, in the woods, with a boy who felt the same way about her as she did about him. And that wouldn't lead anywhere good. Well, maybe it would be good—*okay more than good. It would probably be fucking grand!* But then it would be bad. It would get complicated and messy.

Sam's subconscious—who sounded a lot like Megan—

chimed in. *But what if you stop being scared and it works and it's great?*

What if it did? It still didn't change the fact that Sam was moving back to Boston. She couldn't stay in Ireland. *Could she?* No, she was moving back to Boston and they would both end up hurt if she gave in to her feelings. And Devon didn't deserve that. Hurting him wasn't something Sam could risk.

Sam was already on her feet moving away.

Devon followed, letting the blanket fall to the ground. "Sam, please don't freak out. Just talk to me. Tell me what you're thinking. I can see your mind going a mile a minute."

"I'm thinking you're drunk, or crazy, or both."

"Sam, I'm not. I'm serious. I've felt this way for a long time. A *really* long time."

"Devon! No, you don't. It's only because we're in the woods with this crazy fairytale tent. And you've been drinking whiskey."

"It's not the whiskey."

"I really, really want it to be the whiskey!" she said backing away from him.

Devon grabbed her hands. "Why? Would it really be so bad if we gave this a chance?"

"Yes! We're in a good place right now, Devon. I don't want to screw this up for one night of fun."

"I want more than one night, Sam. I want all your nights. That's what I'm trying to tell you. I don't want to be your almost boyfriend anymore. I want the real thing."

Sam was shaking as she stared at Devon. He seemed so sure of himself. He wasn't raking his hands through his hair and his eyes were clear and bright. He seemed like he'd actually thought this through.

She stared at the beautiful planes of his face illuminated by the crackling firelight. Embers sparked and floated above him like dancing fireflies. The scene was so magical it took her breath away. *This wasn't real. This was a dream.* Sam couldn't end up with Devon James. *Could she?*

"Devon . . ." she started. She was already shaking her head and trying to pull away from him.

"Please don't say no, Sam. Just think about it, okay? That's all I'm asking. Think about giving us a chance. Because I've loved you since I was eight years old. And nothing's going to change that. If you're not ready yet, I can wait."

Sam swallowed hard. But she nodded.

CHAPTER
25

Sam

Sam lay on her back warm under the covers of her comfy bed inside the tent. She had no idea what time it was. She was sure it was late, but she couldn't close her eyes. Not with Devon's words running through her mind. They were like a song on repeat, swelling up inside her chest. All Sam could do was stare up at the winking constellations wishing they held an answer.

After their fireside conversation, they decided to turn in for the night. Devon had promised not to pressure her and she knew he didn't mean to, but sleeping next to him felt like sleeping next to a landmine. *One false move and her world would implode.* It was so strange how they'd spent nights talking in each others beds, but now, sleeping a foot apart, Sam felt like she was crossing a line. *God, she wished he would take it all back.* He hadn't even kissed her tonight, but he may as well have because things were changing. And if things were going to be weird between them, she really, really wanted to have at least one more Olympic kiss.

Their first kiss at Finnegan's kept running through her mind. It happened so fast she hadn't really had time to appreciate it—*well that's a lie, it was a freaking fantastic kiss*—but she hadn't really had time to decide if she wanted it to happen again.

"Sam?" Devon whispered in the darkness, making her jump. "Are you awake?"

"Yeah," she replied.

"I can't stop looking at the stars," he said, still whispering, which made her smile.

"Me neither."

"It just makes me feel oneness, with the universe, ya know?"

She snorted. "Oneness?"

"Hey, don't knock the oneness. The oneness is grand."

She laughed. "You're such a nerd."

"I know," he sighed. "Too bad I'm not a tech nerd."

"Yeah, I guess you're more of a nature nerd."

"Definitely."

She didn't risk looking at him, but she could hear the smile in his voice and it made her smile too.

"Hey, Sam?"

"Huh?"

"I think you like camping."

"Shut up."

"No, you definitely like camping."

"Almost," she said trying not to smile.

"Hey, Sam?"

"What?"

"I'm not pressuring you, but I really meant what I said."

Her chest tightened and she finally asked the question that had been nagging her. "What if you change your mind?"

"About loving you?" He sounded shocked. "I wont."

"How do you know?"

"I just know."

She was silent, refusing to look at the bed next to her. The bed that was illuminated with a bright slice of moonlight as if the heavens were daring her.

"Hey, Sam?"

"What?"

"I really wanna kiss you."

Oh, God! Oh, God! Oh, God! She swallowed hard. "Yeah?"

"Yeah. And I think you wanna kiss me too."

She couldn't resist any longer. Sam turned to look at Devon. He was already looking at her—his face glowing in the moonlight.

"Sam?" he whispered reaching for her hand.

She let him take it. "Yeah?"

"No more almost, okay?"

"Okay."

She held her breath as Devon pulled himself closer to her. He hovered over her, his face blocking out the stars as he gently cradled her head. He hesitated, almost like he was waiting for her to push him away. She didn't. She wanted this. She wanted at least one more kiss. She fought not to close her eyes as Devon finally lowered his face to hers. When their lips met, she let her eyelids flutter closed with a sigh as she clung to the afterglow of the stars and lost herself in his perfect lips.

It was only one kiss, but Sam had been right to worry, because it changed everything. She'd barely been able to pull herself away. They were both panting and breathless, and Devon pressed his forehead to hers like it pained him not to have his lips on hers. They both sat up, staring at each other—pupils wide, breathing ragged. Sam's entire body was on fire. *Holy hell! And that was just a kiss!* Sam didn't think she could actually handle anything more than kissing Devon. But he was like heroine and she was already itching for more.

After the life-changing kiss, Devon pushed his bed against Sam's so they could hold hands and gaze at the stars together. She could tell he wanted to kiss her again, but as long as they were touching, he seemed content enough. Sam lay on her back staring at the sky while Devon traced electric circles on her palm with his thumb. *It was heaven.*

Sam's favorite thing about the tent was the skylight. *Okay it was probably the kiss.* But her second favorite thing was gazing at the stars with Devon. She felt like she could reach up and grab them. She used to pretend she actually could when she was little. It's one of the few things she remembered doing with her mother. Just to be silly, Sam raised her hand and pretended to catch a star between her fingers. Devon reached up too. Then, he threaded his fingers with hers. And it was just the two of them, with the stars in their hands. Sam felt the world stop. Devon was right. The oneness was grand—*everything was grand.*

Sam decided she definitely liked camping. And she definitely, definitely liked Devon. She was tired of being afraid to want him. She took a deep breath and tried to harness her fear. For the first time, she was starting to realize that her fear of making the wrong choice was so much smaller than her fear of never making a choice at all.

She looked over at Devon. He was grinning at her and her chest threatened to strangle her. *This was it. This was Sam's moment.* And she knew with perfect certainty, that she wanted to take it. "Devon?" she whispered.

"Yeah?"

"You were right."

"About what?"

"I don't want to be almost anymore either."

He sat up so fast his covers fell to his waist. "Sam . . . are you serious?"

Her heart was thumping in her chest so hard she worried it might crack open. But she was sure that she wanted the real thing. And she wanted it with Devon. She'd never been more sure of anything in her life. She nodded her head. "Yes."

Devon exhaled her name. It was barely a whisper. He raised a trembling hand to stroke her cheek. She caught it and kissed his palm, then his wrist, then his arm. Then, she was crawling into his lap so she could kiss all of him. Everything was a frenzy and she couldn't get enough. She lay on top of Devon, letting him hold her tightly against him while they pulled at each other's clothes, kissing as if it were the only way to breathe. And maybe it was, because Sam had never felt more alive. *Was this what she'd been missing all these years? Was this what not making choices cost her?*

She wanted more. She wanted everything. And she wanted it with Devon—*now*. Sam pulled his shirt off over his head and started to pull off her own.

"Sam . . ." His voice was husky with desire.

"Yeah?"

"Are you sure?"

"Yeah."

He looked like he didn't believe her, so she kissed him again, deeper and greedily, until he let go of the hem of her shirt. She pulled it over her head, shivering as the cold night air raced across her bare chest. Devon's eyes were tethered to hers. She tried to pull herself back into his lap but he tensed. "Sam, wait."

"What's wrong?"

"Nothing. I just . . . I've wanted this for so long. But I don't want to rush you. I don't want you to think you have to do this."

"I *want* to do this, Devon."

"But, have you ever . . . done this?"

Sam's cheeks flushed and she shook her head slowly. "But I want to. And I want it to be with you, Devon. I want to remember this-us, forever."

His tension eased and he pulled her to him, stroking his hands down her back while he kissed her. She twisted her fingers in his thick hair and pulled him on top of her. Everything escalated to a frenzy of lips and hands again, and soon she was tugging at the waistband of his pants. He sucked in a breath and stilled as her fingers found the band of his boxer-briefs. "Hold on a sec," he said jumping up from the disheveled sheets.

Disappointment flooded Sam. *What had she done wrong?* But Devon was back in a flash with a square foil packet between his fingers. Sam's insides squirmed as she felt her whole body flood with nervous excitement. *This was really going to happen.*

"Do you always carry condoms with you?" she asked mildly embarrassed.

"Yes. I'm a guy."

That was Devon, open and honest, and proud of his manhood. And at that moment, Sam was so grateful for it, because she didn't want this to stop.

Devon slipped under the covers with her and pulled her gently to him, kissing her forehead. "Promise me you're sure." he whispered.

"I Promise."

Devon was patient and gentle. He made Sam feel sensations she didn't know she was capable of. He made her feel warm, and safe, and most of all, loved. When she was with Devon like this, the world stopped rushing ahead without her. Sam felt like she'd finally caught up, maybe even surpassed where she was meant to be. When they were together like this—just Sam and Devon—they were untouchable. They could do anything. They weren't trapped by someone else's plans or expectations. Their future was now! They were in it, and it was endless, in the best way she could imagine.

As Sam drifted off to sleep in Devon's warm arms, she gazed up at the winking stars. Plato said every soul has a companion star they return to after death—*Sam only knew this because one summer Megan had been obsessed with Plato.* But now, as Sam stared at the blank space between the stars she'd picked out for herself, she found she was hoping there might be space for Devon there with her.

CHAPTER
26

Devon

Waking up next to Sam was a dream. Devon felt like he'd captured an angel. Last night had been beyond his wildest fantasies. He'd never expected to have sex with Sam. Of course he'd wanted to, but all he'd hoped for this weekend was time with her—just to be near her. But somehow, between drinking whiskey and gazing at the stars, something had changed. He'd felt the shift in her—like she'd finally let that last little bit of her guard down. And it let all of her flood out, almost overwhelming him—*almost*. But he couldn't get enough of her. If Sam were a well, then Devon wanted to drown in her.

Sometime in the night Sam had curled into his chest and fallen asleep. He wrapped his arms around her, never wanting to let go. He loved the way her eyelashes fluttered against the hollow of his throat. And the feel of her breath softly on his chest. He could lay like this forever, listening to the birds greet the sun while he held happiness in his arms.

Unfortunately, Eggsy had other plans. He wanted breakfast. Devon had already pushed his impatient dog away twice, hissing at him to wait. But finally Eggsy had enough and started howling, rousting Sam from her sleep. Her eyes fluttered open drowsily. Devon waited for her to panic when she figured out where she was. But to his surprise, she didn't shove him away. Instead she grinned, her cheeks glowing pink.

"Morning, kitten," he said, kissing her head.

"Morning," she murmured.

"I've gotta feed the hell hound," Devon said rolling his eyes when Eggsy started pawing at him.

Sam giggled and swatted playfully back at Eggsy.

"Remind me never to bring you camping again, Eggsy," Devon growled as he climbed out of the warm covers.

"Yeah, Eggsy. Don't be jealous. I love you both."

Devon froze, one arm shoved into his heavy jacket. He knitted his eyebrows together in surprise. "*Love?*" he asked.

Sam looked mortified as she tried to stutter a response. "No-well-you know what I meant-I . . . shit." She threw the covers up over her head and hid.

"You *love* me!" Devon teased. He knew she only meant it innocently, but it was too good to let go. Friend-Devon wouldn't let a comment like that slide, so more-than-friend-Devon wasn't going to either. And after last night, they were *way* more than friends.

"I knew it!" Devon continued leaping on top of Sam's bed with Eggsy hot on his heels. "Sam Connors loves me!"

"No!" She squealed when he started tickling her through

the blankets. "I. Do. Not," she managed to get out between fits of laughter. Eggsy had totally forgotten about breakfast and was now pouncing on the squirming blankets like it was his favorite new game.

"Mercy!" Sam screamed and Devon hauled Eggsy off of her.

She popped her head from under the covers. Her toffee-brown hair looked like it had been caught in a tornado and Devon burst into laughter.

"Well, we love you too, Sam," Devon said ruffing up her hair even more, before placing a kiss on her forehead. She blushed. "Let me feed this beast before he starts drooling," he said, pulling Eggsy from the tent. "I'll start breakfast," he called over his shoulder.

Sam

Sam sat huddled under the covers, waiting for the strangeness to take over. After having sex with Devon last night, she expected to feel different when she woke up. And she did, but just not in the way she thought she would. Sam felt stronger somehow, more sure of herself. She expected she'd be embarrassed or feel strange around Devon, but it was just the opposite. Sam felt more connected to him than ever. It was like sex had fused more than just their bodies, but their minds and hearts too. *God! She couldn't believe Megan hadn't told her how magical sex was!*

She stood up and stretched, dressing quickly so she could join Devon outside. She couldn't wait to wrap her arms around him and kiss him, again and again! She sighed, as visions of last night floated back through her mind. *Sex cer-*

tainly changed things. Sam didn't feel scared about anything anymore. All she felt was alive, and hungry. *And maybe a little preoccupied with plotting how she could get Devon back in bed so they could do it again.*

Devon

Sam waltzed out of the tent with a toothbrush in her mouth. She was still in her pajamas and had added a pair of boots and a blanket around her shoulders. Her hair was still a mess, and Devon was sure he'd never seen something so adorable in all his life. She finished brushing her teeth and joined him by the fire. He pulled her into a crushing hug, kissing her head and face all over.

"What's that for?" she asked.

"For last night, for this morning, for having sunshine in your smile, for everything," he said squeezing her tighter. He just couldn't help himself. His chest felt like it had blown wide open and if he didn't hold Sam tight, he might just float away. *How could one person make him this happy?*

"It really happened, right?" he asked.

She laughed nervously. "Yeah."

"And is everything still okay?"

"Almost," she said shyly.

Devon's brows furrowed, wondering what she meant. "What's wrong?"

"This," she said standing on her tippy toes to kiss him.

Devon wrapped his arms around her and lifted her off the ground, deepening their kiss until he forgot where he ended and Sam began. When he finally set her back down they were both breathless.

"Okay, everything's good now," she grinned.

Devon was pretty sure if he were smiling any wider his face would crack in half. "Grand." He handed her a mug of coffee.

"You remembered coffee?" she exclaimed.

Devon didn't drink it, but he knew Sam loved it. "Your dad told me you're dangerous without it."

She laughed. "You still think I'm dangerous after last night?"

"You're even more dangerous."

"Why?"

"Because I'd pretty much give you the world after last night."

She beamed. "Lucky for you I think I'm still on a natural high from last night. I only require coffee and food, for now."

Devon grinned, pulling Sam into another hug, careful not to spill her coffee.

They couldn't keep their hands off each other, and Devon almost burnt their breakfast—bangers and mash—his father's favorite. *And another thing Cara wouldn't let him have.*

Devon and Sam sat next to each other by the fire and ate. He kept stealing glances at her. She looked so beautiful with the sunlight turning her hair into strands of bronze and copper. Then he was staring at her lips. Her perfect, plump, ruby lips. *Good Christ, he couldn't stop wanting to kiss her. Now that they'd started, how would they ever stop?*

"Put that thing away," she said jokingly when she caught him smiling.

It only made him smile more and his heart felt too big for his chest. "Come here," he said pulling her onto his lap. He kissed her again, forcing himself not to get too carried away.

"So, is it safe to say you like camping?" he asked after he traced feathery kisses from her ear to her mouth.

"Yes."

"And what about me?" he asked. "Do you like me?"

"I've always liked you, Devon."

"Liar," he teased tickling her.

She laughed. *Christ, he loved that sound.* And he loved being the one to make her make that sound. He loved making her smile. He loved everything about her. And he wanted to carry her back into that tent and show her all the ways he could love her. But he couldn't—not yet. She still felt as flighty as a bird. Devon could feel her little heart pounding into his chest every time he held her. He wanted to make her feel safe first. He wanted her to be sure about him first. Last night had been perfect—*beyond perfect.* But he hadn't been planning to move so quickly. He wouldn't rush this. It was too perfect. And he'd waited too long. They had all weekend to explore what this was between them. But there was something he did want to know.

"I want to ask you something," he murmured between tender kisses.

"Devon, I don't know if I can handle any more revelations," she mocked. "I mean we already went from zero to I love you. What else is there?"

He grinned. "Well, this will be easy then. Go to the Grad Ball with me, Sam."

"Really?"

"Yes. As my girlfriend. I want to take you on a real date, Sam."

Sam looked up at him, her big blue-green eyes wide. "Girlfriend? Is that what I am now?"

"Only if you want to be."

Her eyes had been bright all morning, but Devon watched a bit of fear creep into them now. "Hey," he murmured, softly taking her chin. "Don't be scared, Sam."

She shivered under his touch. "This feels big," she whispered.

"It is, Sam. It's us. And I know we're worth the risk."

She blinked. He could see her on a precipice and he held his breath, waiting to see if she would jump. *Jump! Please for the love of Christ, jump, Sam. I'll always catch you.*

She slid her hands up his chest. They felt like they were pushing him away and he closed his eyes trying to contain his disappointment. But her hands kept going until they were around his neck and in his hair, pulling his forehead to meet hers. He opened his eyes. He was almost too close to look at her. Her lips brushed his for a moment and then she whispered, "Okay."

Devon disintegrated as Sam kissed him without restraint.

It was like breathing underwater. It was like magic. It was everything.

They were back in the tent, quickly headed for a repeat of last night, when a loud ringing startled them apart and Sam tried to slide from Devon's lap.

"Ignore it," he said pulling Sam back to him. Their lips had scarcely left each other's for the past twenty minutes.

"Devon . . ." she warned. She didn't have to say it. He knew what she was thinking. He was thinking it too. *What if it's your dad?*

But he didn't want anything to ruin this perfect moment. Everything was perfect and he didn't want it to end. But his phone kept ringing. Sam slipped off of Devon and he reluctantly got out of bed to rifle through his pack for his phone. When he saw Cara's name on the screen, his heart stopped.

No! Not now. Not when everything is perfect.

CHAPTER
27

Devon

Everything was perfect. Until it wasn't.

Devon and Sam rushed home after he received the call he'd been dreading. Cara said they didn't have much time. They weren't far away now. They'd run to the car and left everything but their phones and Eggsy behind. Sam still hadn't let go of Devon's hand. She'd taken it when they left camp at a run. And she was still holding it as they drove silently back toward the house.

Devon wasn't ready for this. He knew this was already borrowed time with his father, but he still wanted more. There were so many more things his father was supposed to share with him. Devon wanted his father to see him graduate, get married, have children. He wanted time to make him proud. But there wasn't enough time.

Devon suddenly felt like he was falling into a wide-open abyss and no one was going to reach out and save him. He had no one. His mother had left by choice and now his father was leaving too. *How could this happen? What had he done wrong? Why did he have to be alone?*

I'm not ready. Please, please, please, Lord, I'm not ready. He begged over and over in his mind as tears streamed down his face. He gripped the steering wheel tighter. *I'll do anything. I won't leave his side again. Just give me more time!*

Sam

Sometimes the thing you're looking for is right in front of you. And Sam almost had it—*almost.*

For a few hours Sam had everything. She had Devon, she had happiness, she had a home. She let go of all her doubts and believed that everything would work out. But then, Cara called, and it was gone again.

As soon as Sam and Devon pulled up to the house, she knew it was bad. There was an ambulance with lights on in the driveway. She and Devon barreled into the house through the front doors, with Eggsy chasing them. Thorton caught them in the foyer and sternly told them the dog was not allowed into Henry's room. Devon shoved past the butler like he wasn't even there and jogged down the hallway toward his father's room. Sam apologized and took Eggsy to her room. She didn't know what else to do.

Devon was in Henry's room with Cara and the kids, but she didn't feel right about going in. Even though she lived in Henry's home for months, Sam still didn't know the man that well. Plus, she didn't want to intrude during such a tragic time. And selfishly, she didn't want to watch cancer steal another person's last breath.

Sam searched the house for her father, but he was no-where to be found. She ended up back in her room, stroking Eggsy's head in her lap while she prayed for Devon and his family. Today had started out so good. *Why of all the days did this have to happen today? It wasn't fair.* She didn't want Devon to have to lose his father. She knew how awful saying goodbye to a parent was. It broke a part of you that could never be fixed. And Sam was just beginning to realize that she loved every part of Devon. *What if this broke his kind heart? Or his good humor? Or what if it broke something worse and he couldn't go on?*

Sam had lost her mother as a child and that was hard enough. But she realized she'd been lucky. As a child, her emotional range wasn't very deep. She pretty much bounced from happy to sad to scared to mad. But now, she felt so much more. There were hundreds upon thousands of feelings that flickered through her mind at lightning speed. Especially at this very moment, as she evaluated what this meant for her and Devon's new relationship. Sam put in her ear buds and blasted Adele, trying to silence the doubts running through her head. But there weren't enough Adele songs in all the world to cover the emotions she was going through right now.

There was a knock at Sam's door and she jumped up to answer it.

It was her father, and she knew before he even said the words.

She knew Henry was gone . . . and now, so was a piece of the boy she loved.

CHAPTER
28

Sam

The next few days were awful. Sam had only seen Devon once and when she tried to hug him, he shook his head and held up a hand that stopped her in her tracks. Devon wouldn't even look at her. He stared at his feet holding his temples like his forehead might unhinge if he didn't. He took a shuddering breath and said, "Eggsy . . . can you . . ."

"Of course," she said sparing Devon from having to ask her to care for the dog.

"Thanks," he mumbled and walked away.

He looked so raw and broken. Sam felt her heart crumbling as she watched him walk away, leaving her with a queasy emptiness in her stomach.

Devon wasn't staying in his room. She didn't know where he was staying. Maybe he wasn't staying anywhere. Maybe he was just wandering the halls or the grounds. Maybe he wasn't sleeping or eating. Maybe he would lose twenty pounds like her father had after her mother passed. But wherever Devon was, whatever he was doing, Sam never saw him. She checked his room repeatedly. She even set alarms to check after midnight, but he wasn't there. *He had to sleep somewhere . . .*

But then, Sam remembered not sleeping. After her mother passed away Sam used to hide in her office, like she thought maybe her mother might come back. But that was because Sam was eight. *Where would she hide if she'd lost her mother now?* If only she could figure it out maybe she could find Devon.

Sam asked her father about Devon constantly. But he gave her vague answers like, *dealing with family matters,* or *making arrangements.* The next time she tried to talk to her father, he sat down and actually looked at her. That worried Sam more than anything.

"Sam, sweetheart. I know this has been hard on you too. Thank you for putting on a brave face all this time. I've spoken to Cara, and we agree it's best for everyone if you and I move to our own place."

"She's kicking us out?" Sam cried incredulously.

"No, honey. I suggested it. And Cara agreed. Their family needs some time to adjust. And that will be easier if we're not here."

"But, what about Devon? What did he say?"

"It's not up to Devon, honey."

"But I haven't even seen him."

"I know, honey. You'll see him at school."

"But I need to make sure he's okay. When Mom died .
. ." Sam's voice cracked. "I just have to make sure he's okay,
Dad."

"Okay, honey. After you pack your things you can go
say goodbye."

"What? When are we leaving?"

"Now, honey."

~♥~

Waking up in a house without Devon was a nightmare.

He wasn't across the hall. He wasn't even on the same
property. And Sam hadn't gotten to say goodbye—*not really.*

The day they left, Cara had told her that Devon was
in Henry's office, and when Sam knocked on the door he
wouldn't open it. She could hear him inside, but no matter
how much she begged he wouldn't let her in.

"But I'm leaving, Devon. My dad says we have to leave
now. And, I just . . . I wanted to make sure you're okay."

He didn't say anything.

"I'm sorry. That's stupid . . . I know you're not okay. But
I'm here for you, Devon. Okay? I'm always going to be here
for you."

She waited, but still he said nothing.

"Please just say okay, so I know you heard me."

"Okay, Sam."

Those were the last words he'd spoken to her and she
wanted to erase them. She wanted to go back to him telling
her he loved her and that her smile looked like sunshine. She
wanted to go back to kissing him. She wanted to kiss all his
pain away. She wanted so much more than she ever knew she

could want from Devon, but it didn't matter.

Most days, life doesn't care what broken hearts want—Sam knew that better than most people.

—❧—

"I'm telling you, Meg, something's wrong. He hasn't even been at school. I'm really worried," Sam said into her cell phone.

"What about the funeral?" Megan asked. "You'll see him there, right?"

"No. They already had it and we weren't invited."

"What?" Megan squeaked.

"Family only."

"But your dad's always saying you guys are practically family."

"I know. But Cara's running things now. That's why I'm so worried. What if she's sent him away or something?"

"Sam, I know he called her his step-monster, but it's not like she'd lock him in some tower."

Sam sighed. "I know, but I'm going crazy. I text him and call him and he never answers. I know how bad he's hurting. I just want to help."

"Sam, you know better than anyone how hard this is. And sometimes you just need to let people grieve the best way they know how. Devon knows you're there for him."

"I guess," she said sulking.

"Just keep reminding him. But you can't force him to talk to you about this if he's not ready."

"You're right. But my heart is breaking for him. And we . . . " Sam hadn't told Megan that she had sex with Devon.

It didn't seem appropriate to talk about so soon after Henry passing. And now, it'd been so long since it happened that Sam felt weird bringing it up. And she was beginning to wonder if Devon regretted it. *If she could only talk to him!*

"We what?" Megan asked.

Sam sighed. "Nothing. I just really wish I could talk to him."

"I'm sure you will soon. Now go kick butt today."

"Thanks," Sam replied. But soccer was the last thing on her mind. "I'll call you tomorrow."

"Hang in there," Megan said and disconnected.

Sam tucked her phone in her duffle bag and changed for her soccer match. It was the last one of their undefeated season and everyone turned up to cheer the Lady Eddi's on— *everyone except Devon.*

Sam looked for him anyway. It was habit now to scan the front row of the bleachers for Devon and Eggsy. But they were never there.

It had been three weeks since Henry James passed away and Devon still hadn't returned to school. Apparently, Zander was bringing Devon his assignments. Sam badgered Zander for information all the time, but it was always the same.

"Only family right now, Sam."

"He's not ready for visitors, Sam."

"I'll tell him you asked about him, Sam."

Sam even found herself missing stupid, old Thorton. At least if the James's butler was still driving her to school she could ask him how Devon was. But now that Sam and her father had moved to a little cottage close to school, Sam could walk to Eddington. If the weather was foul her father offered to drive her. But she always walked anyway. She liked gazing out at the valley, remembering what it'd been like hiking it with Devon. Sometimes their camping trip felt like a dream. One perfect day—*not even a day really. More like seventeen hours.*

Maybe that's all Sam was allowed. Seventeen hours of happiness—*one to make up for each miserable year of her life.* Sam instantly felt bad thinking that and tried to take her thoughts back. Her life wasn't miserable. Not all of it. There had been good times. All the time before her mom died. And even a few moments after. Plus, she still had her father. Poor Devon had no one. Sam felt her heart constrict and she thought she might be ill. She really didn't want to play soccer right now. But Coach was blowing the whistle and telling them to start warming up.

Sam jogged up and down the field, imagining she was running all the way to Devon's house. Imagining she wouldn't stop until she was back in his arms.

That's how Sam made it through the game—imagining she was with Devon. She played like crap, but she survived. She was sitting on the sideline pulling off her cleats while the rest of the team celebrated. She felt someone sit down next to her and for half a breath she thought it was Devon.

"Hey, Boston," Zander greeted. "Good game."

"Thanks," she mumbled, her attention already racing ahead to questions about Devon.

"Before you ask, he's still not ready for visitors," Zander said grimly. "But he did ask me to tell you something."

Sam perked up. "He did?"

Zander couldn't even meet her gaze. "Yeah, but you're not going to like it."

"What's wrong? Is he okay?"

Zander sighed. "Nothing's wrong, Sam. But, he . . . he wanted me to tell you that he can't go to the Grad Ball with you."

"Oh." Sam's face fell. Tears started falling in a steady stream as she stared at her socks. She didn't even care that she was crying in front of Zander. She didn't even care about the stupid Grad Ball. She just wanted to see Devon. Nothing would be right until she did.

"I'm sorry, Sam," Zander said stiffly.

"That's okay," she sniffled. "I was just worried you were going to say something was wrong with him. He hasn't been returning any of my texts and . . . I just worry about him going through this alone."

Zander awkwardly put his hand on her back. "I'm sorry, Sam. I know you care about him. This isn't your fault. He's just not ready to face everyone, ya know?"

"I get it," she said, even though her mind was screaming, *but I'm not everyone! I'm Sam! The girl he loves! The girl he had sex with!*

"If it makes you feel any better, I don't have a date to the Grad Ball either."

"What happened to Sophie?"

Zander snorted. "Apparently, Henry's death has inconvenienced her. She said I was spending too much time with my sister. Can you believe that?"

"Yes, she's a bitch."

Zander laughed. "She really is."

"What do guys see in her?"

He shrugged. "Nice tits, great ass."

Sam rolled her eyes.

"I don't know, Sam. We're guys. It doesn't take much."

Sam's heart thudded to a sub-level she didn't even know existed. *Was that what had happened with her and Devon? Was she just easily accessible tits and ass?*

"I know you probably don't feel like it right now, but I'm throwing it out there anyway. If you want to, you could go to the Grad Ball with me."

Sam just blinked at Zander, so he kept talking.

"Me and some of the blokes from the team are going for a bit. Ya know, just for the free booze. Then were gonna skip off to the Garage if ya wanna come with?"

"The Garage?" Sam asked.

"It's a pub in Dublin. Good for blowing off steam."

"Oh. Thanks, but I wouldn't be good company. I'll probably just stay home."

Zander shrugged and stood up. "Well, if ya change your mind . . ."

Sophie

Sophie and Tess were standing on the football pitch waiting for Molly while the rest of the school congratulated the Lady Eddi's on their final victory. But Sophie wasn't really focused on their win. She was busy playing her own game as she watched the conversation happening between Samantha and Zander.

Tess interrupted Sophie's plotting with another annoying question. "Did you really break up with Zander?"

"Yes," Sophie replied without taking her eyes off of Samantha.

"Why? He's so hot."

"Because, I've realized there's someone better for me."

"Who?" Molly asked, joining them.

"That's for me to know and you to find out," Sophie huffed.

She wasn't ready to tell them she had Devon back in her sights. *Or that he'd never really left them.* Sophie always made sure she could back up her claims. That's how she stayed on top at Eddington. She wouldn't tell anyone about Devon until they were officially back together. And now that he was rumored to inherit his father's company, Devon would be an even bigger catch.

"So if you broke up with Zander, who are you going to the Grad Ball with?" Molly asked.

"Don't worry about me," Sophie said with a knowing smile. If everything went according to plan, she'd have the most unforgettable Grad night of them all.

CHAPTER
29

Devon

Devon sat in the back of his father's 1934 Bentley Lagonda tipping back his flask. *Empty. Again.* Yesterday he'd found solace in the Aston Martin. The day before, the Bugatti. Each day he sat in a different car, with a different bottle of whiskey and tried to hold on to the memories he'd shared with his father in each of the cars. They all belonged to Cara now. But she couldn't keep Devon from sitting in them. Besides, the garage had become his favorite hiding place.

No one ever went out to the garage. And its eight bays of windows gave Devon the perfect vantage point to see people coming and going from the house—*not that Devon wanted to interact with any of them.* The only person he wanted to see, he couldn't. He couldn't face Sam. Not when he had all this pain in his heart. It was just as well that she'd moved out. She hadn't given up though. Sam still called and texted every day since his father died. Every message said the same thing. "I'm still here."

She hadn't given up on him. And he couldn't make up his mind if he wanted her to.

Selfishly he wanted to keep Sam forever. But at the same time, Devon loved her too much to do that to her. He was a mess—a giant, broken, disgusting mess. And Sam deserved so much better than that. She deserved the Devon from before. The Devon from the camping trip. The Devon she'd given herself to. Maybe she even deserved someone better than him. But at least that version of himself had been whole and good. This new, broken version only spewed hate and regret and anger.

Devon had never been so mad in his life. Everything made him angry. One second he'd be so furious that he'd trash his room, then the next he'd be in tears for destroying something from his father.

Each day he awoke to a new nightmare. One morning, he'd seen his father in his reflection and wept until he vomited. The next day, he punched the mirror until it shattered and his knuckles were bloody. He was like Jekyll and Hyde. He didn't trust himself and he wouldn't allow that monstrous version of himself anywhere near Sam.

Plus, when he thought about Sam, he thought about their night together. And that made him think about his father, and how Devon should have been by his side instead of off selfishly chasing his desires. He didn't regret his night with Sam, but he couldn't separate it either. Everything was a furious, confusing mess and so far, drinking was the only thing that helped dull the pain. Devon was lost and broken, but he still knew enough to keep Sam safe. And he wasn't safe.

He wanted Sam to be happy. She deserved that. But Devon would never be able to bring her happiness now.

From his perch on the Bentley, Devon saw Zander pull up in his BMW. Zander had moved into the house after the funeral. *At least the bastard had the decency to wait until his father was in the ground,* Devon thought viciously as he watched Zander saunter into the house. *His house. His father's house!*

Sometimes at night, Devon heard Cara and Zander laughing. *Laughing for fuck's sake! What in the hell was there to laugh about?* If Cara had ever loved his father, she wouldn't be laughing. She would never laugh again. She would be just as destroyed as Devon. But no, she was laughing it up with Zander and planning all the ways they would redecorate his house. Like the first thought in her stupid little head was how fast could she permanently erase Henry from existence?

Devon wished they were dead—Zander and Cara. *Why did his father have to die? It wasn't fair!* Henry wouldn't do something like this to Cara if she had died. He'd probably have erected a statue in her honor. But life wasn't fair. And Devon was stuck with Cara and no one left who gave a shite about him.

His phone pinged and Devon stared down at a text message.

SAM: I'm still here.

His finger hovered over the reply button. *Christ, he missed her.*

Devon slid the phone back in his pocket. He couldn't talk to Sam—perfect, beautiful, Sam. He would just ruin her. And if he did that, he would have nothing left to live for. He was barely hanging on as it was. If he hurt Sam, it would kill him, and he'd probably end up doing the world a favor and killing himself.

I could easily do it, he thought looking around at all the cars in the garage. The room was sealed up tight. *It would be easy. Probably only take a matter of minutes . . .*

Devon hopped out of the car and quickly exited the garage before he got any other stupid ideas. He just needed another drink. Just something so he could sleep and not think for a while.

Devon ran into Zander in the hall.

"Jesus! You look like shite, mate," Zander said. He was blocking Devon's path to his room.

"Fuck off," Devon growled.

"I talked to her today," Zander said, not backing down. "She still asks about you." He snorted. "Lord knows why?"

"Did you tell her?" Devon asked.

Zander shook his head and Devon felt his rage bubbling up. But then Zander spoke. "Yeah. I told her."

"Good," Devon said pushing past Zander to get to his door.

"She cried, mate. She fucking cried."

Devon stopped. But he didn't turn around. He couldn't. Something inside of him was tearing and he couldn't breathe.

"Don't ask me to clean up any more of your shite. From now on, if you have something to say to Sam, you say it yourself. It's been three weeks, mate. It's time to start picking up the pieces, or someone else will."

Devon snapped. It happened so fast, he didn't even feel

it at first. It barely registered that he was crushing Zander against the wall by his throat. Words were rushing out of Devon in a hot hissing voice that he didn't recognize. "If you fucking touch her, I'll kill you. Do you hear me, Zander. You're dead!"

But Zander wasn't phased. He pushed back hard. He was shorter than Devon, but broader, built more like a pro rugby player than any teenager had the right to be. He laughed in Devon's face. "Oh, so you do care about her, then? Because I wasn't sure. It seems she's not sure either."

"Leave her alone, Zander," Devon growled. "She's none of your fucking business."

"She is *my* fucking business when she's crying on *my* shoulder every day about you. You've made her my business, making me deliver messages that you're not man enough to. Do you know she walks to school every day, crying over you? And you don't even care. You just sit around feeling sorry for yourself all day."

Devon felt pain shoot through his hand and Zander stumbled away from him, clutching his nose as blood spurted from it. Devon clutched his fist, realizing he'd punched Zander square in the face.

Zander spit blood as he stumbled down the hall. "She's too good for you, Dev."

Devon lay on his bed staring up at the ceiling. His hand was swollen and throbbing. He hadn't bothered to get ice for it. He wondered if he broke something. *It would serve him right.*

Eggsy whined at his feet. Devon rolled off the bed and opened the door, figuring the dog needed to go out. But Eggsy trotted across the hall and paced in circles in front of Sam's door whining even louder.

"She's gone!" Devon shouted.

Eggsy flattened his ears and settled on the floor, stretching out like he was prepared to stay there all night.

"She's not coming back, Eggsy! She left us. Everyone's left us."

Eggsy lowered his head sadly and huffed out an obstinate breath.

Devon sunk to the floor too exhausted to care that he was in a pile of dirty clothes, and he cried. He cried for his father, and how much he missed him. He cried for how much he loved Sam and for how scared he was of losing her. He cried for not being man enough to face her. He cried until he couldn't feel anything at all.

CHAPTER
30

Sam

"Oh my God! What happened to your face?" Sam asked when she saw Zander at school the next day.

"Devon," he grumbled, and then winced from the pain.

"Devon did that to you?" she asked in disbelief. *She'd never seen Devon lift a finger to harm anyone!* "What did you do to him?"

"Thanks for the vote of confidence," Zander replied.

"No-sorry-I didn't mean . . . it's just—"

"It's alright. I guess I wasn't totally innocent."

"Is he okay?"

Zander grunted. "You see my face all black and purple and you ask how's the other bloke? Real nice, Boston."

Sam's face fell.

"Ah, come on. I'm only teasing. He's fine. I think it did him some good to get his frustrations out."

"Yeah, but on your face?"

Zander brushed it off like it wasn't a big deal that his nose looked broken. "At least he actually did something rather than sulking around all day."

"Is that what he does?"

Zander shrugged. "Who knows? All I know is I guess I'm not going to the Grad Ball, looking like this."

"You don't think it'll look better by then?"

"By tomorrow? No. Not unless you got a dress ugly enough to outshine my face."

Sam laughed, "You never know. One might exist."

"In your closet?" he asked.

She shook her head.

"Yeah, I didn't think so. Well, anyway, if ya change your mind, here's my number," he said, swiping her phone and typing his number in.

"You can NOT go to the dance with Zander!" Megan squawked. "I forbid it!"

"You forbid it?" Sam scoffed. "What are you, Queen Cersei now?"

"Ew, no! Everyone knows I'd be Arya Stark. Game of Thrones aside, I'm serious. You're not going out with Zander."

"I didn't say I was, Meg."

"But you were thinking about it."

"I don't know. Maybe. You're the one who's always telling me to go out and have fun. You're going to be here in three weeks and I don't even know where to take you. I've been to Dublin twice."

"I don't care! You're supposed to go to the dance with Devon," Meg whined.

"Yeah, well he doesn't want to go with me," Sam said shortly. "He won't even talk to me."

"But he's in love with you," she protested. Megan still didn't know about Sam and Devon's one night of romance, but somehow she didn't need to. She was convinced they belonged together.

"I don't know, Meg."

"I do! Just admit you love him too! I'm not blind. I spent weeks video chatting with you both and I saw the way he looked at you."

She rolled her eyes. "How did he look at me?"

"Like he hung every star in the sky for you."

Sam burst into tears, because it was true. He had looked at her like that. And she didn't see it until it was too late. And now, Devon was gone, and she didn't know how to get him back.

"Shit, Sam. Don't cry. I'm sorry. I didn't mean to make you cry."

"I know. But you're right. And now he doesn't look at me at all. He won't even talk to me and I haven't seen him in almost a month. I don't know what to do."

"I know, Sam. I wish I could come right now and give you a hug."

"Me too." Sam sniffled. "I just want to come home. I can't do this anymore."

"Don't give up yet, Sam. I know it's going to work out. You guys are meant to be."

"You don't get it, Meg. Maybe we were, but everything's ruined now."

"Sam, it's not ruined. Everything is going to be okay. You just need to give him time and then everything will go back to how it was before."

"Megan, it can't!"

"Why not?"

"Because I had sex with him! And now he won't even talk to me. Nothing is going to be okay."

Megan was speechless as Sam sobbed uncontrollably.

After a while, Megan finally spoke. "Listen to me, Sam." Her voice was soft. "I'm so sorry it happened like this. But please don't give up on Devon. I know you both love each other."

"I don't think I'm cut out for love."

—♡—

After Sam collected herself from her tearful conversation with Megan, she went downstairs to see if there was anything to eat. Her stomach constantly felt empty and raw, but whenever she tried to eat, she lost her appetite. Still, at least going downstairs to pretend to eat gave her something to do.

Sam's bedroom was on the second floor of the little cottage her father rented. It was fully furnished so they were able to move right in, but after a month, she still wasn't used to it. She felt like a nun, living a silent life of exile. *Okay that was a bit dramatic*—but her father was always working so she pretty much felt like she lived alone. He had an office downstairs off of the kitchen. The only other rooms were his bedroom and a tiny living room. But Sam never went in either. They only made her feel more alone. She pretty much lived in her room, making brief escapes to the kitchen for food.

She scrounged around in the freezer. The only thing that looked edible was a frozen pizza. But pizza made her think of Devon. *Pretty much everything made her think of Devon.* Hunger won out. She unwrapped the pizza and put it in the oven, sulking at the counter while it baked.

Sam's father walked into the kitchen smiling. "Hey, honey. I thought I heard someone down here. Whatcha making?"

"Pizza."

"Enough to share with your old dad?"

"Sure."

He sat at the counter next to her, giving her that look. *The one that meant he was trying to think of something fatherly to say.* "How was your soccer game tonight?"

"It was last night."

"Oh. That's what I meant."

Sure. "It was fine. We won."

"That's great, honey."

Grand. Devon would've said it was grand that they won.

Damn it! Now she was thinking about Devon again and her eyes welled up. She tried to get up before her father noticed, but she already felt his hand on her arm.

"Sam," he said quietly. "I want you to be happy. You know that, right?"

She wiped her eyes. "Of course, Dad."

"I really thought you were starting to like it here. But lately . . . I just haven't seen you like this in a long time. And it makes me think . . ." he stopped and pushed his glasses up to rub the bridge of his nose. "It makes me think I did the wrong thing by bringing you here."

"Dad," she whispered, praying her voice would hold

out. "I really, really want to go home."

"Boston?" he asked.

"Yeah."

"Okay, sweetie."

"Okay? Really?"

"Yeah. You said you'd try and you did. You've gotten straight A's and you're graduating next week, right?"

"Tomorrow, Dad. Graduation is tomorrow. I'll have my diploma."

"I'm proud of you, Sam. I know coming back here wasn't easy. I guess I just hoped we were ready to come home. But maybe it was stupid to think Ireland could be home without Elizabeth."

Sam's eyes spilled over. *He actually said her name.* Her father never spoke her mother's name. "It wasn't stupid, Dad."

He pulled her into a hug and she let him. "I love you, honey."

"I love you too, Dad."

"I swear to God, Meg! He said I can come home whenever I want!"

Megan looked concerned. "You're gonna wait 'til I come to visit though, right?"

"Yes, of course, but isn't that the best news? I never thought I'd be so happy that Eddington murdered us with classes for their stupid early testing. But I'll have my diploma tomorrow and after you come visit I can fly home with you!"

"Sam, that's amazing!"

"I know! I'm so happy."

"And that's really what you want?"

"Yes. I just need to leave this semester behind me. It'll be the four months we don't talk about."

Megan smiled tightly. "The term-that-shall-not-be-named."

"Exactly!" Sam smiled. "I feel like I can breathe again."

"You're sure about leaving Ireland, and everything in it?" Megan asked.

"Yes, Meg. It's for the best."

"You know you're going to have to tell him."

"I know. But I don't want to think about Devon right now. I just want to be happy. And I know you think I shouldn't, but I might go to the Grad party thing. At least for a little while. Just to celebrate that this is finally over and I'll have my life back."

Meg forced a smile. "You should. You deserve to be happy, Sam."

CHAPTER

31

Devon

Devon felt twitchy and hollow as he drove himself to school Friday morning. The headmaster had sent a note home to Cara requesting Devon show up for final exams today if he wanted to be eligible for graduation. Apparently, even Eddington thought Devon should be done mourning by now.

He hadn't kept up with any of his course work even though Zander had been bringing it home. Devon didn't see the point in returning to Eddington. His fate was sealed. He didn't need a diploma to be chained to his father's company for the rest of his life. He tried arguing with Cara about it, but she told him attendance today was mandatory and threatened to have Thorton drive him to Eddington if Devon wouldn't do it himself.

Devon gave in. At least if he drove himself he could leave as soon as exams were over, or maybe even sneak out early. Once Devon pulled onto campus he knew he'd made a mistake. He should've taken a different car. Everyone recognized his Defender and a group of girls were already pointing and whispering.

He sighed and took another sip of liquid courage in the form of his father's best whiskey. It would take all the strength Devon had left to get out of his car. One sip wasn't enough. It didn't even keep his hands from shaking anymore. If anything, the whiskey just made his pounding headache even worse.

Devon waited until the bell rang and the parking lot was empty before heading inside. He shielded his eyes from the bright morning light when he got out of the car. He hadn't been outside much these days and he'd stupidly forgotten his sunglasses. He glowered up at the cloudless sky. It was a rare blue-sky morning, just like it had been on the last morning he'd spent with Sam. A flicker of anger for everything he'd lost flared up within Devon's chest as he thought about that day—the day everything he loved had been stolen from him.

Why? Why had he been given those few short hours of bliss if it was all going to be taken away? He'd rather have had nothing at all, than been left with an ashen husk where his heart used to be.

Devon glared up at the bright sky in disgust and shook his head.

Even the sun is against me, he thought as he trudged toward the school, his hands shoved deep in his jacket pockets.

❧

Devon was surprised he was still standing by lunch. He'd bombed his first exam and skipped the second one because he knew Sam would be there. Instead he hid in the lavatory and drank the rest of his father's whiskey.

He hadn't even meant to go to lunch, but somehow he ended up in the cafeteria by habit. It was like his body was just going though the motions.

Devon was following the flow of students filing past rows of tables in a trance until something vivid caught his attention. *Laughter.* But not just any laughter—*Sam's laughter.* Devon honed in on the sound, his feet carrying him toward it. But what he saw stopped him dead. He was a boulder in a stream—students parting on either side to get by him, jostling him in the process. But all the while, Devon stood stone still and watched Sam—*his Sam*—laughing with Zander.

And then, he broke.

The last remaining thread that had been holding Devon together finally frayed beyond repair. And when it snapped, Devon lunged.

Sam

Sam was standing next to Zander's lunch table, which consisted of half the boys' soccer team. She was listening to him talk animatedly about plans for Grad night. Ever since she told him she wanted to go, he hadn't stopped talking about it.

"Maybe I can get us a limo or something," Zander mused.

"Oh, you don't have to do that. We're just going as friends."

"Of course, but if you're really leaving us, then we have to send you off with a bang. Ya know, something to remember us Micks by. Am I right, mates?"

Sam laughed as Zander's teammates boisterously agreed.

"I still can't believe you're leaving us, Boston," Zander exclaimed over the ruckus.

"Yeah, it's time."

"Ah, well. Save your goodbyes until tonight. I'll pick you up at eight," he said handing Sam a ticket to the Grad Ball. "Good luck on the rest of your exams."

Sam was about to wish him the same when someone slammed into Zander from behind, smashing him into his lunch table. She screamed and stumbled backwards to avoid getting clipped by the flailing limbs. When she regained her balance she realized it wasn't someone—*it was Devon!*

She yelled his name and tried to get to him, but Devon was being attacked by three huge boys from the soccer team. That should have stopped Sam, but it didn't. All she could think of was getting to him. This was the first time she was seeing Devon and there was definitely something wrong. He looked thinner and his eyes were wild with sunken blue shadows beneath them.

Devon had Zander pinned to the lunch table and refused to let him go even though Sean Dougherty had Devon in a headlock. Sam tried to get through to Devon, but he was screaming profanities at Zander through clenched teeth and saliva.

"I told you to stay the fuck away from her!" Devon screamed. "I told you—"

"Devon!" Sam screamed. It was like he didn't even see her.

Terror gripped Sam as she helplessly watched Devon struggle. He didn't look familiar at all. *This wasn't her Devon.* This Devon looked like he escaped a psych ward. She didn't know what to do, but if she didn't get his attention soon he was probably going to pass out. His face was turning violent shades of red as Dougherty tightened his chokehold.

Sam did the first thing that came to her. She grabbed a nearby lunch tray and slammed it as hard as she could onto the table next to Devon and Zander. It worked. Food sprayed across the boys and the deafening crack of the tray startled Devon enough that he looked at her. As soon as their eyes met he let go of Zander. He slumped in Dougherty's arms, his frightened gray eyes closing.

~♡~

Sam was sitting in the nurse's office waiting for Devon to wake up. The nurse told her he was fine, sadly, just intoxicated and disorientated. She'd cleaned him up and let him lay down in the back. Then, after Sam had sobbed for twenty minutes in the waiting room, the nurse took pity on her.

"I've been young and in love too," the nurse said. "Go sit with Mr. James until he wakes up. But don't let me catch ya getting flirty back there."

"Yes, ma'am."

Currently, Sam was holding Devon's hand, stroking the calloused underside of his long fingers. She noticed the knuckles of his right hand were covered in cuts and bruises. She noticed a lot of new bruises on him as tears filled her eyes. She barely recognized the boy in front of her. *How could she have let this happen to him?*

She was so angry with herself for not being there for Devon. She shouldn't have let him push her away no matter what he said. She knew how bad he was hurting. The bruises on the outside were nothing compared to how he must be hurting on the inside.

Sam brought his hand to her lips, kissing each knuckle. She couldn't stop crying and her tears splashed his hand, leaving a splotchy trail down his wrist. He finally began to stir and she leaned over him, stroking the side of his face and whispering to him. "Shhh, you're okay, Devon. I'm right here. It's Sam."

He looked up at her with confusion. "Sam?"

She smiled and let out a bottled up breath. *God, it was so good to hear his voice.* "Yes," she whispered, bending to kiss both his cheeks.

"Sam?" he asked again.

"Yes, Devon. It's me."

She hugged him, laying her head on his chest. He hesitantly put one arm around her and held her against him. Sam breathed in deeply. He smelled more like whiskey than himself, but still, he was here. *Her Devon was still here.* She could feel him underneath the pain as she listened to his heart hammering in her ear.

Suddenly, he stiffened and she lifted her head to look at him. "What's wrong?"

He just shook his head and tried to push her away.

"Devon . . ."

"No, Sam. Don't." He pushed himself up so he was sitting. "I-I can't do this, right now."

"Do what?"

"You! Us! This! I can't even look at you."

His words left shrapnel in her heart. "Why?" she asked, tears welling in her eyes again.

"Because it hurts! Everything hurts, Sam."

"I know, Devon. I promise you I know how bad it hurts, and that's why you need to let me help you."

"I can't," he muttered swinging his legs over the bed and grabbing for his shoes.

"Where are you going?"

"Away from you."

"I know you're hurting right now, Devon. But please don't push me away."

"Leave me alone, Sam."

"Stop!" She yelled. Devon finally turned and looked at her. "I know this sucks, but that doesn't mean you get to be an asshole. I'm trying to help you."

"I don't need your help, Sam."

"Look at yourself," she yelled. "You clearly do."

He scowled at her. "Oh, and how are you gonna help me, Sam? Flirting with Zander? Going out with him? Is that your idea of helping me?"

"No-I-I wasn't flirting with him. We're friends."

"Friends that go out to dances and pubs? I know how your friend-rules work."

"That's not fair, Devon."

"You're not going with him, Sam. He's no good for you."

She narrowed her eyes at him. "Oh and you are?"

"I'm a hell of a lot better than that wanker."

"Maybe you used to be. But right now I don't even know who you are."

He laughed, but it sounded wrong, desperate. "Then why don't you just forget about me like everyone else."

"Because, I don't want to! Because I care about you, Devon. But you have to let me in," she pleaded.

He turned his back on her. "Sam, if you know what's good for you, you'll stay away from me."

"But—"

"Sam! I'm trying so hard not to hurt you. Please, I just can't do this right now."

"If you don't want to hurt me, stop pushing me away!"

"Sam, look at me. I'm a fucking mess. And if I let you in I'll ruin you too. I'm trying to do the right thing."

"Well you're not! All you're doing is hurting us both."

"Maybe I am. But I just need more time, Sam. Is that so much to ask?"

"No," she said quietly.

Devon looked at her. He was standing across the room, fully dressed, opening and closing his fists, like he wasn't sure what to do next. She hated seeing him like this. He looked so pained and drawn. It was like a parasite was eating him from the inside out, feeding on his pain and suffering.

"I won't go out with Zander if you don't want me to," she offered.

Devon let out a rattling laugh. "I don't care what you do, Sam. But you should know, Zander's just using you to hurt me."

Pain seared through her tattered heart. *How could he be so cruel? Just because he didn't want her anymore didn't mean no one else would.* "Really? Because the way I see it, you're the only one who's hurting me."

Devon

Devon watched Sam's face harden. He'd finally done it. He'd finally pushed her far enough. He could almost see her mind snap shut as she straightened her spine and walked away from him, slamming the door on her way out.

Once the door was shut, Devon sank to his knees and

thought of all the things he wished he could say to her. But wishing wasn't enough.

He'd done the right thing letting Sam go—even if it killed him. He knew it was better this way. He couldn't ask her to love him when he was like this—so full of hurt and anger. This way he couldn't poison her with his hate. Even though a tiny voice rose up in him, whispering, *but maybe you love her more than you hate everything else.*

Devon scrubbed his hands over his face trying to push the thought away. No matter what he felt for Sam, it wasn't enough. He wasn't enough for her. And he never would be. She deserved so much better.

Devon signed himself out of the nurse's office and left campus. He didn't care about his exams. There was no way he would pass them in the state he was in anyway. He drove home and snuck into his own house. He knew Cara would have a fit if she caught him home this early. She'd probably make Thorton drive him back to Eddington and tie him to a desk. Devon stopped outside the door to his room. He didn't want to go back in there. Everything was destroyed in his room. *But Devon was beginning to realize that everything was destroyed no matter where he went.*

He pushed the door open and sunk onto his bed, wishing for the black numbness of sleep to carry him away.

CHAPTER

32

Sam

"I'm telling you, Meg, you didn't see him. He's not even the same person anymore," Sam said as she finished pinning up her hair.

"That doesn't mean you have to go out with Zander."

"I'm not going out with just Zander. There's a bunch of us going. And besides, Devon was extremely clear that he wants nothing to do with me and doesn't care what I do."

"Sam . . ." Megan's face was stuck in her, I-disagree-with-you, scowl.

"What? That's what he said."

"I doubt it."

"Meg! He literally said, *I don't care what you do, Sam.* And he's so egotistical that he can't even comprehend that anyone else would want to hang out with me."

"What does that mean?"

"He said he thinks Zander's only using me to hurt him."

"Well, is he?"

"No! Devon is the only one who's hurting people. He practically smashed Zander's face in for the second time and he wouldn't even talk to me. I know he's hurting, Meg, but he clearly isn't ready to face things. Until he is, I don't think anyone can help him."

"Yeah but—"

"No buts! Can you just be on my side? I'm going out tonight and I really wish everyone would stop trying to tell me what to do."

"I'm sorry. I'm not trying to tell you what to do, Sam. I'm just worried."

"Well, there's nothing to worry about. I'm going to a party with some friends, like a normal teenager. Now, I need to finish getting ready. Zander's gonna be here in twenty minutes. I'll call you tomorrow."

Sam disconnected her video chat with Megan and finished getting ready. She slipped on a cute lacey black skater dress she'd bought on her shopping spree with Devon. It had a plunging neckline covered with sheer black mesh, an open back and a short flouncy skirt with pockets. Sam gave herself a once over in the mirror. She looked good—and not like herself at all.

She knew it was childish, but she wanted to look good tonight, if only to prove to herself that she was desirable after what Devon said to her. *Did he really think just because he had been okay with being her almost boyfriend that meant no one else would ever want to date her for real?*

"Arrogant prick," she mumbled under her breath.

Sam finished tying the bows on her strappy heels when

she heard a car horn beep. She looked out her window to see a massive stretch SUV with a half dozen soccer players hanging out the windows.

Shit!

Sam raced downstairs before her father came out of his office to see what all the commotion was. "Bye, Dad! Love you," she called as she rushed out of the house.

Devon

It was dark by the time Devon woke up. He felt groggy and a bit hung over. He decided a shower was in order. The steam helped clear his head, but then all his memories from earlier that day came rushing back. He'd been a complete wanker to Sam. Devon turned the water cold to try and drive away his queasiness. But he suspected feeling ill had much more to do with what he'd said to Sam, than too much whiskey.

He dressed as his stomach growled. He hadn't eaten anything today. He checked his watch. Almost ten. *Perfect.* Cara and the kids would be in bed by now and the kitchen would be empty.

~❧~

Devon sat on the kitchen counter eating the last of a sandwich he found in the refrigerator. It seemed Cara was rationing his food now, because he found three sandwiches with his name on them. He'd been too tired to defy her by making something else, so he ate the sandwich with the newest date on the label.

As he finished his meal, Devon let his mind wander back to when he'd first brought Sam to the kitchen to make pizza. It felt like a lifetime ago. The memories made his chest tight. And when Devon wondered what Sam was up to at the moment, his eyes stung.

Probably snogging Zander, he thought wickedly. He couldn't really blame her if she was. Devon had practically driven Sam into Zander's arms with the way he spoke to her in the nurse's office.

Christ! Devon knew pushing Sam away was for the best but it still hurt like hell.

Devon hopped off the counter and put his plate in the sink. He had to get some fresh air. All this thinking about Sam, and what would never be, was making him crazy.

Devon was about to open the door to his bedroom when he heard a whine behind him. He turned to see Eggsy come padding out from Sam's room. Devon shook his head at the dog. "What are you doing in there? I told you she's not coming back."

Eggsy whined morosely.

"Yeah, I miss her too."

Devon walked to Sam's door intending to shut it, but he found himself peering inside. It didn't even look like her room anymore. Cara removed every trace of Sam. The white comforter, the twinkling fairy lights, the fluffy pillows, all erased.

"That bitch," he huffed stepping inside the room. First his father and now Sam. It was like Cara wanted to erase everything that had ever made Devon happy. *Why did she hate him so much?*

Devon found himself rifling through the room for any sign that Sam had ever been there. He just wanted one thing to hold on to. One thing so he knew what they had was real—even if it only lasted a short while.

The only thing Devon found was the adapter he'd loaned Sam when she first moved in. It was still plugged into the wall near the nightstand. Devon leaned over to unplug it and noticed a notebook wedged behind the nightstand. He pulled it out. It was the spiral bound kind Sam used to take notes in class. She must have forgotten it when she moved out. Devon smoothed the bent pages back and froze when he read what Sam had written.

It was a list.

And it was about him.

Devon James: Pros & Cons.

In the Cons column she'd written:

Always thinks he's funny.
Always thinks he's right.
Stubborn.
Moody.
Used to put spiders in my hair.
Used to call me Spam.
Too good looking.
Spends more time on his hair than me.
He scares me.

But in the Pros column there was only one thing written. And when he read it, it changed everything.

He scares me because I'm in love with him.

Devon blinked and read the sentence over and over again.

Holy shite! Sam loved him! That changed everything. Or at least it could. Devon had always known he loved her. But she'd never said it back, not even after he told her on their camping trip. Well, she sort of did, but she was joking. *Wasn't she?* But if she loved him this whole time . . .

His mind flashed back to video chats they'd had with Megan. She was always teasing Sam and saying "Don't be scared, Sam." And every time Sam's face would flush pink and she'd cut Megan off. *Was this what Megan was talking about?*

Devon still thought he was a right foul mess, and Sam deserved better. But if she loved him too . . . Maybe she didn't care. Maybe she was just as mad for him as he was for her. He knew they could never go back—that Devon would never be the light and carefree boy he was before. But maybe, just maybe he could be some version of himself that Sam could love. Maybe there were enough pieces left of him. And maybe she would want to help put them back together.

Shite! He had to try.

Devon quickly took a photo of the list on the notebook and sent it in a text message to Megan.

DEVON: I need your help.

He pressed send and raced across the hall to get changed.

His phone was already ringing before he reached his door.

CHAPTER
33

Sam

The Garage was awesome! They made awesome Appletinis! And Appletinis made Sam awesome at pool!

"I win!" Sam yelled blowing on the tip of her pool stick like it was a smoking gun. "You have to buy me another drink, Z."

"I think you might want to finish that one first," Zander said, trying to steady Sam as she leaned against the table.

She grinned at him and knocked back the remaining green liquid in the martini glass. "Finished!" she called triumphantly.

Zander laughed. "Not quite what I meant, but okay."

"I'll get this one," Dougherty called from the bar. "Besides, I already called next game, Boston. Quit hogging the table."

"Make me," she taunted.

Dougherty smirked and brought her another Appletini, snaking his arm around her waist when she took it. "I'd be happy to," he said thrusting his hips suggestively against her.

"Dougherty, give it a rest," Zander warned.

But Sam only laughed and slinked out of Dougherty's grasp. "I can take care of myself, Z."

"Yeah, *Z*, she's a big girl," Dougherty taunted.

Sam started racking the balls for the next game and Zander threw his hands up, joining the rest of his friends at the bar.

"Who knew you were such a craic, Sam," Dougherty purred.

She laughed giddily. "I did."

"Well, why've ya been hiding all this time?"

"Dunno," she slurred. "What're we playin' for?"

"How 'bout a kiss?"

Sophie

Sophie sat in a dark corner of the bar watching Dougherty at the billiards table with Samantha. He was putting on quite a show. She scowled at Samantha impatiently. Tonight was the night everyone would see Samantha Connors for the little slut she was.

Devon

By the time Devon got to Dublin it was almost midnight and there was no parking. Everyone was out celebrating the end of term. He had to park twenty blocks from Temple Bar district. He ran all the way to the Garage, feeling like his lungs were going to burst. He prayed Megan was right about Sam being here, because she wasn't picking up her phone.

After Devon caught his breath, he went to work scanning the packed crowd. Once inside it took a moment for his eyes to adjust in the dark haze of the bar. He didn't see Sam, but he spotted Zander and his crew.

Devon marched over to them. "Where is she?" he growled, eyeing Zander's bruised face like he wanted to take another crack at it.

"Who?" Zander asked.

"Don't play games with me Zander. I know she came out with you."

"Yeah, she did. But I haven't seen her in a while."

"You fucking lost her?"

"I'm not her keeper, Devon. We're just friends."

"If you're so worried about her, why don't you ask your mate Dougherty where she is?" Both Devon and Zander whirled around to see Sophie standing a few feet away, her arms crossed and face twisted into a conniving sneer.

"What's that supposed to mean?" Devon asked.

"I saw them go into the toilet together," she said coyly. "But that was a while ago. You might not want to interrupt. They should be almost finished."

Devon glared at Sophie and made his way to the toilets. He tried the mens. It was empty. Next he knocked on the ladies.

"Just a minute," someone called back. It was a man's voice—*Dougherty.*

"Open the fucking door, Dougherty."

"Fuck off!"

Zander was standing at Devon's side now. They both

looked at each other for a moment and then ran at the door. They shouldered it until the lock splintered off the wood and the door swung open. Sam was crumbled on the floor with Dougherty standing over her, his pants around his ankles.

Rage rippled through Devon so strong he could taste it. *Dougherty was a dead man!* Devon was going to kill him. And he was going to do it with his bare hands, right here and now, if he'd hurt a single hair on Sam's head. But first he had to get to her. He had to make sure she was alright.

Devon raced toward Sam, but Dougherty must've thought he was coming for him, because he cowered and started babbling.

"I didn't touch her, I swear. She just passed out."

Sophie strolled into the bathroom behind them. "I always knew she was just another slut. You can't possibly want anything to do with her now, can you?"

Devon didn't turn around. He didn't care about Zander and Sophie's problems. All he cared about was Sam. He was crouched next to her on the floor trying to get her to open her eyes. "Sam, angel. Sam, can you hear me?"

"Devon!" Sophie stomped her foot. "I'm talking to you!"

Devon turned to look at Sophie. *Was Sophie seriously talking to him?* He surveyed the scene. Zander was glaring at Sophie, while he held a squirming Dougherty, his arms pinned behind his back. Sam was still limp, her head in his lap. Devon shook his head and turned his attention back to Sam, who was murmuring incoherently. *Thank Christ! At least she was breathing.* But she was sloppy drunk. He'd never seen her like this.

"For Christ's sake, Devon! What do you see in her?" Sophie yelled! "She's a drunken slut! You're too good for her. All of you are. What do I have to do to prove it to you?"

What do I have to do? A dark thought clawed its way into Devon's mind as he slowly turned to face Sophie. *Sophie was evil, but this . . .* He stood up and walked toward her. At first she smiled, like she'd finally gotten through to him. But as Devon got closer his hate was undeniable and Sophie began to back away.

"What did you do to her?" Devon growled.

"Nothing," she hissed. "I didn't have to. Look at her."

"Yes, look at her. She looks like she's more than a little drunk. And Sam can really hold her booze. She must've had what, ten or so drinks to be this messed up."

"She only had three," Zander said, still restraining Dougherty. "I was keeping track."

"What did you do, Sophie?" Devon asked again.

"Nothing!"

"I don't believe you." Devon growled. Sophie shuddered as he snatched her purse from her hands and shoved her into a bathroom stall while he searched through it. He pulled a small amber prescription vial from it, straining to read the label. "Flunitrazepam?"

Devon threw Sophie's purse on the ground and hauled her out of the stall. "What the hell is this?" He was gripping Sophie's wrists hard and she started to cry.

"Fuck me! You said it was just roofies, Soph," Dougherty yelled. "Oh, Christ. What did I give her?"

Zander squeezed Dougherty's arms tighter behind him. "Start talking."

"Sophie made me do it," Dougherty blubbered.

"Shut up, Dougherty," Sophie hissed.

"No! I'm not taking the blame for this. You said it was

just roofies. You promised it wouldn't hurt her!"

"That's what Flunitrazepam is, you idiots," Sophie yelled. Everyone looked at her. "Look it up," she spat.

Devon took a photo of the prescription label and searched it on his phone. "She's right," he said, reading the results he found online.

"Why'd you do it?" Zander asked.

"Because! Ever since she showed up, it's all you two ever seem to talk about. *Sam* this, *Sam* that. She's not special. And she's not good enough for you, Devon. You're supposed to be with me!"

"You?" He laughed. "You broke up with me as soon as I quit the team."

"That was a mistake."

"And was dating me a mistake too?" Zander asked.

"Yes! I only did it to make you jealous, Devon."

"And all of this?" Devon asked pointing to Sam and Dougherty.

"Zander was supposed to catch her with Dougherty. I knew Zander would tell you. And Dougherty was supposed to take pictures so I'd have proof she's just a slut that doesn't care about either of you."

"Well, mission accomplished Soph. We all know who the crazy one is now," Devon said turning back to Sam.

Sophie grabbed his shoulder and Devon shoved her off. "If you ever touch me or Sam again I'll go to the police about this. Now get the hell out of here before I reconsider."

Sophie frowned and looked like she was going to say something, but Devon's scowl stopped her and she ran out of the bathroom while she still could.

Devon gently hoisted Sam into his arms and carried her

from the bathroom. Zander followed him with Dougherty. "What do you want me to do with him?" Zander asked.

"I wasn't gonna hurt her, I swear," Dougherty whimpered. "I was only trying to pose her like Sophie said, but I couldn't get her to stand up."

"I don't care," Devon growled pushing through the crowded bar with Sam cradled to his chest. And he didn't. The only thing that mattered was Sam. And making sure she was safe.

～♡～

Devon had only made it two blocks when Zander pulled up in his car.

"Let me give you a ride," he called.

Devon didn't want to take the help, but he also didn't know if he could carry Sam another eighteen blocks.

"Fine." Devon carefully laid Sam on the backseat and slid in next to her, holding her head in his lap.

"Where to?" Zander asked. "Home?"

"No, I think she needs to go to the hospital."

"For roofies?" Zander asked.

"I'm not taking any chances."

"Right."

Zander navigated traffic quickly, pulling into the ER bay at St. James Hospital. After the nurses took Sam back, Devon and Zander gave their statements and filled out the paperwork the best they could. Devon gave the nurses Mr. Connors' phone number and paced around the waiting room while they tried to reach him.

"Boys," a tired-looking nurse called. "We've reached Mr.

Connors. He's on his way."

"Thanks," Devon replied. He turned to Zander. "I'll wait for him to get here. You can take off."

"I'll wait with you."

Devon shook his head.

"I don't mind," Zander said, sitting back down.

They both sat silently in the waiting room. Zander finally turned to Devon and spoke. "I didn't have any idea Sophie was planning this. I swear to it. I never would've let her hurt Sam."

Devon was hunched over, his head resting in his hands. "I know."

He didn't like Zander and he disliked the thought of him with Sam even more. Zander was many things, but Devon had never known him to be someone who had to drug his dates. Sophie, on the other hand, had always been vindictive and possessive. There were plenty of rumors about her viciousness. Sophomore year, while they were dating, Sophie shaved off a girl's eyebrows at a sleep over because she caught her talking to Devon in the lunchroom. The summer before that she got another girl drunk and took pictures of the poor girl in her underwear with a bunch of blokes and plastered them all over the internet until she dropped out of Eddington. The girl claimed Sophie drugged her and she didn't even know any of the guys. Of course Sophie and her bitchy friends said the girl was lying and just pissed the photos had gotten out. But after what Devon had seen tonight, he was certain all the rumors about Sophie were true and he found himself wishing he hadn't let her off so easily.

"I should have made sure Dougherty didn't get any photos of Sam."

"He didn't," Zander replied. "I wiped his phone before I let him go."

"Good thinking." Devon shook his head, still not quite believing how bad this was. "Sophie's fucking batty."

Zander huffed a breathy laugh. "Certifiable." He shook his head. "Well, at least I don't feel bad about dumping her now."

"You broke up with Sophie?"

"Yeah. She was giving me hell for spending so much time with Cara and the kids after Henry died. Said I wasn't putting her first. I told her if she couldn't see that family needed to come first right now then I didn't need her in my life." Zander sighed. "She told everyone she dumped me. I let it go. You know how she is. Didn't seem worth it to argue. Makes sense now that I know she was only ever using me to get back at you."

"But I don't get it. She dumped me as soon as she heard I wasn't football captain."

"Yeah, she was worried she'd lose status if she wasn't dating a baller. But I knew she still had her eye on you. When she saw you snogging Sam at Finnegan's she flipped. Chewed my ear off about it for an hour after you left."

Devon shook his head. "Christ, she's crazy."

"Yeah. If she'd just been honest about her feelings she could've probably had either of us."

Zander's words hit home. *How could he fault Sophie when Devon himself had been dishonest about his feelings too?* Of course he hadn't deliberately tried to hurt people, but he'd still managed to mess things up pretty bad anyway. He'd definitely hurt Sam. Devon rubbed his temples. "I just keep thinking Sam wouldn't have even been in this mess if it wasn't for me."

"Don't blame yourself."

"Who else can I blame?"

"Dunno. But that girl in there loves you, Devon. She asked me about you every day you were home. I know you care about her too. I see what staying away is doing to you. We all do. Cara's worried sick about you. She keeps redecorating the house because she doesn't know how to talk to you and it's the only way she can keep busy. She's driving me mad. I really hate being everyone's in-between man. We all just need to talk to each other. We're family."

Devon looked at Zander like he had two heads. "Cara's worried about me?"

"Christ, Devon. Are ya that daft? I know you don't like her, but she's not a monster. You lost your father, but she lost her husband, too. You're not the only one who feels alone in that big old house."

"What about you?" Devon asked.

"What about me?"

"Do you still hate me?"

"Devon, I've never hated you. I've been jealous of you, but I'm not gonna kick a man while he's down. Christ, what do ya think of me?"

"I just always thought you hated me."

"Sometimes I think I might have. But I was wrong. I more hated myself. Maybe even Cara a little. I felt like she left me for your dad and a big house. And I always had to struggle for my place in life while I watched things just handed to you. But it wasn't your fault. I know that now. It was just life."

"So what do we do now?" Devon asked.

Zander laughed. "Hell if I know. Try to put our mess of a family back together. That's all Cara wants."

"Really?"

Zander nodded.

"Do *you* want that?" Devon asked.

"I think being a part of the family might be nice."

"What about all the things you said about stealing Cor-Tec?"

"I was just trying to take the piss outta ya. I got it into my head that I had a shot with your girl, but I know better now."

Devon smirked. "Well, I really have no interest in my father's business. Maybe, if you're open to it, you could help me run it."

Zander raised his eyebrows and then extended his hand. "I'd be honored."

Just then, a frantic-looking Mr. Connors came racing into the waiting room. "Where is she? Where's Sam!"

The nurse quickly tended to him before he could get any closer to Devon and Zander.

"You better get out of here, mate," Devon said after Mr. Connors was escorted back to Sam's room. "He's probably going to lay into me when he gets out."

Zander nodded. "Want a ride home?"

"I can't leave yet. I need to make sure Sam's okay."

"Then I'll wait with you."

CHAPTER

34

_____

Sam

Sam was lying in her bedroom when she heard a knock on her door. It was Sunday morning and her father had been doting on her since she came home from the ER early Saturday morning. He was worried because all she did was lay in bed and cry. *But what else was she supposed to do?* Her life was an episode of *Gossip Girl*. Her so-called friends had drugged her in a potential date-rape revenge scheme.

All Sam wanted to do was get on a plane to Boston. But her father suddenly refused to let her out of his sight. He'd gone into overprotective mode since he saw her in the hospital bed. *It was hard to blame him.*

"Dad, I'm fine. You don't have to check on me every fifteen minutes," Sam called.

"Uh, it's me," called a familiar voice.

Sam sat bolt upright as Devon's face tentatively peeked into her room.

"Can I come in?" he asked.

"I have nothing to say to you."

He walked into the room anyway and shut the door behind him. He sat on the edge of her bed. "That's okay. I have something I need to say to you."

Sam glared at him. She'd woken up in the hospital room alone and confused and all she'd wanted was to see Devon. She'd sworn he was with her, but when she opened her eyes he wasn't there. And now that he was here, all she wanted was for him to leave.

"I need to apologize to you, Sam. I don't even really know where to start. But I'm sorry. I was wrong to push you away. And I was wrong not to tell you how I really feel. I never wanted to hurt you, Sam."

She turned away from him, hating that he could still make her cry. But her stupid heart seemed hell bent on not giving up on him.

"Sam, I don't want to lose you."

She scoffed. "It's a little late for that."

"Please don't say that."

"Oh, now that I've finally got your message, you've changed your mind?"

"I was wrong, Sam. But I was hurting and I didn't want to hurt you."

"That doesn't make any sense at all."

Devon ran his hand through his stupid, perfect hair. "I know. I was being an idiot, okay?"

"And you're not anymore?"

"Some thing's have changed."

"Oh really? Like what? You're no longer an idiot?"

"I'm trying not to be"

"I'm sorry, but it's not enough."

"But—"

"No! Did you not tell me you loved me and change your mind? Did you not tell me to leave you alone? And that people only date me to get back at you? Did you not leave me alone in a hospital?"

"Sam, no!"

"Devon. You apologized. I don't forgive you. Now please leave."

"But I need you, Sam. What happened to always being there for each other?"

"That ended when you let your friends drug me and abandon me in a hospital."

"I didn't let them. And I didn't leave you. The doctors wouldn't let me back to see you because I wasn't family. I was in the waiting room the whole time. Just ask your dad."

"I don't care, Devon. You hurt me. And I can't . . . we can't go back to how things were before."

"But you love me."

Sam's eyes bulged. "What?"

"I found your notebook. The one you made the list in. And I talked to Megan."

"Good, then I'm sure she told you she's the one who made me make the stupid list."

"Yes, but she said you meant what you wrote."

"Now you're turning my last friend against me too?"

"No, Sam. I didn't know how you felt. It changes things."

"No it doesn't. And besides, it was just a stupid list. It didn't mean anything."

"Don't do that, Sam. I know it did. It meant something to me. And Megan said—"

"Despite what Megan thinks," Sam interrupted. "She doesn't know everything. I may have thought I loved you. But not anymore and it doesn't matter anyway. I'm going back to Boston."

"What? No. You can't. Sam," he begged. "This is us. I can't let you go!"

"What are you going to do? Roofie me again?"

"Sam, please don't do this. Don't give up on us."

"There is no us, Devon!"

"Then don't give up on me. Just give me another chance. I was hurt and I messed up. Just give me one more chance and I promise I won't let you down ever again."

"I can't, Devon. It's too late. Ireland was a mistake and so was everything that happened with us."

"Don't say that, Sam. The way I feel about you is not a mistake. That night in the tent wasn't a mistake. You know it too. And I know it scares you. It scares me too. But it scares me more to lose you. Don't give up because you're scared to take a risk."

"I did take a risk, Devon. And it was a mistake." Tears streamed down her face and Devon moved closer to wipe them away. She cringed when he touched her and he dropped his hand to his lap. "I'm not scared anymore, Devon. I'm not anything. There's just too many highs and lows. And I can't do it. I'm sorry."

"I'm sorry too, Sam. I'm sorry because I know that this could work and this could be grand. And I know you know it too. We're so close and you're just giving up. How can you quit on me when we've gone through all of this? We've gotten through all the bad stuff. Now it's time for the good. We're almost there, Sam."

"That's just it, Devon. Almost isn't enough."

Devon

Devon didn't know what else to say. He couldn't catch his breath. *It wasn't supposed to go like this.* He was supposed to be able to apologize and win Sam back. It had worked with Zander and Cara. *They'd forgiven him.* He was finally getting his life back together. He almost felt whole again. He just needed the missing piece. *He just needed Sam.*

He pushed off of her bed and paced her room, running his fingers through his hair desperately trying to think of anything to make her change her mind. *But what else could he say?* He'd thrown himself at her mercy. He couldn't make her want him, no matter how wrong he thought she was.

"Sam, I don't know what else to say. I'm in love with you. And I'm not gonna stop. I'm sorry for everything I've put you through. But you have to let me make it up to you."

"I don't have to do anything," she said. "Please leave, Devon. I don't want to have to ask you again."

He stood open-mouthed staring at her. He was at a loss. He could see her mind was made up as she crossed her arms. He wasn't going to win any battles today. But that didn't mean he was giving up. He just needed a new strategy.

"Fine. I'll leave. But I'm not giving up on us. I love you, Sam."

"Goodbye, Devon."

Sam

As soon as Devon left, Sam exploded into hysterics. She was practically hyperventilating by the time her father came upstairs to check on her.

"Sam! Honey, what's wrong?" he cried when he opened the door to find her frantically throwing clothes into her suitcase.

"I'm going back to Boston. You can't make me stay here, Dad!" she wailed. Sam had balled her hands into fists and was flapping them with each word. "I. Can't. Stay. Here!"

Her father ran over to her, wrapping his arms tightly around her until she stopped flailing. She was still shaking in his arms while he stroked her frazzled brown hair and tried to soothe her. They both sank onto her bed and her father rocked her back and forth like she was a child again until she caught her breath.

"Baby, what's wrong?" he asked.

"He broke my heart, Dad." Sam sniffled letting a whole new barrage of tears free. Admitting how much Devon had hurt her made everything hurt worse, and Sam couldn't stop hiccupping and sputtering. "I just really want to go home."

Her father kissed her forehead. "Okay, baby. We'll go home."

"Now?" she asked.

"Yes, honey. Whenever you want."

"I want to go now."

"So you're really coming home?" Megan asked.

Sam was still puffy-eyed, her voice raw from crying. "Yeah. I just bought my ticket. I leave tomorrow morning and my dad will be back next weekend after he ties up some loose ends here."

"Where are you staying?"

"I sorta told him your mom said it was okay to stay with you. Is that cool?"

"Yeah of course. Hold on." Megan left the screen for a moment. "Ma! Sam's staying here tomorrow."

Sam heard a voice in the distance respond. "Okay, hun."

Megan came back and gave Sam a thumbs up and a wide grin. "So you're really coming back for good, huh?"

"Yep."

"Well, I'll be glad to have you back, but I can't say I'm not a tiny bit disappointed I didn't get to visit Ireland first."

"You're not missing much," Sam muttered.

"Oh come on. You can't hate a whole country just because of one bad apple, Sam."

"It was more like a whole school full of bad apples."

Megan rolled her eyes. "So, did you tell him you're leaving?"

"Yeah."

"What'd he say?"

"I don't know. He said I'm sorry a lot. But it's not enough."

"But you love him, Sam."

"Yeah, thanks for telling him, by the way."

"I'm sorry but I was just trying to help."

"I really wish people would stop saying that."

"I know you're mad now, but what if in like three weeks you're not mad anymore? Are you sure you want to just walk away?"

"Yes. I can't live like this, Meg. It's killing me. My heart feels like its been trampled."

"That's because you're in love!"

"This isn't love. Love isn't supposed to hurt like this."

"I think it is. I think that's the only way you know it's real."

"Megan, I really don't want to have this conversation again. I just went through it with Devon a few hours ago. I don't need to be convinced that I was in love. I know I was. But I know it's over now, okay? Everyone just needs to move on."

"If you're really sure."

"I am."

"Okay. I'll see you tomorrow, Sam."

CHAPTER
35

Devon

Devon woke up early Monday morning. He hadn't really been able to sleep anyway. Ever since his conversation with Sam, his stomach was in knots. He still couldn't believe it had gone so wrong. When he got home he was a mess. He must have looked as wrecked as he felt because Cara took one look at him and refused to leave his side until he told her what happened.

Cara was actually really kind, and a good listener. Devon felt bad for never giving her a chance all these years. Things had been better between them since that night at the hospital with Sam. Zander had finally driven Devon home after Mr. Connors told him Sam was okay. When they got home, Cara was waiting up for them. The three of them had a heart-to-heart and Cara pretty much told them both that they weren't leaving the house again unless they all pledged to be honest with each other and start trying to behave like family.

He and Zander had begrudgingly agreed. Devon secretly loved having someone mother him. He hadn't felt that kind of love since his own mother left. It weakened his defenses and he'd spilled everything to Cara—his unhappiness with her redecorating and hatred of Eggsy, feeling trapped by his father's company, his feelings for Sam. By the end of the night—*well, actually it was morning*—they'd patched up a lot of their differences.

It turned out Devon had Cara all wrong. Like Zander said, she was just as lost as Devon after Henry's passing. She was redecorating because everything reminded her of Henry and made her cry. And she was leaving food with his name on it because she wanted him to eat something but was afraid to be too pushy. And she promised Devon they'd find a suitable replacement for him at Cor-Tec, because the only thing Henry had truly wanted for Devon was his happiness.

With things going so well between him, Cara and Zander, Devon had decided to try and fix the last missing piece of his life. He had to wait until Mr. Connors finally agreed to let him come over and talk to Sam. He'd sent Devon away the first time, but by Sunday, Devon had worn him down. *Although now he sort of wished he hadn't.*

He'd been so sure that once he finally had a chance to talk to Sam, everything would right itself. They were Devon and Sam—his love for her had survived across continents. He couldn't have ruined everything with a few weeks of foolish thinking. *Could he?* He'd only been keeping his distance because he thought he was protecting her—that she was better off without him. But he knew how stupid that was now. Grad night had proven they needed each other. Thinking Sam was in danger was the only thing that snapped Devon out of his self-loathing.

After Devon told Cara how terribly his conversation with Sam had gone on Sunday, she suggested he write her a letter. She thought it might be easier for him to get his feelings across to Sam if he wasn't there to argue with. Devon thought it was actually a brilliant idea, but every time he sat down to write, he got stuck on the first sentence. The only thing he managed to write was, *I love you.* But each time he stared at those three little words, he heard Sam's voice telling him it wasn't enough.

Now, as the sunlight streamed into his bedroom, Devon realized he must have nodded off in the midst of writing, because he had ink on his hands and heard paper crinkling beneath him when he rolled over. He sat up, hanging his legs over the side of his bed, rubbing the sleep from his eyes. He tried to take a deep breath, but he felt wrung dry—his insides all twisted and brittle. *He couldn't live like this.* He needed to make things right with Sam. He'd told her he wasn't giving up, and he'd meant it.

Devon got out of bed and took a quick shower to wake himself up. He dressed with renewed determination. He was going to write that damn letter and it was going to perfect, because he loved Sam and love was always enough.

He was just sitting down at his desk to lay his heart out on paper when Cara burst through his bedroom door, with Zander right behind her. Eggsy snarled at them and Devon leapt up to restrain him.

"Good, you're dressed!" Cara said breathlessly, keeping one eye fixed on Eggsy.

"Lucky for all of us," Zander teased.

Cara gave Zander a look of death. "You shouldn't be joking. This is your fault."

"How was I supposed to know why he needed the car?" Zander replied defensively.

"Is someone going to tell me what's going on?" Devon asked.

Cara spoke. "You need to go to Sam's house immediately. Her father called an hour ago requesting to borrow our car service to the airport."

The color drained from Devon's face. "What? She's leaving?"

"I didn't know it was for Sam," Zander said apologetically.

"She said she was going back to Boston, but she didn't say she was leaving today. I thought she meant at the end of the school year," Devon replied.

Zander shook his head. "Last I talked to her she said she wasn't coming back next term."

"I confirmed with Thorton the car's for Sam," Cara said.

"Christ!"

"Well, what are you waiting for?" Cara squawked, practically shoving Devon out the door. "Go get your girl!"

Sam

"Bye, Dad. I love you," Sam said giving her father a big hug before getting into the back of the town car.

"I love you too, honey. Call me as soon as you land," her father said for the hundredth time.

"I will, Dad. I promise."

"I'm sorry I'm not coming with you," he said again. "It's just the—"

"Dad, it's okay." Sam knew he was hosting a big web

conference right when her plane took off, but she was too eager to get back to Boston to change her flight time. Plus, she didn't want him to change his mind about letting her go. Getting back to Boston had become like a shuttle launch, she had to take the window of opportunity before it disappeared. "I'll see you next weekend, Dad," she said blowing him a kiss and shutting the car door.

He stood in the driveway and waved to her until she couldn't see him anymore. It was odd for him to be so clingy. She wasn't used to having him worry about her so much, but ever since the hospital, it was like a protective mama bear had hijacked her usually oblivious father. He was upset that she didn't want to wait one more week for him to fly home with her, but he hadn't argued with her.

After Sam had told him how she felt about Devon, her father had been making an effort to be more understanding. And he hadn't said any of his token poster sayings either. She'd expected him to say, *you're too young to be in love*, or, *you're better off without him*. But he didn't. Instead he apologized for not setting a better example for her as far as healthy relationships were concerned. He'd even tried to talk about her mother. But after he'd said, "I wish your mother were here. She would know what to say," Sam had stopped him.

She could see how much it hurt him to talk about her mother, and she didn't see any reason for both of them to be hurting. Besides, Sam wasn't strong enough to pick up the pieces if her father fell apart too. She was barely holding herself together.

Sam was hoping she'd feel better this morning, but as the car wound through the rolling green hills toward Dublin, she still felt hollow. Devon's words kept haunting her. *I'm in love with you. And I'm not gonna stop.* She'd wanted to hear him say those words every day since his father died. *So why, when he finally said them, was it not enough?*

Sam wished she had an answer. She still loved Devon. If she didn't it wouldn't hurt so much to leave him. But the problem was, it hurt to stay too. Ireland would always remind Sam of the things she'd lost—her mother, the senior year she was supposed to have, and now, her first love.

Sam put in her ear buds and cranked up Adele, finally understanding what she'd been singing about all this time.

CHAPTER
36

Devon

Devon skidded to a stop in Sam's driveway, sending a shower of gravel against the cottage. He pounded on the door until Mr. Connors answered.

"I need to talk to Sam," Devon pleaded.

"I'm sorry, Devon—"

"Please, you don't understand. I'm in love with her."

"Devon . . ."

"Sam!" Devon yelled, trying to look past Mr. Connors. "Sam!"

"She's not here. She already left for the airport."

Devon was sprinting back to his car when Mr. Connors called after him.

"You'll never catch her."

"I have to try."

Devon prayed while he drove. He prayed for traffic for

Sam. He prayed for open roads for himself. And most of all, he prayed he wasn't too late for one more chance with her.

When Devon got close to Dublin his prayers were answered. *Well, one of them.* Traffic was backed up on the M50 and being re-routed through Dublin due to an accident. When he turned onto Ormond Quay, a long road that ran along the River Liffey, traffic slowed to a standstill. This was it, now or never. Devon got out of his car, ignoring the honking and shouting behind him. "Do or die, Devon," he reminded himself as he ran along the scenic sidewalk that followed the river. That's when his second prayer was answered. There, ten cars ahead, right next to the famous Ha'penny Bridge, was a black town car with plates he recognized.

Devon started screaming and waving his hands wildly, not caring about the strange looks he was getting. "Sam! Sam! Wait!" In a few more steps, he was pounding on her window breathlessly. "Sam!"

She looked so startled at first he thought she didn't even recognize him. But he didn't wait for an invitation. He opened the door and slid in next to her.

"Devon! What are you doing here?"

"You can't go, Sam. I love you and I know you love me too. Don't leave. Please. Just stay and we can work this out."

"No! I already told you I don't want to."

"Sam, please," he begged, reaching for her hands. "We can't be over."

"We never even started, Devon." She pulled away from him.

"But—"

"Sorry to interrupt, Master James, but in or out?" Thorton said, glancing at them in the rearview mirror. "Traffic is moving."

"In," Devon replied stubbornly.

"Out!" Sam shouted.

"I'm not leaving, Sam. Not until you hear me out."

"Fine, then I'll leave," she said furiously exiting the car.

For a moment, Devon and Thorton just stared at each other in shock, and then Devon jumped out of the car and stormed after Sam.

He caught up to her on the Ha'penny Bridge, catching her by the wrist. She whirled around, but instead of looking angry like she had in the car, her face was streaked with tears. Devon couldn't stand it. He didn't want to be the reason she was so upset. But he couldn't let her go either. He took both of her hands and dropped to his knees. "Don't go, Sam," he begged. "Please? Just stay."

"Why?"

"Because I love you. And I'm nothing without you. Please, Sam. You're all I have left. And I have to believe that you still love me too."

She sniffled but didn't object.

Devon got slowly to his feet and cupped her face. "Sam," he whispered. "Tell me I'm wrong and I'll let you go. It'll kill me. But if it's what you truly want, I'll let you go."

"You're not wrong," she whispered.

Devon's heart soared. She was still here, his Sam, the one that loved him back was still holding on.

"I do love you. But it's not enough. It's not a reason to stay."

"Yes it is. There's no better reason. I've found the person

I love. She's standing right in front of me. And I can't let her go. Not now, not ever. If you leave, I'll follow you. Just say the word, Sam. Just tell me this is what you want too and I'll come with you. Anywhere you want to go. All I want is to be with you."

"Devon . . ." Her lip quivered as her watery blue-green eyes gazed up at him. His heart was pounding in his chest. He'd never felt more alive or more terrified. He was so close. He could feel Sam reaching for him. But something was holding her back. He pulled her closer with trembling hands, bending his forehead to meet hers. He breathed in her scent and shivered. "Sam." He murmured her name like a prayer. "You told me once that almost isn't enough. And you were right. So here I am, Sam. I'm all in. Now it's up to you."

Sam

Sam's heart was pounding. This was it. They were back at the tent, back before the phone rang, back with their futures wide open ahead of them. Devon loved her. He truly did. *What else could she want?* He was willing to follow her back to Boston. She could have it all. She only had to stop being afraid to want it. But that meant opening her heart up to be hurt again. And it was still in tatters. Her heart was still in the ICU. Could she really ask it to take on more so soon. As if in response, her heart pumped faster. It was strong enough. *She* was strong enough.

Sam reached her hands up, twisting them around Devon's neck. She was staring at him. His expression was so open she could see their whole future in his eyes.

"Devon, I love you. I love you so much it hurts," she whispered.

"You do?"

"Yeah."

"So, does this mean . . . are you in this with me?"

"I don't know how to get out." She grinned lopsidedly. "So yeah, I'm all in."

Devon

Devon wrapped his arms around Sam and sighed into her toffee-colored hair. "Oh thank Christ!"

Sam giggled as Devon pulled her off her feet, holding her tighter than he thought possible, peppering her with kisses. Her feet were barely back on the ground when his lips found hers. Devon kissed Sam like she was air and his lungs had been starved for oxygen. He kissed her like his life depended on it, and maybe it did. Because for the first time since his father died, Devon felt like someone had opened that window in his chest again, flooding him with light and air and warmth—flooding him with love.

A burst of applause from onlookers broke their lips apart momentarily. Sam blushed, but didn't let go of Devon. She gazed up at him, eyes shining. "Thank you for not giving up, Devon." Then she added more softly. "I was just scared I wasn't enough."

Devon pulled her closer. "You were always enough, Sam. You're more than enough. You're everything."

EPILOGUE

"Oh come on!" Megan begged. "You guys owe me."

She was bouncing up and down on Sam's bed as she and Devon poured over Boston University's sophomore course catalog.

"We owe you?" Devon asked, winding his arms around Sam, who was sitting in his lap. "How's that?"

"Because, when the three of us rented this apartment it was all, *This is gonna be fun, Meg. We're gonna have amazing adventures, Meg. It'll be like the three amigos, Meg.*"

"Have we not been amigos?" Sam asked pretending to be hurt.

"You two have! You spend like every waking second together. I hate being the third wheel. We need to go out and do stuff so *I* can meet someone."

"We do stuff," Devon said.

"Yeah watch movies!" Megan retorted.

"You're a film major!" Sam laughed. "You're the one who drags us to the movies."

"Yeah but you promised me adventures." Megan pouted as she pulled the course catalog away from Sam and Devon and started flipping through it.

"We've gone on adventures," Devon argued, trying to hide his smirk. "We've done all the cool Massachusetts stuff."

"Ew, we did all the tourist stuff that I did on fifth grade field trips. I want four-leafed clovers, and fiddles and magic. I want real adventure!" Megan said, shoving the course catalog back under their noses. She'd folded the page back to the study abroad section and circled the Ireland exchange program in pink highlighter. "Please?" she squeaked bouncing even faster.

Devon and Sam glanced slyly at each other, trying not to give away their secret just yet. They'd already signed up for the program the minute they saw it while registering as freshmen. They signed Megan up too without her knowing. It was a hard program to get into and you had to sign up a year in advance. They'd been put on the waiting list until two weeks ago when Sam got an email saying the three of them had been accepted. Apparently, thanks to Zander. He pulled some strings and said that he needed three interns to help him at Cor-Tec, which he was running fulltime. Zander had even fabricated some film documentary nonsense so that Megan would have a reason for interning at an international software company. It was clearly obvious that he had a crush on Megan. Zander was always making up excuses to Skype with Devon and then asking if Megan was around. It was adorable.

Now Devon and Sam were just toying with Megan. They loved her to death, but it was kinda fun to watch her squirm a bit.

"I don't know?" Sam started. "I'm not sure I want to go back to Ireland."

"Yeah, me either," Devon replied.

"But I'd give *anything* to go to Ireland," Megan whined.

Sam and Devon grinned at each other. Sam would give anything to go back there too . . . well *almost* anything, she thought as she laced her fingers with Devon's.

"We're in!" they said in unison.

THE
END

**Want to go on your very own
Almost Boyfriend study abroad?**

Here's a list of the places in the book that you can actually visit.

- Finnegan's of Dalkey – Dalkey, Ireland
- Brown Thomas Department Store – Dublin, Ireland
- The Garage – Dublin, Ireland
- Ha'penny Bridge – Dublin, Ireland

To my readers,

I want to personally thank you for taking the time to seek out this great little indie book. Writing is truly my passion. I believe each of us can find a small part of ourselves in every book we read, and carry it with us, shaping our world, our adventures and our dreams.

Following my dream to write frees my soul but knowing others find joy in my writing is indescribable. So thank you for your support and I hope your enjoyed your brief escape into the magic of these pages.

If you enjoyed this story, don't worry, there's plenty more currently rattling around in my rambunctious imagination. Let me and others know your thoughts by sharing a review of this book. Reviews help shape my next writing projects. So if you want more books like this one be sure to shout it from the rooftops (or social media.) ;-)

ABOUT THE AUTHOR

Award-Winning author, Christina Benjamin, lives in Florida with her husband, and character inspiring pets, where she spends her free time working on her books and speaking to inspire fellow writers.

Christina is best known for her wildly popular Young Adult series, The Geneva Project.

Her best-selling novel, The Geneva Project - Truth, has won multiple awards and stolen the hearts of YA readers. Packed with magic and imagination, her epic tale of adventure hooks fans of mega-hit YA fiction like Harry Potter, The Hunger Games and Percy Jackson.

Christina loves to read and write across genres. YA is her favorite but she's a sucker for a good love story. Don't miss her romance, paranormal and historical fiction, as well as the multiple anthologies she's been a part of.

To learn about new books and more fun stuff, follow her at:
FACEBOOK
@ChristinaBenjaminAuthor

TWITTER
@authorcbenjamin

INSTAGRAM
@authorcbenjamin

PINTEREST
@authorcbenjamin

WEBSITE
www.christinabenjaminauthor.com

Made in the USA
Middletown, DE
18 April 2022